The Winds of Wharhalen

Tom Nelson

First Edition

Oshawa, Ontario

The Winds of Wharhalen
by Tom Nelson

Managing Editor:	Kevin Aguanno
Acquisitions Editor:	Sarah Schwersenska
Typesetting:	Tak Keung Sin
eBook Conversion:	Agustina Baid
Cover Design:	Robert Robbins

Published by:
Crystal Dreams Publishing
(a division of Multi-Media Publications Inc.)
Box 58043, Rosslynn RPO, Oshawa, Ontario, Canada, L1J 8L6.

http://www.crystaldreamspublishing.com/

All rights reserved. No part of this book may be reproduced or transmitted in any form or by any means, electronic or mechanical, including photocopying, recording or by any information storage and retrieval system, without written permission from the publisher, except for the inclusion of brief quotations in a review.

Copyright © 2008 by Crystal Dreams Publishing

Paperback	ISBN-10: 1-59146-090-5	ISBN-13: 9781591460909
Adobe PDF ebook	ISBN-10: 1-59146-091-3	ISBN-13: 9781591460916
Microsoft LIT ebook	ISBN-10: 1-59146-093-X	ISBN-13: 9781591460930
Mobipocket PRC ebook	ISBN-10: 1-59146-094-8	ISBN-13: 9781591460947
Palm PDB ebook	ISBN-10: 1-59146-096-4	ISBN-13: 9781591460961

Published in Canada. Printed simultaneously in England and the United States of America.

CIP data available from the publisher.

Table of Contents

The Karpoans 5
Engrid 11
Raiders 15
Kaine 21
The Secret 35
Vartan 41
Eylese 49
The Race 63
Joal 85
The Quarry 97
Kira 111
Braslon 123
Ritola 139
Attalia 149
Cecel 155
The Resistance 167
Zironon 177
The Mission 183
Tasha 195
Ej Tauk-Zar 205
Torin 213
The Return 223
Reunion 229
Toulon 239

CHAPTER ONE

The Karpoans

The sparse growth along the wind-swept ridge provided little cover. The thick, contorted trunks of the trees, dwarfed by meager rainfall, grew at odd angles as they competed for sunlight. These survivors were a hardy race, tested by the harshest conditions in Killarassee. Their shallow roots clung to the face of the rock along the snaking spine of hills known as the Karpoans, the vague boundary between the relatively civilized lowlands and the barbarous mountain territory of Wharhalen. All the borders in the Empire were vague. The Empire of the Old Kings itself had always been a loose aggregation of lands with shifting loyalties to individual warlords. Every thirty or forty years, however, power would be consolidated to extract a measure of cooperation from far-flung regions, always emanating from the sprawling city of Attalia.

    The Tabar Ridge was far from Attalia. Along this ridge, the remote villages that comprised this region had little contact with the world outside the Karpoans. The harsh environment alone made it difficult to scratch out a living; compounding this was the menacing presence of the roving bands of raiders that extorted food and supplies

The Winds of Wharhalen

from the villagers in exchange for protection from other bandits.

The flinty sky streaked with wind-driven swatches of light seemed to brush the peaks of the hills. Partially concealed among the stunted, gnarled trees and scrubby undergrowth was a young man of about nineteen years. His gangly arms and legs were a marked contrast to the stubby limbs of the centuries-old dwarfs that he was attempting to hide behind. When finally he felt it was safe to rise to his full stature, it could be seen that the youth was taller than average, thin, but well-proportioned. He was fair with blue eyes, and thick, straw-colored hair that fell stubbornly across his forehead. The boy, whose name was Locke, cupped his hands to his mouth and simulated the call of the Teevit, a small scavenging bird common in the high elevations. After a few minutes, a second man emerged from the scrub, this one leading four horses in single file. Two of the horses, stout, shaggy ponies really, were laden with bulky packs. The other two, larger and sleeker but still sturdily built, carried only light riding saddles and small packs.

The second man was a good bit older than the first, with a hint of gray mingling with the dark brown of his hair and beard. He probably wasn't as old as he appeared, but he was obviously still strong and vital. The harsh life offered by the Karpoans tended to chase away the freshness of youth if one were lucky enough to survive childhood at all. "The pass looks clear," said the younger man to his companion in a hushed tone of voice.

"It'd better be. I don't want to spend another night shivering on this plateau."

The narrow pass that lay below them was a likely place for an ambush by bandits. Beyond the pass was an open and nearly treeless valley. At the other end of the valley was the village that Locke and his companion, Jocar, hoped to reach before nightfall. There, they knew they would be able to sleep with a roof over their heads, and, in Jocar's case, have a woman to warm the blankets. Locke recalled from the last

1 - The Karpoans

time they'd come this way that Jocar knew a woman named Angalika who lived there. Locke had been traveling with Jocar for a little over two years, selling implements of steel to the mountain villagers, who, for the most part, were still using iron tools and weapons. On the packhorses, the two traders had knives, swords, and arrow points, as well as plowshares, chisels and ax heads. The mountain people had little in the way of gold to exchange for their wares, but were always willing to barter for the valuable steel, which they were unable to obtain by any other means. And Jocar was inclined to accept most anything they offered him that he could in time haul out of the mountains and sell elsewhere.

Getting through the pass was still no assurance of safety. Encounters with bandits were one of the constant risks that traders in the hills continually faced. At least in the open valley, where visibility was good in all directions, there would be little danger of surprise. Most Killarasseans regarded the Karpoans as a desolate place. But Locke, who had grown up exploring the rugged terrain, with its hidden valleys and occasional grassy meadows, its cold streams and spectacular views, adapted easily to the seasonal changes and always enjoyed the wonder of discovering new vistas. Although the sun shone infrequently, when it did, the light it cast on the hillsides revealed an ever-changing palette of subtle colors.

It was late summer, and the valley was still green with the short, resilient grasses that provided a welcome cushion for the horses' feet. Negotiating the rocky mountain paths was difficult, and the toll on their legs was extreme. Locke's mount, which he had named Arawae, after the large raptor of the highlands, was sure-footed and had a calm demeanor. She also had astonishing speed on the flats, which had enabled Locke to outrun bands of raiders twice in the last month. Locke had raised her from a foal and was training her as a yearling when his father died. He loved that mare as much as anything that lived, but, consequently, his thoughts of her training would always be tinged with sadness.

Wind swept through the valley as it always did, but in the daylight hours it wasn't cold. However, it would be different in a few months, Locke thought, when the iron-gray clouds of winter would bring snow almost every day. It was late afternoon when they approached the village nestled into the hills. There were cook fires visible and the plumes of wood smoke drifted toward the two tired travelers. Log and mud huts with thatch roofs were scattered randomly up the slope, their backs built into the hillside to block the biting northern winds of the winter months.

"Where are we staying tonight?" asked the boy, innocently.

"Angalika's door is always open to us, Locke."

"And her bed?"

The comment didn't get a reaction from Jocar, who simply pretended not to hear.

The two traders' arrival garnered little attention from the women, old men, and children that Locke saw as they rode on the dry path that wound through the village. Most of the groups of hunters were still out on the slopes of the Karpoans, and those that weren't hunting were probably patrolling the surrounding ridges, looking for raiders. Locke and Jocar knew though that they had been under scrutiny for many miles before they'd arrived in the village. Furthermore, even when all the young men were back in the village for the night, they would still make up only a small percentage of the village population. The raiders recruited heavily, and the intense fighting between bands ensured that most men would never grow old. In addition, this village, nameless like nearly all the others in the remote north, had no stockade fence. Building a fence would be regarded as a hostile act and would have been, in any case, pointless. Before a fence could be completed, it

1 - The Karpoans

would be burned to the ground along with all the houses. The tenuous relationship between the raiders and the villages was always one based on mutual benefit, unbalanced as it might seem.

Jocar stopped in front of a house familiar to Locke where two young girls were playing outside. They were dressed in tattered, grimy clothes, and their feet, a full shade darker with dirt than their legs, were bare. They stopped what they were doing to stare at the visitors, and then, the older of the two wiggled her hand shyly and said, "Did you bring me anything, Jocar?"

Jocar got down off his horse and said in his best mysterious voice, "Well, let's see what might be hidden in the secret saddlebag."

He produced two small, carved wooden animals and presented them to the wide-eyed children. Just then, a woman appeared in the doorway of the house. She was plain, but not unpleasant looking, with long hair and pale skin, shiny with perspiration. Her clothes were drab and worn, and their loose fit gave a shapeless appearance to her small body. Angalika smiled a little at the man kneeling beside her two daughters, and the two girls quickly scurried off with their prizes. Jocar walked up to her and spoke a few words that Locke could not hear, and then motioned for his friend to put the horses in the small barn down the hill from the house.

Once he'd gotten to the barn with the animals, Locke removed the large packs from the ponies and unsaddled the riding horses. He wiped them down with handfuls of straw and gave each of them water. He had to make two trips to the small stream, which made its way down the hillside toward the valley below. At this time of year, it was little more than a trickle, and so it was with a good bit of effort that Locke managed to fill two buckets each trip. When he was satisfied that the animals' needs had been tended to, he left the animals contentedly munching on hay, and well deserving of a night's rest.

The Winds of Wharhalen

By the time Locke left the barn, the sun had dipped below the tops of the hills, leaving a faint coral glow in its wake. The mountain air cooled rapidly and the boy took one last look at the broad, hill-encased valley before him. The girls had preceded him into the house and were continuing whatever fanciful game they had been playing outside. Inside the house, Jocar was sitting on a bench by the heavy, rough-hewn table, and Angalika was filling bowls from the large iron pot that hung over the fire. The stew was a vast improvement over the fare that had sustained the two travelers over the many days on the trail. Offering equal gratification to the weary traders was having a roof over their heads and a warm fire within.

After the meal, and once the girls had finally settled down for the night, Locke lay on soft hides on the floor, lingering on the ragged border between wakefulness and sleep. Later that night, coming from the other side of the one-room house, the boy could clearly discern the softly restrained sounds of passion coming from the sleeping area of Jocar and Angalika.

CHAPTER TWO

Engrid

The rider barely noticed the tree branch that flicked her cheek as she raced along the narrow path through the woods. Her focus was on the massive fallen trunk that lay ahead and barred her way. She urged the huge gray stallion on, and he responded eagerly with a powerful ground-devouring stride. The girl's gloved hands, firm in their control, moved in perfect rhythm with each surge of the steed's magnificent head. As the wind swept across her face it whipped her long blonde hair like a battle flag. There was no fear in horse or rider, only the exhilaration of speed and the confidence that comes with being young and invincible. The barrier loomed ever larger, and the cadence of hooves on the path quickened in the girl's ears. As the horse gathered strength in his powerful muscles for the effort it would take to clear the obstacle, the rider leaned slightly forward to remove her weight from the animal's back. Her sensitive hands allowed her mount's head its freedom at the precise moment of take-off and for an instant, the hooves were silent as the tandem was airborne over the jump. When they hit the path on the other side, they galloped away under the canopy of trees that isolated horse and rider from the rest of the world.

The Winds of Wharhalen

As Engrid trotted her horse back to the stables, she sighed deeply as another morning ride came to an end. An attendant hurried out to meet her, but she waved him off as she dismounted. She was not anxious to resume her duties as Queen of the Empire right away, preferring instead to prolong her time at the stables grooming her own horse. Her rides in the woods allowed Engrid a temporary escape from the royal responsibilities that threatened to smother her.

Engrid Warrener was only twenty-three-years old, blonde, willowy and fair. She had grown up in faraway Tairellia where her father, Willander, lived in exile from Killarassee. He had been taken to Tairellia as a young boy by Menaslas, his guardian, after the death of King Jonas, Engrid's grandfather. There had been a long and bloody war in Killarassee, with a powerful warlord, Zironon, eventually overthrowing the king. When he grew older, Willander married a Tairellian girl, Felixia, and resigned himself to spending the rest of his life in his adopted land. When Engrid was born, she was raised as a warrior, as were all Tairellian children. By the time she reached her teens, Engrid was not only an expert horsewoman and archer but her skill with a sword rivaled even that of her best male counterparts.

However, Engrid's education was not limited exclusively to fighting skills. She was also schooled in history, mathematics, writing, and military tactics. Her education in Killarassean history fell to old Menaslas, and that was the subject that interested her most. Her thirst for more information about her father's native country soon became an obsession, centering for the most part on the rebellion that had claimed the life of her grandfather. Over time, Zironon had proven to be a durable tyrant, spreading his poisonous influence over the entire Empire of the Old Kings. By the time Engrid was eighteen, she had decided that it was her destiny to go to Killarassee and help bring down Zironon and restore the monarchy. A resistance movement had formed in Killarassee, and she secretly helped supply the rebels from Tairellia. Nearly four years later, the pent-up fury of the people had consolidated behind the leadership of a former bandit leader named Kaine, and the warlord's government was ultimately toppled.

Kaine, realizing his shortcomings as a politician, and recognizing the value of a charismatic Queen, allowed Engrid to assume the throne. However, he also knew that true power would always rest in the hands of the strong, and, to that end, he agreed to remain as commander of the army. The new regime was besieged by problems almost from the outset. Dangerous foes of the new Queen worked to undermine her power while simultaneously bartering for their own personal gain. Meanwhile, ethnic groups from the far reaches of the Empire staged uprisings against local Regents while rogue commanders maneuvered to gain influence with armies that hadn't been paid for many months.

In addition to Kaine, there were only two other men that Engrid fully trusted. Cecel, the huge Gruenlander, was an able leader and was honest and forthright. His fighting skills were legendary, and he was unfailingly loyal. However, for all those qualities so highly valued by the young Queen, Cecel had no political aptitude. The subtle underlying motives of power-brokering completely bypassed the workings of his honest and uncomplicated intellect.

The Queen's other Officer-at-Arms, Joal, was more astute. The native Killarassean had been a thief nearly all of his thirty-one years. A small and wiry man, he had now, seamlessly, adapted his crafty and devious mind to political intrigue. His advice on the subtle shifts in power, and concealed motives in and around Attalia was invaluable. It seemed like Joal knew everyone. As such, he had access to a steady flow of information from confidants in places Engrid, in her idealistic naiveté, didn't even know about.

One immediate concern following the successful rebellion that had brought Engrid to the throne was the ability of the Royal Army to respond to the numerous threats with which the Queen was now faced.

The Winds of Wharhalen

It contained a core of professional soldiers, but many of those that had fought in the rebellion were simple farmers and tradesmen who'd never intended to continue to be warriors once the tyranny of Zironon had been extinguished. Eventually, Kaine convinced Engrid that she needed to use some of the treasury that had been amassed during the warlord's reign to raise a larger standing army to ensure the security of the new regime.

Several months later, that newly-formed army was needed in the south as a local warlord named Vartan moved on the city of Ritola and briefly laid siege to the castle there. The small force that defended it might have been able to hold out longer had Vartan not been able to bribe someone to open the gate from the inside. The citadel fell quickly and immediately upon taking control the warlord had the Queen's Regent hanged. Engrid, with the counsel of Kaine, decided to send Cecel to lead a crusade that would travel from Attalia to Ritola to attempt to persuade Vartan to relinquish the city and control of his army. Vartan proved to be a stubborn adversary, though, and dug in for a long siege instead. Unfortunately, Cecel, never one to command his troops from the rear, was seriously wounded in one of the initial attacks on the walled city, and the Royal Army soon thereafter retreated in ignominy and disarray. This was a serious embarrassment to the Queen, and so it was decided that the only alternative left to avoid losing control of the south was to have Kaine lead an army of additional troops to secure Ritola.

However, the decision to have Kaine leave Attalia was not an easy one to make. Having Kaine at her side served to deter many of the Queen's enemies from thoughts of insurrection and bolstered the credibility of her fledgling regime. But to appear to cower in Attalia and not respond to the threat that Vartan now posed would be viewed as a sign of weakness. Thus, Kaine rode out of the city at the head of a full legion to assume command of the southern army.

CHAPTER THREE

Raiders

Locke and Jocar set up their wares in the center of the village, and a few men wandered over to inspect the much-coveted steel implements. There were a small number of trades, mostly to villagers who had planned to obtain a particular item ahead of time and had had the foresight to bring the appropriate amount of goods to trade. By late morning, the customer supply had dried up though, and Jocar decided it was time to move on. There was no point in staying any longer there when it was going to take days to reach the next place where they might have an opportunity to make trades.

And so, after loading up the packhorses, they rode out of the village without bothering to return to Angalika's house. Locke assumed that Jocar and the woman had said their good-byes earlier, and, in any case, they would be back again before the winter snows blocked the passes. As they rode, he casually said to his friend, "Are either of those two girls yours?"

Jocar shook his head. "They were both born before I met their mother. The father was forced to leave them and ride with one of the raider bands. He never came back."

The Winds of Wharhalen

"Have you ever thought about staying here with her permanently?"

Again the other man shook his head. "Look at this place. There's no getting ahead here. It's even worse in the winter. Eventually, I'd end up like the girls' father. Angalika is a good woman, but there aren't enough men to go around."

The boy glanced back at the lonely cluster of houses on the hillside and thought about the village where he'd grown up. Locke's parents lived in a place similar to the one the two traders had just left behind them. His father had a forge and spent the better part of each day firing iron and hammering out implements for his own use and to trade to his neighbors. He also raised some crops and had a few animals, mostly goats. There were horses, too, and Locke had learned much about them from his father. The rest of what he knew about horses he learned from long days spent on the hillsides and meadows observing the way the animals behaved when they weren't around people.

Locke was one of three children but had been the only one to survive. His sister died of a fever in infancy; his little brother drowned in a flash flood at six. When his mother first fell ill, Locke was just beginning to learn the blacksmith trade. It happened shortly after she'd returned from a neighboring village. She had gone there to help care for her two nieces while her sister was recovering from an illness. During her sickness, Rafe, Locke's father, sent his son to stay with some people who lived outside the village while he stayed home to care for his wife. Four days later, Locke's mother was dead and was buried shortly thereafter on a hillside overlooking the river.

One week after his wife's death, Rafe came down with the fever. Anticipating that his son would soon be alone, he asked Jocar, who had long been a friend of his, to take the boy as an apprentice. Jocar was in need of help, as his previous partner had died when his

3 - Raiders

horse stumbled on a steep mountain trail, and both horse and rider had plunged to the bottom of a deep ravine. Thus, Jocar agreed to his friend's request and stayed in the village long enough to help Locke bury Rafe beside his wife.

Death was a frequent visitor in the harsh Karpoans, but losing both parents within a period of two weeks was a truly crushing blow to Locke. Subsequently, he retreated deep within himself for many months and spoke hardly at all. This was not troublesome for Jocar though, who was himself a man of very few words. And the long rides between settlements in the mountains afforded Locke the time to sort through things in his mind. The companionship of Jocar eventually grew to be of some comfort, and the two soon became friends. At the same time, Locke found his mentor to be a good man who never cheated those with whom he traded. He knew, too, that Jocar always made sure that Angalika and her daughters always had enough gold or trade goods to get along, although he did this quietly.

It was a good day to travel. The wind was behind them and intermittent slashes of blue broke up the iron-gray sky. Their horses were rested, and they had restocked their food supplies. And so the valley was quickly crossed, and the two traders soon were starting up into the hills that surrounded it. As they climbed, Locke again looked back at the vibrant green of the valley floor, framed by the horseshoe-shaped rim. This was a familiar landscape to him, and so it brought him some comfort. His parents were buried in a similar place, their graves overlooking a river that cut a verdant swath through the dry hills.

Suddenly, his eye caught some movement behind them and to the right. He shouted to Jocar, who was in front of him. Together, they quickly assessed the situation. It was unmistakably a band of raiders, still nearly a mile away, but moving rapidly in their direction. "Let's go. Once we get through the pass, we might be able to elude them by hiding among the rocks." Jocar urged his horse up the slope, pulling the balky pack pony along behind. With the treacherous footing and the steep incline the pace was excruciatingly slow. Several times Jocar's horses lost their footing and dislodged stones that would cascade down the path toward Locke's mount. Finally, they reached the narrow pass where they knew they would be most vulnerable. With its high walls, there was no way to go but forward, but, at least, the floor was relatively level and firm.

Locke and Jocar negotiated the pass without incident but when they emerged at the other end they had no idea how close their pursuers were. And, they still had to climb the scrub-covered hills overlooking the pass before they would be on the plateau. There, they could make better headway and perhaps even find a place to hide. Just then, the first of the bandits emerged from the pass. Jocar had arrived with his pack pony at the crest, but Locke was still struggling to get his up the hill. His only chance to escape now was to turn the pony loose and hope that Arawae could outrun any that persisted in the chase. The mare scrambled quickly up the remainder of the slope and, urged into a gallop by his rider, soon passed the other two animals. "Turn the pony loose!" shouted Locke.

The boy continued to flee, and the next time he glanced over his shoulder, he saw that Jocar had finally let go of the lead rope on the pack pony, but was only about twenty-five yards ahead of the raiders. Locke didn't see it happen, but when he looked back again, Jocar and his mount were on the ground, and the horde was all around them. When he stopped and turned Arawae around, part of the band started to ride toward him. Fear instantly gripped him and, for a moment, he stood frozen on the spot. Then, with the assassins only seconds from overrunning him, he wheeled Arawae around and fled.

The rocky, boulder-strewn plateau was dangerous even at a walk. At a gallop, it was suicidal. Still, fear drove the boy on. At one point, he could hear the hoofbeats of his pursuers right behind him.

3 - Raiders

This sound alone would have been enough to cause Arawae to speed up without his rider's urging. But urge her on Locke did anyway, and soon he could only hear one set of hoofbeats. Eventually, the mare began to tire. Nearing the point of complete exhaustion, her pace slowed to a walk, and then she stopped altogether. Locke knew that she had no more to give and to continue to drive her on would kill her. The boy didn't bother to look back though, for he knew there was no one behind them when he got down off his horse and fell to the ground. He struggled to choke back the sobs that wanted to come pouring out. Part of him wanted to cry tears of relief that he had escaped death that day. But what of the tears that he felt should be shed for Jocar, his only friend? As the sun was setting behind the dark hills, the sound of Arawae's rapid breathing was all that interrupted the lonely silence.

The next morning, as soon as the dim light of the cloudy dawn would allow, Locke retraced the steps of the chase. Several times he strayed in the wrong direction, his path the day before having had no definite course. Finally gaining his bearings, he eventually found the trail that he and Jocar had taken. It wasn't long after that that he saw the scavengers. His stomach seemed to collapse within him, and he spurred Arawae forward at a gallop. The large black carrion-eaters scattered, and allowed Locke to see what he'd feared—Jocar's body lying on the rocks, disfigured by the scavenging flock. Nearby, the head, tail, legs and entrails of his friend's horse were also left as a grotesque reminder of the previous day's tragedy. Locke thought to himself that Jocar's mount must have been injured when it fell, since it was unlikely that the bandits would have otherwise slaughtered a perfectly sound horse for food.

Locke began the grim task of trying to bury Jocar's body in the rocky ground. He had no shovel, just the knife from his pack and a large flat rock. By early afternoon the unpleasant job was finished, and the boy got back on his horse and started to ride south. He knew he

The Winds of Wharhalen

should go back and tell Angalika what had happened, but a gnawing fear of the bandits wouldn't let him ride toward the valley. He wanted to put as much distance between himself and the Karpoans as possible. Brutality and death had snuffed out the last remnants of light from a region that now seemed to Locke as desolate as so many others saw it.

The wind, sweeping down across Wharhalen from the North Sea, which had seemed so warm two days ago, now had a chill to it. The weather was changing. The very air seemed to be pushing him out of the Karpoans and toward the lowlands of Killarassee.

CHAPTER FOUR

Kaine

The dusty ribbon of road stretched out toward the southern horizon. Another long day of travel lay ahead for Kaine and the Queen's legion as they moved closer to Ritola. Their progress was painfully slow in the eyes of the commander, who was more accustomed to swift, mounted strikes rather than the deliberate crawl of an expeditionary force comprised of infantry and archers. However, he realized it would do no good to move the mounted forces on ahead, for, alone, they could do little in the type of battle that awaited them. Also, dividing his army would subsequently leave the slow-moving foot soldiers vulnerable to attack. And so, the massive force, commissioned with the task of expelling the warlord Vartan from Ritola, plodded on.

The long days in the saddle had given Kaine plenty of time for thought. Some of these thoughts were of the future that he hoped to spend with his wife of a year and a half, Myleia. So far, their love had survived a separation of nearly five years when the treachery of her father had forced them apart. Certainly it would be able to endure this

The Winds of Wharhalen

hopefully brief campaign deemed necessary for the unity of the Empire.

If only Kaine's wandering mind could stay focused in the future. Instead, it kept getting tugged back into the whirlpool of the past, a place that held little joy. Eventually, his reflections brought forth images of his youth spent in Galen, a small village near Attalia. There he grew up without brothers or sisters, raised by his mother alone. He was told that his father had been killed before he was born, having died a hero's death. He'd accepted this with some measure of pride and did his best to help his mother, whose life in the poor village was difficult.

Kaine had always been a resourceful youth, using his shrewd mind to get the most from meager resources. While unable to acquire any real wealth, his abilities at bartering ensured that neither he nor his mother would ever starve. When he was older, he began to range farther and farther from home in his trading ventures. Soon he had ties that extended well beyond the borders of Killarassee. And it was on one of his journeys to Khotau, far to the east, that Kaine met Myleia. He was in his mid-twenties at the time, handsome and confident with dark, curly hair and a ready smile. The lands far to the east of Killarassee were advanced and prosperous when compared to those in the west and south where progress was mired in a feudal system controlled by land-holding nobles. From ports in Khotau and Bakkah, ships were able to transport goods along the coast of the North Sea, and even as far as Toulussia and Shardansk. But the combination of the Karpoan mountain range and the savage Wharhalen territory made overland travel and trade difficult between east and west, as well as having created separate cultures. And yet there were some adventurous travelers who'd been willing to bridge the gap, and Kaine was one of them.

4 - Kaine

He was having dinner at the home of a merchant named Moussaud one night and was seated across the table from the host's daughter, a beautiful young woman still in her teens. She had long black hair with the luster of onyx, and brown, almond-shaped eyes. Throughout dinner, she never spoke, but their eyes met several times, and Kaine was encouraged when the faintest of smiles crossed her delicate lips. Although there were many other people at Moussaud's house that night, Kaine's eyes could only see the girl whose name he soon learned was Myleia. After dinner, he found her alone on the balcony looking out over the city of Kuensah where a thousand lanterns in the windows of houses kept the dark at bay. There, as they talked, time melted away, and far too soon, the guests began leaving. By then, though, the enchantment was complete, and as he walked back to where he was staying that night, through the streets of the exotic city, so far from home and intoxicated by the lingering scent of her perfume, Kaine could think of nothing else but the lovely girl he had just met.

In the ensuing days, Kaine returned often to the house to see Myleia, but he was careful to do this only when her father was gone. When he could visit, they would walk in the colorful and fragrant gardens surrounding Moussaud's home, which had previously seen many generations of royalty but now was owned by a man who made his fortune selling cloth. Sometimes they would venture out into the city, where they would stroll among the vendors in the marketplace. There, Kaine would buy small gifts for the girl, which would magnify many times over for her in value because of the special moments that they represented. Often they would buy bread and cheese and fresh fruit, and then go out of the city and sit on a hillside for hours overlooking a meadow and talk, enjoying the warm afternoon sun. They were always careful to return to the house before Moussaud did, but, in spite of their discretion, the cloth merchant was aware of their every movement, for he had eyes and ears throughout the city. He

The Winds of Wharhalen

considered their friendship a harmless diversion for his daughter, but, on the day when Kaine came to ask permission to marry her, Moussaud's expression immediately grew dark. "You have neither wealth nor position. Myleia will marry a prince or a king, and such a marriage will thereby double my fortune. God has bestowed great beauty on my daughter, and beauty commands a high price. As a common trader, you cannot afford her. That is just the way life is."

 Disappointed but not surprised at this harsh appraisal of the situation, Kaine decided to discuss with Myleia the possibility of leaving her father's home in secrecy and going with him to Killarassee. Of course, they both knew this would be a drastic and dangerous course but, as is usually the case with young lovers, passion totally obscured reason. However, when Kaine tried to visit Myleia the next day, he was turned away by a guard at the front entrance, and told that he was no longer welcome at the house. His disappointment of the previous day quickly turned to anger and then despondency as he confronted the prospect of never seeing the girl again. That evening, as he sat in his room considering his options, his thoughts were interrupted by a knock at the door. It was Nazre, a servant girl from Moussaud's house. Appearing nervous, she handed him a note, and without speaking, hurried away. Kaine's heart beat faster as he realized that the note was from Myleia and that she had arranged for a secret rendezvous for later that night.

 The hours seemed to pass ever so slowly for Kaine as he waited to leave for the meeting place. Over and over, he calculated the time it would take him to reach the house, as he didn't want to risk arousing suspicion by arriving early and loitering in the area too long. When he did leave, he had to restrain himself from running on the nearly-deserted streets as he made his way through the city. At the back of Moussaud's gardens there was a hidden gate obscured from view by a large hedge which grew untended along the back of the property.

4 - Kaine

When Myleia was late, he feared that her plans had been discovered. The minutes seemed to pass like hours, and soon the slightest sound would cause his hand to tighten around the hilt of his dagger. Finally, a voice came from inside the garden walls, saying his name. Upon his reply, the gate opened, and he slipped inside.

To Kaine, Myleia had never before looked so beautiful, standing there in the moonlit garden, dark hair falling across her shoulders and wearing a long robe covering her nightclothes. For a while, he had feared he might never see her again. She was trembling as he took her lithe young body in his arms and held her in a tight embrace.

"I argued with my father," she said after a time. "He said we couldn't see each other any more."

"Then we must go away together, to a country where your father has no influence."

"That is what I hoped you would say, but you must realize there is great risk involved."

"No risk greater than that of possibly losing you."

This declaration instantly brought tears of happiness from the girl, and as each paused on a lovely cheek, Kaine gently kissed them away.

They resolved to meet at the gate the following night. From there they would leave on foot and go to a spot just outside the city where Kaine would arrange for horses to be waiting. By horseback, they would then cross the border into Bakkah where Myleia would be less likely to be recognized. From there they could board a ship in Harock, sail to Velesko, then make their way south to Killarassee. Kaine spent most of the next day making arrangements and buying a few of the things that they would need for their journey. He had friends in

The Winds of Wharhalen

Kuensah, a city steeped in greed, and as long as a person could pay, few questions were asked.

While she and Nazre were making secret preparations for her departure, Myleia tried to keep up the appearance of a normal day. Nazre was the only one in the house that Myleia could trust; the two young women had grown up together and subsequently formed a close bond of friendship. When it finally came time to go down to the garden, Nazre accompanied her mistress. The plan was nearly spoiled, however, when a guard heard them leave the house and enter the garden; but when he came to investigate, Nazre managed to convince him that she was alone. While the servant girl diverted the guard's attention, Myleia hid in the bushes until all had settled down again. When she eventually arrived at the gate, Kaine was already there waiting. A quick embrace, a tender kiss, and the two young lovers slipped away into the darkness.

Using back streets and paths to avoid attracting attention, they wove their way to the river. Following its banks was a horse path that led south toward the market street bridge. They were able to move quickly along the path, somehow managing to avoid the clusters of unsavory characters that normally gravitated to this old part of town. At one point, however, the couple's progress was temporarily delayed by two brash individuals who happened to catch sight of the young Myleia. Having no time for diplomacy, Kaine quickly grabbed the bolder of the two and sent him plunging over the side of the levy and into the river. However, the second man, seemingly unconcerned about the plight of his friend, tried to take advantage of the distraction and seize the girl. Kaine recovered quickly and, dagger in hand, stepped between the attacker and Myleia, who had deftly managed to avoid capture. In the meantime, Kaine's burly opponent had also produced a blade but, to his misfortune, was too slow for the agile young Killarassean and was subsequently left on the path, bleeding from a fatal wound.

4 - Kaine

When Kaine and Myleia reached the bridge, they hurriedly crossed it and left the city behind them. In less than an hour they came to the first crossroad where, hidden in the trees, were the horses that Kaine had arranged for. From there, they rode to the northwest toward Bakkah, fleeing the light that had begun to show on the horizon behind them. It was necessary to rest the horses every hour, for Kaine knew that having one of them break down would surely spell the end of their scheme. At the same time, they both realized that the girl's absence would soon be noticed, bringing about an extensive search and the subsequent closing off of all possible avenues of escape.

The excitement of freedom had taken hold on Myleia, and Kaine saw an elevation of spirit in her that had never previously been revealed in Moussaud's house. She was radiant. Her cheeks were flushed with color, her long black hair flowed untamed in the wind, and her smile was irrepressible. As lovely as the caged bird might have been, it was far more beautiful in flight.

They crossed over into Bakkah sometime during the morning. It was impossible to tell exactly when they crossed, for there was no delineated border visible, or marked change in terrain. Kaine had brought some bread, cheese, and fruit, as well as water, and as the sun neared its apex, they stopped to eat. If either feared capture, they didn't speak of it as their vision was focused on dreams of a life together. After a while, refreshed by their respite, they continued on, reaching the port city of Harock by mid-afternoon.

Kaine made arrangements for them to board a merchant vessel for their passage to Velesko, but it wasn't scheduled to sail until the tide turned several hours later. Neither wanted to spend time aboard the ship at anchor when they knew they would, by necessity, be later confined to it for many days during the voyage. Kaine also felt that, since boat docks would be the first place that a search would begin once Moussaud realized that Myleia had run away, they should wait

The Winds of Wharhalen

until the last minute to board. And so, they ventured off, away from the dock area where they would be conspicuous and found a sandy cove tucked neatly into the rocky coastline far away from town. There they spent the balance of the afternoon, savoring their time alone together. For all their concern, they could have been the only two people on earth. Reluctantly, they left the cove to return to the ship by the appointed time. The hours spent on the secluded beach had provided a quiet and welcome interlude amidst the tumultuous journey of the escape. But now they knew they must re-enter the turbulent waters of that exodus. They arrived back at the docks in plenty of time for their departure from Harock, and Kaine was careful to observe the ship at a distance, looking for signs of a search. When all seemed as they had left it, Kaine and the girl continued across the wharf, and headed quickly up the narrow wooden planks to the deck of the vessel. However, when they reached the top, they found the ship's captain with a man whom Kaine immediately recognized as one of Moussaud's guards. Kaine quickly grabbed Myleia's arm and spun her around, but just as they started back down the ramp, they came face to face with three more armed men waiting at the bottom. Trapped, they had no choice but to surrender and be returned to Khotau to Myleia's father.

Moussaud knew he could have had Kaine killed, but didn't wish to make relations with his daughter even more difficult than they already were. So, Kaine was convicted of killing a citizen of Khotau (the man on the riverbank during their escape) and sentenced to imprisonment on the island of Elkabar, two miles offshore. The proceedings could not even have been described as a formal trial. Kaine was simply told by Moussaud what crime he had committed, what his punishment would be, and then whisked off in chains by two guards who had instructions to kill him instantly if he tried to escape. Figuring that killing him during an escape attempt was what his captors wanted, Kaine cooperated completely during the transfer to the prison on Elkabar. There he languished for months in a dirty, windowless cell

4 - Kaine

where the passage of time eventually became blurred in the workings of his mind.

Kaine would have thought that he had been forgotten completely if it were not for the jailer that brought him food and water once daily. But even then he had no contact with the man, for the meal was simply shoved through a slot at the bottom of the door. On the first day, he was instructed that if he wanted to be fed the following day he needed to return the tray back through the slot when he was finished. Further efforts to communicate with the man proved futile, and, eventually, he quit trying.

At several weeks' intervals (Kaine lost track of how many exactly), he would be taken from his cell by two guards and placed in another cell at the end of the corridor. Each time this happened, the light, although not strong, stung his eyes. The holding cell had a window in the door, and another, high on an outside wall. Then, when he was returned to his cell, the straw on the floor was new, and the stench that had accumulated from his own wastes had been reduced. Kaine deduced from the work detail that he passed in the corridor during one of these exchanges that the cleaning of the cells was done by other prisoners, perhaps those that had somehow earned the privilege of getting out of their own cells for a time.

The second time Kaine was placed in the holding cell he noticed that under the straw on the floor near the outside wall was a heavy wooden panel that lay flush with the stone. He also thought he could hear the sound of water rushing somewhere beneath the floor. Kaine surmised that the opening below the panel was used for discarding waste. Also, during this second transfer, he began counting in his mind the time that elapsed from when he was placed in the holding cell to the moment when the guards came to retrieve him. During the third transfer, he found that the duration he was kept in the holding cell was nearly the same as the previous one. While he was

The Winds of Wharhalen

counting, he would also scour the stone walls of the holding cell for fragments of rock that might be useful to him. There weren't many, but one day he did find one fairly substantial piece that he quickly hid in his clothes just as the guards were returning.

Time passed even more slowly for Kaine in the weeks that followed as he anticipated the next time he would be transferred to the holding cell. Thoughts of Myleia were all he had to sustain him through the endless days and nights that now melted together in lonely darkness. When the next transfer occurred, he could feel his heartbeat quicken as the door to his cell opened and the guards summoned him. However, when he reached the door and began to turn right to go toward the familiar outside cell, he was roughly shoved in the opposite direction and taken to a dark, windowless room at the other end of the corridor. It was then that he noticed that a different set of guards than the ones who'd gone with him on the previous transfers now accompanied him. Despair wracked his mind as he crumpled to the floor in the damp, dark chamber in which he'd been placed. All the pent-up energy that he had hoped he could use in an escape attempt suddenly flowed out of a body that now felt limp, weak, and emaciated from his long captivity. The frustration became nearly unbearable for Kaine and he suppressed a sob as it rose from his chest and lodged in his throat.

Many more months passed and each subsequent transfer took Kaine to the inside cell where his efforts to find a means of escape proved futile. One day when Kaine was roused from sleep by guards that opened his cell door, in his stupor, he nearly forgot to pick up the makeshift tool that he had fashioned out of the fragment of stone taken from the original holding cell. Grinding it against the rough surface of the walls had, over time, produced a short, wedge-shaped pry bar of sorts. Therefore, when he shoved it into his clothes, he did so almost carelessly, for hopes of ever again having an opportunity to escape had long since left him. The guards were talking loudly between them and failed to notice his actions. It was then that Kaine realized that these were not the same guards that had been executing the recent cell transfers, nor were they even the original ones. Hope suddenly rekindled in his now-alert mind, and as he reached the door, his excitement rose when the guard turned him to the right! Still busy talking between them, the guards escorted Kaine to the outside room of many months ago.

As soon as the holding cell door closed behind him, Kaine began his count. He had decided that any risk was worth taking to avoid spending the rest of his miserable existence in the prison. If he died in the shaft under the cell, then that would be the end of it. And so he began to work feverishly with his stone tool, struggling to lift the heavy wooden panel far enough so as to get his hands under the edge. Again and again he failed, and he swore as his hands began to bleed from the effort. With his time running out, the panel suddenly gave way ever so slightly, and he slipped his fingers under the edge.

With the panel now separated from the floor, he was quickly able to get the fingers of his other hand under it as well. By now, he had lost track of his count but felt certain that the time had run out and the guards would be back at any second. With strength that he didn't know he still possessed, he managed to lift the panel and throw it back on its hinges with a thunderous crash. With his arms up to protect his face, Kaine allowed himself to fall, feet first into the rushing water in the drain far below. The last sound that he heard before he hit the water was the opening of the cell door.

The drain tunnel sloped sharply under the outside cell as it rushed toward its termination point somewhere beyond the prison walls. Carried along in the flow, Kaine braced himself for impact with objects as yet unknown. The sides of the pipe were rough, and at one point his shoulder and head slammed against the stone, leaving him momentarily dazed. There was no way to arrest his descent, however, and he continued to be carried along on the cold torrent. He didn't know if it was night or day, having long since lost track of such things, but when the pipe finally expelled him and he dropped into the first outdoor air he had felt in months, it was into darkness. It was also into the sea, and Kaine exulted that he had not landed on rocks.

The night quickly became his ally, since a search with boats would surely be mounted soon, and the blackness in the channel between the island and the mainland would make it difficult to find a lone swimmer. Even though he had a badly bruised left shoulder and a large bump on his head, he still swam powerfully. The cold water was invigorating, but he realized that if he stayed in it too long it would eventually kill him. He rested on his back when he had to, and from that position he could hear the voices of search parties from the prison in the distance. Once when he looked back he could see the light from lanterns over the water. When he finally dragged himself up on a rocky stretch of beach, he was totally exhausted and nearly numb from the cold water temperature. However, he knew that word of his escape would soon reach the town by boat, so he couldn't tarry long by the water, for that would be the first place that would be searched. Of course, no one knew for certain whether or not he'd survived the escape, and he doubted if the authorities would have much enthusiasm for a prolonged hunt. After all, it was really Moussaud's personal motives that sent him to prison in the first place.

Kaine decided that he would stay in hiding for a few days until the search was abandoned and then go to Moussaud's house to find Myleia. The wait was especially difficult now that the girl he loved was again so close at hand, but he'd become used to waiting. However, it was different this time; for this time he had the freedom to walk among the trees and smell the fresh air coming off the ocean. In addition, this time he had hope; not just the hope that had sustained him in his prison cell, but real hope that he would once again be able to hold Myleia in his arms.

4 - Kaine

Kaine decided to go to the house first, but keep a discreet distance away and watch for Myleia. Days went by and the surveillance proved fruitless. People came and went from the house every day, some familiar to Kaine and some not, but there was no sign of Myleia. By the fourth day, he had decided that the daughter of Moussaud was being held somewhere out of sight within the house and that he would need to break in to free her. He decided to put this rescue attempt in motion that same night and was about to abandon the day's watch when suddenly he observed the servant girl, Nazre, leave by a back door. He waited until the girl was clear of the grounds and followed her as she walked to the marketplace. Hiding in a space between two buildings, Kaine snatched the surprised young woman as she passed, lifting her off her feet and transporting her to a place where they could not be observed.

When he turned her to face him, Nazre was too frightened at first to even attempt to recognize her abductor. Holding her firmly by her shoulders, he said, "Nazre, do you not know me?"

Initially, the girl stared blankly, but then a glimmer of recognition crept into her features. "Kaine?" A gasp escaped her mouth as she tried to bring her hands up to her face. Her expression reminded Kaine of how ghastly his appearance must have looked to the girl after his months of captivity. His hair and beard were long and shaggy, and the lack of food and sun had made him pale and gaunt. His pleading eyes, however, soon caused the girl's initial look of revulsion to turn to one of pity.

"Where is Myleia? Is she all right?"

Nazre hesitated. Kaine pressed on. "What has happened?"

"She is gone," answered the girl reluctantly.

"Gone? Gone where?"

"Across the northern sea to marry a Toulussian prince."

"How did this happen?"

"Moussaud arranged it soon after you…"

"At great personal profit, I'm sure."

Nazre nodded. "Moussaud is now the richest trader in Khotau. He's been appointed Archann and now has a fleet of merchant vessels. He is extremely powerful."

Kaine released the girl from his grasp. Then with a faint wave of his hand he dismissed her. She hurried down the street toward the busy market but stopped and turned to look back at Kaine as if she wanted to say something. But her lips remained silent, although Kaine thought he saw a tear glistening on her cheek just as she again turned away and continued on.

Kaine left Khotau that same day, never to return. He was now a fugitive with a powerful enemy. He was without money, possessions or influence. In time, his body would recover from the ravages of his imprisonment; the damage done to his heart though would not heal quite so easily.

CHAPTER FIVE

The Secret

Weakened by his imprisonment, destitute, and now a fugitive, Kaine left Khotau defeated. He worked his way back to Killarassee many months later, only to find his mother gravely ill. So advanced was her condition that she could barely recognize her son nor fully comprehend the ravages of his awful imprisonment. Since the poor woman knew she was dying, she felt compelled to tell him the real story of his father. As a young girl she'd worked in the castle of Zironon in Attalia. At that time, she was engaged to marry a young farmer who lived near the village. One day when she was finishing up her work, Zironon assaulted her. She struggled with every fiber of her small body, but the warlord, intoxicated from an afternoon of drinking, beat her until she was forced to succumb to his foul advances. Following the attack, she was unable to hide the bruises, and when the young farmer saw her, he couldn't control his rage. In spite of her pleas, he went to the castle to avenge the wrong that had been done. The next time she saw him was when Zironon's guards hung his body from the castle gate as a warning to others that might have plans to assassinate the warlord.

The Winds of Wharhalen

All these things Kaine's mother confided to him from her deathbed. But the most painful revelation was still to come. She told him that until that horrible day in the castle, she had been a virgin. Kaine was born nine months later. There was no question that Zironon was his father. This terrible secret had tormented her for twenty-five years, and she felt that before going to her grave she should reveal the truth to her son.

After his mother's death, Kaine left Galen for good. However, thoughts of the terrible injustice that she had suffered at the hands of Zironon continued to torture his soul. He longed for revenge but felt powerless as how to exact it. He remembered how he had failed when he'd attempted to challenge the cloth merchant Moussaud and so how could he even consider succeeding against Zironon, who was infinitely more powerful? He wandered about aimlessly for months seeking answers to seemingly unanswerable questions. Why was evil so strong in the world? Why did it seem that those in powerful positions always preyed on the weak instead of helping to make their lives better? Do evil men have an advantage in gaining power, or do they become evil after they've attained power? In his growing cynicism he doubted that virtue could ever push back the darkness that so far had seemed to cast its sinister veil over everything in his life.

It was around this time that Kaine met Joal. It occurred in the sprawling, walled city of Attalia one night when Kaine was walking on a street near the outer wall. The city's rim was a lawless place but it suited Kaine's sour disposition and reckless mood. A commotion in a dark corridor between two buildings caught his attention and as he investigated, Kaine saw a man engaged in a desperate struggle to fight off four attackers. The beleaguered fighter was smaller than any of his assailants but had thus far managed with the tenacity of his counterattacks to keep his larger adversaries at bay. His only weapon was a barrel stave, but so far it had taken a bloody toll. Swinging

5 - The Secret

furiously and connecting again and again, he was carving an ever-widening circle around him. The little man's courage impressed Kaine, and, on an inexplicable impulse, he picked up a broken wheel spoke and joined the melee. Approaching from behind, he struck at the back of one attacker's knees, causing them to buckle. Startled, the other three men momentarily lost their focus on the lone fighter. Quickly, a second man was down, the barrel stave crashing into the side of his head. The odds now even at two on two, the remaining assailants quickly lost their nerve and slipped away into the shadows. Leaving the two injured men on the ground, Kaine and the gritty battler also vacated the scene.

Some distance from the location where the fight had taken place, the two new acquaintances slowed their pace to a walk, once confident that no pursuit was imminent.

"Why were those men so mad at you?" Kaine inquired.

"It was a dispute over possession."

"You stole something from them."

"I don't like that word. It sounds so…"

"Dishonest?"

"Yes, dishonest. I consider myself a procurer of previously claimed property."

"Well, you probably have a lot of enemies then. I think we'll part company now, before another group of them finds you."

"I have a lot of friends, too. I now count you among them. What is your name?"

"Kaine."

"I am Joal," the smaller man replied with a nod. "Perhaps we will see each other again."

"If so, I hope I am heavily armed."

The Winds of Wharhalen

Joal smiled, and then vanished into the dark.

Two days later, Joal spotted Kaine in one of the many nondescript taverns that lined the back streets in the south quarter of Attalia. He went over to where Kaine was sitting, pulled up a chair and started a conversation as if the two were long-time friends. Suddenly concerned for his personal welfare, Kaine began looking around with apprehension, figuring that trouble usually followed the little thief around like a hungry puppy. A few minutes later, Joal produced a small pouch and shoved it across the table. "What's this?" said Kaine, glancing quickly around to see if anyone had noticed the act.

"I was able to get a good price for the …'acquired' object; this is your share for helping me."

"I appreciate your integrity," said Kaine, fully aware of the irony of this statement, "but it isn't necessary. After all, I had nothing to do with the theft of the object."

"But, without your intervention, not only would there not have been an object to sell, I more than likely might not even be sitting here at this table, able to make this offer."

"Perhaps that is true," answered Kaine, shoving the pouch back. "However, I have no intention of getting involved with a petty thief and getting my hand chopped off."

"How do you know that my endeavors are petty?"

"I don't, but even if they were on a grand scale, I still wouldn't be interested."

"Are you quite sure you wouldn't…"

Kaine held his hand up in such a way that it stopped Joal in mid-sentence. The subject was not brought up again, but the two nevertheless continued to talk for another two hours, the conversation covering many topics, none of which Kaine could later recall. They met

5 - *The Secret*

many more times after that, always, at the insistence of Joal, at a different tavern. They eventually became friends, Joal providing a diversion from the pervasive loneliness that had been the major part of Kaine's daily existence since the loss of Myleia and his mother. The thief may have been as cynical as Kaine himself, but he was also clever, funny, and had the ability to keep the conversation going even when the introverted Kaine became silent.

One day Joal brought up the subject of stealing from Zironon.

"What did you say?" asked Kaine abruptly.

"Sorry, I wasn't suggesting that we…"

"Actually, Zironon is the only person that I *would* consider stealing from."

Joal's eyes suddenly brightened at this surprising revelation from his friend. "Zironon is the only person in Killarassee *worth* stealing from! He has already bled everyone else dry," he replied with a smile.

It was then that Kaine and Joal hatched the plot to steal, little by little, Zironon's ill-gotten wealth. To Joal, it was the ultimate caper, a challenge worthy of a master thief. To Kaine, it was the revenge that he needed to salve the discontent that he harbored against men in power, and especially against his father. His *father!* The very word had become a trigger for the rage that churned inside him. That the warlord's blood flowed in his veins made him feel unworthy of good things ever happening to him. However, little did the two conspirators know at the time that the plans they made that night would lead to events which would eventually spell the end of the warlord's reign.

The Winds of Wharhalen

CHAPTER SIX

Vartan

Kaine surveyed Vartan's defenses around Ritola. This was a different type of warfare than that with which the former rebel was accustomed. Leading light mobile units on hit-and-run raids, then disappearing while the enemy searches for you, was one thing. Planning an assault on a walled city was quite another. Ritola had grown up below an ancient castle built into the side of a mountain with three sides protected naturally by craggy peaks. The only approach to the city was across a wide, nearly flat valley floor that stretched about two miles out from the walls. Kaine concluded that his army wasn't large enough to be successful in overcoming his opponent's heavy fortifications, which included an outer curtain wall, and an inner castle wall that would have to be overcome once they breached the wall around the city. However, a long siege could tie them up for years. But if they attempted an assault on the city and failed, it would be a staggering defeat for the new Queen. Such a failure would then serve to embolden her enemies and plunge the Empire into greater chaos. Such an environment would give rise to more warlords that would vie with each other for power. In time, one might even become strong enough

The Winds of Wharhalen

to attempt to topple the monarchy again, as Zironon had done more than thirty years ago.

Therefore, Kaine decided to try negotiation first. If Vartan would swear his allegiance to the Queen and agree not to attempt to extend his power, Ritola could be shared. Indeed, Kaine realized that a diplomatic solution would surely strengthen the new government's position in the south, whereas a protracted war would only deplete the Queen's fledgling army. A precedent for this had previously been set when Engrid's grandfather, King Jonas, the most powerful ruler in the history of the Empire, managed to coexist with the warlords during his long reign.

Kaine called together his Officers-at-Arms. There were Drobek and Karolic, holdovers from Kaine's renegade days when they'd launched raids against Zironon from hideouts scattered all over Killarassee. Drobek was an able fighter who had smoothly made the transition from thief to leader. Karolic, on the other hand, wasn't quite as polished, and was still inclined to let his sword do his thinking. A third officer, Sauric, had been with the original rebel band of the future Queen. Captured during the battle at the Temple of the Old Kings, he had been sentenced to die by Zironon. That changed though when Kaine assassinated the old warlord and set in motion the events that would ultimately put Engrid on the throne. Sauric was a tough, resourceful leader, battle-hardened from years of resistance fighting.

Kaine, now in his thirties, had a much different look than he'd had in his trading days when he'd met Myleia. And the change went deeper than just the physical changes normally attributed to the passing of years. Still powerfully built and handsome in a rugged sort of way, now there was always about him a dark, brooding aspect to his countenance. Gone was the disarming smile, since replaced by a grim, impenetrable cynicism. Once he'd gathered his officers together, he told his assembled men that he planned to send his herald to set up a

6 - Vartan

meeting with Vartan. After a long silence that Kaine perceived as a sign of disapproval, Karolic said, "Vartan won't negotiate. He's a barbarian."

Drobek spoke up and added, "Even if he agrees to your terms, you won't be able to trust him."

Kaine then looked at the third officer. "Sauric?"

Sauric paused for a moment before answering. "I guess it wouldn't hurt to try. Your only other choices are to either let him have Ritola or lose an awful lot of men trying to get him out."

"Either way, I'd like to know who I'm fighting," replied Kaine. "Let's find out what he wants."

And so, Kaine sent his herald, a young man named Darian, to the gates of the city on horseback under a flag of truce. However, he never got to deliver his message. As Kaine and his Officers-at-Arms watched from the ramparts of their encampment, Darian was hit by an arrow shot from atop the wall. Before he fell from his saddle, he was struck again, and then again.

Kaine struggled to fight back the sickness that now rose in his stomach. He couldn't speak, but inwardly he cursed himself. Karolic and Drobek had been right. Only a fool would trust a barbarian. Furious with himself, he retired to his tent to suffer alone with his self-recriminations.

Kaine had made a terrible mistake, and the cost had been dear. He had tried to be a diplomat, a role that did not suit him. It was not a role that he would assume again. Instead, he would crush Vartan and all of his followers. There would be no terms or compromises. But before he could take Ritola, he knew he would have to recruit a larger army. He also knew that the coffers that Zironon had left behind were full from decades of squeezing the Empire dry and this wealth must now be used to strengthen the new regime. Kaine had brought a large amount of gold with him to offer bounties to entice men to enlist with

The Winds of Wharhalen

his army and support a long campaign. At the same time, he also knew it would take time to train the new enlistees who would now comprise this larger army. Eventually it would be able to dislodge Vartan from his city stronghold; but, in the meantime, the best that Kaine could do was to contain him.

Meanwhile, Vartan wasn't just entrenched in Ritola waiting complacently for Kaine's next move. To the east, near the border with Karkesso, Vartan's brother, Patrov, was amassing a huge army that would soon be on the move for Ritola. If he were allowed to reach the city, not only would their combined armies be nearly invincible, Vartan would then have supply lines that stretched all the way to the inland sea. With a constant flow of goods then readily available to the warlord, control of the south would be lost, and it would ensure that the Queen would have to contend with a strong rival to her power in the Empire. Cecel already knew of this new threat from the east and had warned Kaine about it. Therefore, Kaine realized he could not afford to let Vartan and Patrov unite. At the moment though, he lacked a large enough army to stage an all-out assault on Ritola; so he turned his attention to Patrov.

Kaine's scouts had placed the distance of Patrov's army at about a hundred and fifty miles and not yet on the move. His plan was to take approximately two hundred cavalry and use hit-and-run tactics to harass and delay Patrov, thereby giving Drobek more time to train the growing number of Royal Army recruits.

Kaine's detachment slipped away at night, two days after the failed attempt at negotiations. One by one, men and horses were swallowed up by the dark countryside as they filed out of camp. They continued at a walk until daybreak; by then they were fifteen miles from Ritola. After that, Kaine's horsemen devoured ground at a gallop, covering nearly five miles at a time between rest stops. In less than a week after leaving Ritola, they reached the location where Patrov's army

6 - Vartan

had been sighted. And to Kaine's good fortune, Patrov had chosen the place for his encampment poorly. Instead of creating a wide open buffer on his perimeter that would have made an approach difficult, his camp was surrounded by hills and forest on two sides with a stream on a third. Kaine decided to stage his attack from the nearest hill, then escape into the woods.

The first assault came at dusk while Patrov's unsuspecting soldiers were settling in for the night. Half of the horsemen that Kaine had brought with him were mounted archers. This was an unconventional tactic in much of the Empire, but during his travels Kaine had seen it used successfully in Bakkah. At Bakkah, the tribesmen there fought Zironon's men to a standoff for years by employing swift mobile units of bowmen riding horses. When he'd begun to build up the Queen's standing army, he'd also begun training a segment of his cavalry in this mode of fighting and this was to be their first test. On Kaine's signal, one hundred archers rode over the crest, raced down the slope, and sliced into the encampment like a knife. The effect was total surprise. Engulfed in chaos, some of Patrov's recruits failed to even get to their weapons before they were cut down. Within five minutes, the damage was done. With only a handful of casualties themselves, a hundred of Kaine's men had killed nearly their own number of enemy soldiers. The horsemen then rallied for a dash into the nearby woods. By the time Patrov could mount a counterattack, the raiders had vanished into the welcoming darkness.

With Patrov's camp on alert for further attacks, Kaine used the following day to move his cavalry to the north in order to stage their next assault from a different direction. Furthermore, expecting the pursuit to be better organized the next time, Kaine set a trap. The other half of Kaine's cavalry was comprised of armored knights who could fight with lances or swords. Attacking the north wing of Patrov's camp with deadly efficiency, they once again disengaged after about five minutes, as had the mounted archers, and then retreated for the safety of the woods. However, Patrov's cavalry was ready this time and followed close behind. But Kaine had previously positioned his archers around a clearing, and when the pursuers entered it, they were cut down in a barrage of arrows. A second torrent of shafts brought down many of those who didn't immediately flee, and then Kaine's knights, who had doubled back after crossing the clearing, fell upon the confused survivors with their swords. The victory for Kaine would have been a satisfying one had it not been for one tragic aspect: Karolic, leading the heavy cavalry into the midst of the enemy camp, during the battle, was dragged from his horse by several soldiers and killed.

Nevertheless, the raid was a humiliating defeat for Patrov. He angrily sent out his horsemen to search for his tormentors, but years of being chased by Zironon's men had made Kaine as elusive as a fox. Hit and hide was the tactic that the former thief knew best. Eventually, these types of raids had a demoralizing effect as Patrov's soldiers became fearful and apprehensive. Desertions soon started to deplete the ranks faster than recruits could be found to fill them. Since Patrov resented the idea of being pinned down in a vulnerable encampment, the large army he commanded, consisting mostly of infantry, began to move toward Ritola.

Although Kaine's maneuvers had been successful in harassing Patrov and weakening his ranks, he realized Patrov would still be able to join Vartan at Ritola in a matter of weeks. But Kaine nevertheless continued to shadow Patrov, striking every few days at his flanks while his army was on the move, and at the fringe of his camps when he stopped. Patrov elected to keep his army moving roughly parallel to the Sundsgard River not only in order to have a continuous source of water available, but also so that he wouldn't have to cross a wide, deep channel with his army. Consequently, when they made their camps, it was often on the banks of the river.

6 - Vartan

One day as rain moved into the area and fighting had come to a standstill, Kaine was observing Patrov's encampment from a hill which overlooked the river valley. The tents he saw spread before him covered a huge area in the flood plain with a gentle bend in the river wrapping around it. Kaine, as was his custom, searched for the tent of Patrov and finally located it close to the riverbank at the bend. Since the river offered protection on one side and the entire army buffered it on the other, it seemed a secure site. However, as Kaine continued to study the scene before him, the same thought kept repeating itself in his mind — the entire army on one side of Patrov's tent and only the river to protect him on the other side! Soon, a daring plan started to form and as soon as Kaine returned to his camp, he called Sauric into his tent. "I want you to get some of the men together and build a raft."

Sauric looked at him quizzically.

"We're going to snatch Patrov right out of his camp. We'll see how well his army functions without him."

Sauric's men immediately set to work constructing a crude raft made from logs lashed together and within hours were pushing it into the river downstream from Patrov's encampment. Kaine and Sauric climbed on and poled the raft up the river for about a half mile where they abandoned it, leaving it concealed at a bend about a hundred yards downstream from Patrov's camp. It had been difficult working against the current, but in about two hours they'd been able to secure the craft to a small sand bar well-hidden by tree limbs. The two men then swam the rest of the way to Patrov's camp and emerged from the river in the inky blackness of the storm-shrouded night. The pounding rain helped them by drowning out any sound of their approach to Patrov's tent, and, to add to their good fortune, there were only two guards posted outside Patrov's tent. Anyone else who might have thwarted Kaine's plan was huddled under cover from the soaking downpour. Once they neared the tent, Sauric slit the throat of the first guard and Kaine took

The Winds of Wharhalen

out the remaining guard with a blow to the head. Kaine then slipped quickly inside the tent and woke the sleeping Patrov. Vartan's brother raised his head momentarily but was immediately rendered senseless by Kaine's cudgel. Kaine had considered trying to take Patrov prisoner without knocking him out but decided that they would never be able to get him away from his camp and back to the raft if he was struggling. Unconscious, bound, and gagged, Patrov was then carted to the water's edge and pushed in. Keeping the face of his limp body above water so that he didn't drown, Kaine and Sauric glided with the current downstream to the place where they'd left the raft. Quickly loading their prize on to the simple vessel, Kaine and Sauric pushed out from the sandbar and drifted back to the spot from which the raft had been launched and their men were waiting with horses. By the time Patrov's army discovered he was missing the next morning, Kaine and his cavalry were well on their way back to Ritola. Kaine realized that there was always the chance that his captive could die en route from his head injury, but, in that event, his army would still be without its leader. And, if he did survive until they reached Ritola, he could be extremely valuable for barter. Kaine also hoped that once Vartan became aware his brother had been captured and wasn't coming to his aid, he might be more likely to surrender to save his own life, as well as that of his brother. Unfortunately, by the time they reached the encampment at Ritola, Patrov was dead.

And so Kaine's bold plan had only partially succeeded. There would be no bartering. Soon after Kaine's return, a man was sent out from the camp of the Royal Army to Ritola with Patrov's body strapped to the back of his horse. Stopping short of the killing range of the arrows, he cut the body loose, let it drop to the ground, and rode back to camp.

The siege would go on.

CHAPTER SEVEN

Eylese

Locke sat at the edge of the meadow watching Arawae graze on the long grass. It was late morning, and they had stopped to rest and replenish their water supply at a small stream that meandered around the little peninsula. The sun's rays were warm on his face, but the soft blades of grass still felt cool between his toes. His boots lay beside him, as did Arawae's saddle. The songs of birds surrounded this peaceful place, far from the Karpoans.

The past three weeks had given Locke plenty of time for reflection. The gradually changing landscape was all that he had to distract his thoughts from the events he'd left behind. The terrible image of Jocar's ravaged body lying on the plateau had burned itself so deeply into his consciousness that not even sleep would afford him respite. Once a night he would awaken from a nightmare in which he was being chased by the same murderous bandits that had taken his only friend's life. Escaping the Karpoans had been easy compared to that of trying to erase the painful memories that still continually plagued his mind. It probably would have helped the young man were he to have had some reason for optimism about his future. Noisome

The Winds of Wharhalen

recollections are more easily buried by hope. Instead, his aimless wanderings only served to further reinforce the lonely desolation that had now become his life. Locke called to Arawae, and the bay looked up but made no effort to move from where she was grazing. The young man called again, but the mare was being stubborn. It was indeed a lovely spot, and Locke shared his companion's reluctance to leave. Finally, he walked over to the horse, which, in anticipation of having her meal interrupted, grabbed a few more mouthfuls of grass. The boy lifted her large head and, cradling it in the crook of his arm, stroked her forehead. Soon they were off again on their journey, of which neither knew the destination. The ride, ever southward, had taken Locke past a few villages in the rugged mountain region and past the larger settlement where he and Jocar had often traded, one which lay in the foothills and was the terminus of several trails that led through the mountain range and on to the North Sea. Locke was tempted to linger there since its busy marketplace and skilled craftsmen offered numerous opportunities for him to find work. However, he longed to put more distance between himself and the mountains, and, besides, everything about the settlement reminded him of Jocar and at the time, he didn't feel like answering the inevitable questions about his friend's fate.

The rolling hills next gave way to wide stretches of grassland that eventually became dotted with forests. The area north and west of Attalia was sparsely populated, and had Locke not passed a few small herds of sheep and goats and their herdsmen, he might have thought he was the last person left on earth. The abundant grass of the lowlands provided ample forage for Arawae, and clear, running streams supplied water for both of them. Locke had bought some food on the outskirts of the settlement, but that was many days ago, and his dwindling supplies were quickly becoming a serious concern.

That afternoon, on a day in which he had yet to see another human so far, Locke steered Arawae toward a large grove of trees that would get them out of the afternoon sun. The canopy of interlacing treetops created a wonderful mosaic of light and shadow within the quiet grove. Even Arawae's footsteps barely disturbed the peaceful setting, muffled by the deep cushion of moist, leaf debris. Locke had never seen anything quite like this before, and he was so enthralled by the majesty of the gigantic trees that, at first, he failed to notice a young woman whose drab attire blended in with the surroundings. She was standing motionless, and had it not been for the fair skin of her face and hands, which stood out even in the low light, he might have missed her altogether. When he did discover her Locke was a little embarrassed at first, since she had obviously seen him ride into the grove and had more than likely been observing him for some time. Recovering his composure, he rode closer and noted that she was close in age to his own and holding a basket of mushrooms. He smiled and said "Hello," to which the girl shyly nodded in response. Locke studied her carefully and found the features of her face quite pleasing. She had long brown hair, which fell loosely about her shoulders and a few freckles that graced her pale skin with the slightest glow of pink on the cheeks from having been out in the sun. Her plain clothing, though modest, was unable to conceal the appealing curves of her body. Her large brown eyes were disarming and held the young man speechless for another awkward minute. Finally, he summoned up the courage to try again. "Do you live near here?"

The girl nodded again.

"Well, is there a village nearby where I can restock my provisions?"

This time the girl shook her head.

"Then where do you live?"

"I live at the castle. You are on Lord Toulon's land," she replied.

The Winds of Wharhalen

"It's nice to know you can talk. You're the first person I've seen in days. I can talk to my horse, but she doesn't answer me."

"She's beautiful. Does she have a name?"

"Arawae. So who is this Toulon? Are you related to him?"

"No," she responded somewhat emphatically to the last question, and Locke thought he noticed a slight look of repugnance come over the girl's face. "Lord Toulon is a very wealthy noble. You could ride the rest of the day and not come to the end of his holdings."

"So, why do you live with him?" Locke got down off his saddle. Now that he had the girl talking, he wasn't eager to have the conversation end.

"I don't really live *with* him. I'm a servant."

"Does it pay well?" he said jokingly.

"It doesn't pay at all," she lamented. They were walking together now, with Locke leading Arawae.

"Why do you stay?"

"I have no choice. I'm obligated."

"Do you mind if I unsaddle Arawae? I had intended to let her rest in this grove."

"Go ahead. It is not I that would have you skewered for trespassing in Lord Toulon's fief."

"Skewered? Would he really? I guess I'll just have to take that chance though since you say that I couldn't reach safety in a day's ride in any case. You said obligated. How are you obligated?"

The girl sat down at the base of a large, spreading tree and watched Locke unsaddle his horse. "My mother died when I was twelve, and I had five brothers and sisters. My father couldn't care for

7 - Eylese

us all, so the ones that could be placed as servants were. Master Toulon gives me food, clothes and a place to live. In return, I must serve him for ten years."

"Ten years? How many years do you have left?"

"Five."

"Is there no way out before that?"

"My debt could be bought out with fifty gold coins. But even if that were to happen, where would I go? What would I do?"

Locke wanted to comment on what a dreary outlook that was, but, at the same time, he didn't want to make the girl feel bad, so he changed the subject. "What's your name?"

"Eylese. You haven't told me who you are."

"Locke," he said, turning Arawae loose and sitting down beside the girl. "What are your duties for Lord Toulon?"

"During the day I work in the fields or gather things for the kitchen. In the evenings, I help prepare the meals."

"Do you have any contact with your brothers or sisters?"

A look of resigned sadness came across her face. "No. I was the only one brought here. And since I was the oldest, I was the first to go. But, since I have been here, I have heard that the others have gone too. My father has also left looking for work."

A prolonged silence ensued. Locke was at a loss for things to talk about since so many subjects seemed to make the girl unhappy. Finally, Eylese came to his rescue. "Where have you come from?"

"The Karpoans."

A bewildered look came across the young woman's face as she processed this answer.

The Winds of Wharhalen

"It is a mountain range on the border with Wharhalen."

"I've heard of that. But aren't they really far away?"

"Yes. I've been traveling for three weeks."

The girl's eyes widened further. "What are you doing here?"

"Just traveling."

"People don't just travel," she said with skepticism in her voice. "You must do something else."

"I used to be a trader in the mountains. My partner was killed by bandits, and I have been riding south ever since."

"How awful. Where are you going?"

"I don't know."

Eylese seemed anxious to ask more questions but resisted.

"I had better get back," she said finally. "I've already been gone too long."

As the girl picked up her basket of mushrooms and started to leave, Locke was seized with the feeling that he didn't want her to go. "Will you be back here again tomorrow?"

Eylese stared at the ground for a moment, then looked up at Locke and searched his eyes. "I might be." With that, she hurried out of the grove, leaving the young man alone again. Even though the girl had departed, she still filled his thoughts. He stayed there under the cool canopy of trees for a while longer, recounting over and over all that they'd talked about. Her image was etched in his consciousness, and he realized he couldn't calm the agitation within him. And, he further realized that even if he could have, he wouldn't have wanted to.

Locke decided to move out of the grove and into a deeper wooded area about a half-mile away. It was secluded and had a small

7 - Eylese

stream that gurgled over a bed of rocks. If it was as the girl had said, that Lord Toulon fiercely protected his lands, Locke wanted to avoid well-traveled areas. This was a new experience for Locke as he had never before had to worry about riding on land that had been set aside and claimed by one man. In the Karpoans, there were no lords, just peasants and bandits. He had heard of warlords that jealously guarded specific territories in Wharhalen, but figured that they were nothing more than better-organized bandits. When he inspected his provisions, he saw that he was running low with only a small hunk of dried meat and a couple of hard rolls left to eat. But on this night food wasn't foremost in his mind as he went to sleep listening to the sounds of the stream, and as the name "Eylese" kept finding its way into his thoughts.

Locke woke to a cacophony of singing birds and the sun casting checkered shadows through the dense canopy of leaves. He washed in the cold water of the stream and munched on the last of his stale bread. He had decided the night before that he would explore the area around the grove where he had talked with the girl. Since he was planning to return to that place in hopes she would be there again, he wanted to be well-acquainted with it in case he had to make a quick escape.

Locke walked Arawae in a wide circle around the grove and then ventured out in four directions, like the spokes of a wheel, and rode for some distance in each. On one side he found that the creek of his previous night's campsite meandered back to the grove and passed within about fifty yards. This would be especially valuable information if he needed to conceal his trail. On the side adjacent to the one with the creek lay a broad rolling meadow with few trees. The other two sides were more densely wooded with thick underbrush, saplings, and tangled vines. He realized these areas would be difficult to negotiate in a hurry.

The Winds of Wharhalen

On his return from the last of the four "spokes," he heard a noise coming from the direction of the grove and stopped. The well-trained Arawae stood absolutely still as Locke listened. He dismounted, tied the reins to a log to prevent the mare from browsing, and moved closer to the large trees. When he reached the perimeter, he saw the source of the sounds. A ranger, leading his horse, was examining the footprints left by Arawae the day before. This inspection went on for several minutes and then was interrupted by Eylese's arrival with her mushroom basket. The two exchanged greetings, and then the ranger appeared to question the girl. The conversation continued for a while with Eylese finally pointing toward one of the paths that led out of the grove. The ranger, apparently satisfied, got back on his horse and rode away, not in the direction the girl had indicated, but the opposite way.

Locke continued to observe the girl as she went through the motions of gathering mushrooms, but he also noticed that she frequently looked around and seemed distracted. Locke wanted to go to her before she left the grove, but waited cautiously for the ranger to get far away. Finally, without a word, he walked back to where Arawae was tethered. The fine horse was waiting patiently and nodded her head up and down on Locke's return. Back in the saddle, he rode slowly into the grove as if he were just arriving for the first time. Eylese's face brightened as horse and rider came into view, but then she discreetly dropped her gaze so as not to appear too eager.

She raised her head again as Arawae came to a stop and held out her hand to the horse's muzzle as she walked closer. "Hello, Arawae," she said, as if the horse had arrived by itself. "I'm glad your owner has brought you back to see me today." She looked up slyly at Locke. "A ranger was just here. He was examining your footprints."

"Yes, I saw him leave," he answered, now that she had mentioned it first. "Did you talk to him?"

7 - Eylese

"I told him that I had talked to you yesterday and that you had mistakenly wandered into the fief. I said you were on your way to Callanco."

Locke nodded silently, studying the girl's expression.

"Why did you come back?" she added.

"I came to see you." Locke thought he saw her blush slightly as she lowered her eyes beneath long lashes.

"In case you did come back, I knew you wouldn't have time to ride all the way to the village to get provisions, so I brought some food and drink." As Eylese was speaking, she produced a large piece of cloth from her basket and began unfolding it on the grass. Next, she took out a long loaf of bread, a hunk of cheese, part of a roasted fowl, and a bottle of dark, red wine.

Locke remained atop Arawae and watched in amazement. As he watched the girl arranging the items on the cloth, he couldn't ignore the hunger in his belly, in spite of the other unfamiliar sensation deep within him. Finally, he dismounted, took the bridle off of Arawae so she could graze, and then stood awkwardly as if waiting to be told what to do next. Fortunately, Eylese obliged, patting the place next to her on the ground and saying, "Well, sit down and eat!" Her voice had a playful ring as she handed Locke a knife and pushed the fowl over to him to carve.

His initial caution beginning to dissolve, Locke ate heartily, saying little until he had sated his hunger and thirst. Feeling satisfied and a little flushed from several glasses of wine, he lay back upon the grass and gazed up at the canopy of tree branches that filtered the light from the noonday sun. Eylese then reclined on her side next to him, propping herself up on one elbow and combing her fingers through the long grass in front of her.

"Thank you," he said simply, "that was wonderful."

The Winds of Wharhalen

"I'm glad you came back. I would have had to throw all this food away if you hadn't. I certainly didn't want to have to smuggle it back into the kitchen."

"I would be glad I came back even if you hadn't brought the food."

The girl smiled sweetly and blushed again. And then, looking toward the mare grazing nearby, she said, "Is Arawae fast?"

"I've never seen a horse faster. I wouldn't be alive right now if she hadn't been able to outrun the bandits that killed my friend."

"There's a race in Callanco three days from now. The prize is a hundred gold pieces."

"A hundred!"

"Yes, many of the nobles raise horses just for the purpose of racing at Callanco. For them, the money is nothing. They just want to be able to boast that they have the best horse."

"Can anyone enter?"

"I've never been there, but I think so."

Locke was turning thoughts of a race over and over in his mind when Eylese said, "I'd better go back now. Keep what's left of the food." She gathered the corners of the cloth and handed the bundle to Locke.

He purposely folded his hands around hers as he took the food from her. "Will I see you again tomorrow?"

"If I can," she answered. "If I don't come, it won't be because I don't want to." She was trembling slightly as she turned her face upward to look into the face of the taller boy. Locke tilted his head downward and kissed her softly on the lips. She smiled and kept her eyes closed for a moment as he looked at her and waited for a reaction.

7 - Eylese

She then slipped her hands from his and hurried toward the edge of the grove. Turning briefly, she started to say something, then simply waved her hand and ran away down the path.

That night, in the young man's mind, thoughts of racing Arawae in Callanco mingled with the nearly constant image of Eylese. His shallow sleep was filled with dreams, but, in this instance, because the principal figure of these dreams was the girl, he would smile when he later recalled them. He awoke early, and since his excitement was preventing him from returning to his dreams, he washed the sleep from his eyes in the stream and prepared to leave his campsite. He satisfied his hunger with bread and cheese from the day before, washed down with the cold clear water from the rushing creek. What was left of the bottle of wine had been consumed the previous night, and a slight morning-after headache accompanied breakfast.

The rest of the morning passed like an eternity as Locke waited for the sun to rise high enough in the sky to signal the time to make an appearance in the grove. When he arrived, Eylese wasn't there yet, which was no surprise, since the boy knew he was early. He waited patiently at first, but after about an hour and a half, he began to be concerned that she might not come. He remembered that she had said "*If* I can." Locke knew that the girl's life was not her own, under the present circumstances, and suddenly wanted more than anything to be able to take her away from her captivity here. He wanted her with him as he traveled freely, searching for a new life to replace the one he had left behind in the Karpoans. Another hour passed, and Locke's hopes of seeing Eylese began to wane. He dozed off under a tree and slept lightly for a time, and when he came to full wakefulness, it was late afternoon. He got up, stretched his long arms and legs, and then walked over to Arawae. She pressed her soft muzzle against his chest, and he stroked her neck. Locke slipped the bridle on to the mare's head and was preparing to mount when he heard a rustling in the woods behind him. He swung quickly into the saddle so that he could make a hasty exit from the grove if the ranger appeared but then saw the familiar figure of Eylese coming through the trees. His spirits again soaring, he dismounted and walked toward the center of the grove to meet her. Immediately, he sensed that something was wrong. The gaiety was gone from her step and her head was down. As she looked up, he could see that her eyes were red and swollen from crying. Locke stopped, but the girl ran the last few steps and threw herself into his arms. She held him in a tight embrace and between sobs said, "I was afraid you wouldn't be here."

When the young woman's crying had subsided, Locke took her by the arms and asked, "What's happened?"

Eylese winced at his grasp and involuntarily pulled away. She gingerly pushed up the sleeves of her dress to reveal fresh bruises on both arms.

"Tell me who did this."

"If I tell you, promise me that you won't rush off and do something foolish."

"All right, I promise to think carefully before I do something foolish."

Eylese smiled through her tears at this silly statement then began slowly. "Lord Toulon had guests at the castle last night. We were serving the evening meal when I bumped into one of the other girls and dropped a tray of food. Master Toulon yelled at me and said I was stupid and clumsy, and had me place my arms on the table. He then took a cane and struck me across the wrists again and again."

"The bastard!" Locke hissed, the blood rising to his face.

"He made me spend the night in the barn, and today I was forced to carry water to the animals until my shoulders ached and my hands were bleeding."

7 - Eylese

Locke took the delicate hands in his and examined the raw, blistered palms. He gently took each to his mouth and kissed them.

"When they finally let me stop, I slipped away to come here. I can only stay a few minutes though or they might come looking for me."

"Has he hit you before?"

Eylese nodded.

Locke was silent for a moment. "I have been thinking since yesterday, and I would like to try to win the race in Callanco. If I succeed, I will come back and buy your freedom. Then you will be free to come with me, or if you choose, go your own way."

The girl's eyes shone brightly through glistening tears. "Oh! I want more than anything to be able to go with you!"

"Then it is settled. If I don't win, I will return for you anyway, and we will come up with another idea."

Without another word, the girl put her battered arms around Locke's neck, and he encircled her slender waist in a tight embrace. They kissed, this time a long and tender kiss. Finally, Eylese began to draw away. "I have to hurry back."

"I will be back in three days," exclaimed the young man. "I will wait for you here in the grove. Just remember, whatever happens, I will be back." Locke was still holding the girl's hand. She slowly slipped her fingers from his and hurried off toward the edge of the forest. She paused briefly and waved a reluctant good-bye. "Good luck!" she called, the music having returned to her voice.

The Winds of Wharhalen

CHAPTER EIGHT

The Race

Locke set out for Callanco with mixed emotions struggling for space inside his head. He hated leaving Eylese in the service of Toulon where she'd been so badly treated. And, the thought of someone striking the sweet, innocent girl filled him with rage. But the upcoming race offered an opportunity to free her from her bonds within a few days. In no other way could they gain the necessary money so quickly. Locke had never been in a formal race, although he knew that his mare possessed unnatural speed and courage. Even when they weren't outrunning bandits, Locke loved to feel the power surge beneath him when Arawae would reach full stride galloping across an open plateau. She was nimble, too. Riding in the hills had made her legs strong, and she could turn so sharply that an unwary rider would be left on the ground. Despite this, she had never run against horses that had been bred and trained specifically for racing. As quick and explosive as the mare was compared to the stock in the Karpoans, Locke didn't really know what they would be facing in Callanco. The doubts were there in his mind, but the boy suppressed them. It was much more pleasant to think about Eylese.

The Winds of Wharhalen

Locke arrived in Callanco late the next morning. It was a typical village, with most of its activities revolving around local agriculture. A market was located at its hub, where the surplus produce of farms owned by the local Lord was brought to be sold to the peasants. The fiefs were self-sufficient entities with all the various industries owned by the noble. In return for their services, the peasants were protected by the Lord's Men-at-Arms. It was a system that had been in place since the era of the "New Kings," having survived throughout the years when the warlord Zironon was in control of Attalia. Governing of the sprawling Empire had always been tenuous, with anyone succeeding in it needing the cooperation of the nobles.

Locke proceeded immediately to the market where an agent had been located to take entries for the race. He found the tent quite easily as it was conspicuous by its lack of agricultural products on display. There were a handful of men standing nearby, but they too differed in appearance from the farmers and merchants working in the market. These men stood around engaged in idle discourse, and Locke surmised that they were either owners or riders of racehorses, in Callanco only for the race. Wagering was undoubtedly going on, he thought, but that didn't concern him. He was there to win the gold and to thereby claim the prize that was most important to him: Eylese.

As he walked up to the tent leading Arawae by the reins, Locke felt that all eyes were on him. Or was it his horse that the men were looking at? He looped the reins around a post, confident that the mare would stay where he left her. Nodding at a couple of the men who were standing near the opening of the tent, Locke walked in and was immediately confronted by a man who greeted him with obvious disdain.

"I'd like to enter the race."

A scornful half-smile crossed the man's face as he said, "It will cost you eight gold coins."

8 - The Race

Locke fingered his leather pouch, knowing that he only had six, all that was left of what he and Jocar had possessed when they were attacked. "What if I give you six and this dagger?" he asked, drawing the weapon from his belt. "It is worth at least two."

The man replied curtly, "You can do that if you want, but it still won't get you into the race. It will take eight gold coins to get you in."

"How long are you going to be here?"

"Until the end of the day. When I leave, the entries are closed."

"I'll be back." Locke turned on his heel and left the tent. When he was back outside, three of the men he'd seen earlier were now standing by Arawae, looking her over from nose to tail. As he approached, one of the men, hefty in build and dressed in the fine clothes of a noble said, "Do you want to sell her?"

Locke shook his head and said simply, "No."

"I'll give you ten in gold."

Locke felt a surge of pride that someone would offer such a sum for his horse. "Thank you, no."

"Twelve."

The young man smiled. He had never held twelve gold coins in his hands at one time in his life. "It's a fair offer, but I don't want to sell her."

The well-dressed man shrugged but didn't say anything more.

Locke felt a tinge of self-reproach as he led his horse away. Although he had never possessed twelve gold coins before, he knew now that the mare was probably the single most valuable thing that he would ever own. But a more pressing matter was how he was going to obtain the extra two gold pieces he needed to enter the race.

The Winds of Wharhalen

He actually still had a few small silver coins in his pocket that reduced his need slightly, but finding enough work to make up the difference in such a short time wasn't going to be easy. The first thing he did was to go to a merchant stand that he remembered passing on his way in to the market. He offered the dagger for sale to the dark, leathery-skinned man he found there. The man took the dagger and examined it closely. "Eight," he said.

"Silver?"

The man nodded.

"Ten."

The merchant shook his head.

Locke held out his hand to reclaim his property.

The man, still holding the dagger, hesitated, then said, "Nine."

Reluctantly, Locke nodded his assent. The merchant opened a small box under the counter and counted out nine silver coins. Locke was sure that the wily trader would later sell the dagger for much more. Still, he also knew that the dagger was the only thing in his possession of any value to sell other than Arawae, and he saw no other recourse. The nine that he received plus the three that he'd found in his pocket still left him eight short (ten silvers equaling one gold coin).

After leaving the booth, Locke next began asking the farmers if there was any work to be had. Most simply shook their heads; others tried to sell him vegetables. Late in the morning, he encountered a man who, eyeing him cautiously, said he would pay him for an afternoon's work in the fields near his home tomorrow.

Locke told him that he must find work today because he needed the money today.

"Tomorrow. Today, I sell produce."

8 - The Race

"I won't be able to work tomorrow because I will be in the race."

The farmer stepped back and looked at Locke in disbelief. Then he looked at Arawae. He turned and said a few words to his wife, and then motioned for Locke to follow him. He then hitched up a bony old horse with sleepy eyes and slowly climbed into the cart. At the same time, Locke mounted Arawae and followed as they rode out of the marketplace and down a dusty road. Several narrow country lanes later, they came to a rolling, rocky field bordered by low, stone fences. The man, white-haired and thin, like his horse, handed Locke a set of saddlebags and an iron bar that he took from the back of the cart and said, "I will give you three pieces of silver when you reach the corner with this fence."

Locke threw the saddlebags across the back of his horse and started picking up stones and placing them in the compartments on both sides. When the bags were filled, he led Arawae to the unfinished part of the wall and began stacking the stones. The farmer then got back up on his wagon and started back for the town. He turned briefly and shouted to Locke, "There is a creek over that hill where you can get water."

The work wasn't complicated, but by mid-afternoon, Locke's legs and back ached and his hands were blistered and bleeding. Arawae worked uncomplainingly, of course. Locke wondered, though, at the toll this labor was taking on his mount for the race that was to take place the next morning. He also wondered where the additional five silvers he still needed were going to come from. There were numerous times that afternoon in the glare of the hot sun when he questioned the sanity of this whole venture. But he continued to work and when he heard the creak of the farmer's wagon coming down the road later that afternoon, he was just finishing up the fence at the corner of the field.

The Winds of Wharhalen

The man looked approvingly at the work that Locke had accomplished, then took three silver coins from his purse and placed them in a dirty, blood-encrusted hand. "You'd better come up to the house and clean up those hands."

Locke answered, "Thank you, but right now I need to get back into town. I still need five more silvers, and I still don't know how I'm going to obtain them."

The farmer shrugged, and Locke turned to go. Then the young man stopped for a moment as if gathering his thoughts. He turned back to the man and said, "I realize you don't know me, but I wonder if you would listen to a proposal."

The old man, whose wife was still sitting in the cart, cocked his head slightly to one side with a wary look.

"If you would advance me the five silver coins that I need to complete my entry in the race, I will give you ten if I emerge the winner."

The suspicious look on the farmer's face turned to one of incredulity.

"And if I fail to win the race, I will work two days for you to repay my debt."

The man studied Locke intently for a long time, but the boy's blue eyes were unwavering.

"All right."

Locke's countenance brightened.

"One condition, though. That you return tonight to have a meal with us. I assume you have no money for food."

Locke smiled sheepishly. He took the five additional coins from the man and said, "Thank you. I will keep my word."

8 - *The Race*

"What is your name? If I am to endure the wrath of my wife for giving away money, at least I should know to whom I gave it."

"Locke. And you?"

"Sebastian," said the farmer, extending a large, bony hand.

Locke winced noticeably when the two men shook hands. "How are you to hold the reins of your horse tomorrow with those hands?"

Locke looked at his palms and had no answer.

"When you return tonight, we will treat them as best we can, and tomorrow we will bind them."

Locke then mounted Arawae and rode back to Callanco and arrived at the marketplace just as the man that he had talked to before was closing the race tent for the night. "Wait. I have my entry fee now."

"Entries are closed."

"But you are still here, and I have the money." Locke tried to keep his voice from sounding angry.

"You are too late; I have closed the entries."

Locke, in no mood for officious nonsense, grabbed the man by the shirt and with both hands nearly lifted him off the ground and backed him up four paces. "I have worked all day and sold everything I own to have enough money to enter this accursed race. You will accept my entry, or I will leave your lifeless body on the ground right here."

The suddenly tractable official nodded his assent whereupon Locke released his hold on the man's shirt and allowed him to retreat into the tent. The book was signed and initialed, the money changed hands, and Locke turned to leave.

"You have no chance, you know. You have wasted your money," came the words from behind him.

The Winds of Wharhalen

"I have no chance if I don't try."

On the way back to Sebastian's farm, doubts began to creep into the boy's thoughts. He felt he was probably deluding himself by thinking that Arawae could compete with the fine race horses of the wealthy lords. But the attempt was nevertheless worth taking. He could conceive of no other way for him to accumulate fifty gold coins. He would then have to go back to the fief of Lord Toulon and figure out another way to continue seeing Eylese. It was nearly dark when Locke finally returned to the small, log and mud house of Sebastian and his wife. The old farmer came out as he approached and led him to the barn where Arawae would spend the night. Before going into the house, Locke washed the dried sweat and dust from the mare's body and rubbed her vigorously with a cloth. He also gave her fresh water and hay, then patted her side before walking with Sebastian to the house. The food that Sebastian's wife, Isa, prepared was simple fare, but to Locke it was wonderful beyond description. Two years of riding with Jocar, then subsisting on what he could carry with him along the trail for the past three weeks, had made him especially grateful whenever he could get hot, freshly-prepared food. Add to that a powerful appetite generated by moving rocks all afternoon and Isa, a round, kindly woman, had in Locke a very appreciative dinner guest.

The meal was consumed in relative silence, but, at its conclusion, Sebastian initiated a conversation by asking his guest a few questions about his recent past. Locke told of the time spent trading in the hills with Jocar. The part concerning his partner's death came haltingly, and Sebastian didn't probe any further. He then asked how Locke had ended up in Callanco on the day before the big race with the unlikely goal of claiming the prize. Locke saw no harm in telling the farmer and his wife about Eylese; so he replied that there was a girl who would spend at least the next five years of her life bound to service to a cruel master if fifty in gold were not paid to secure her release.

8 - The Race

"So the money is not for you, but instead to buy the freedom of a girl."

"Yes."

"This girl must be quite special."

"Yes, sir, I believe she is."

The eyes of the farmer met those of his wife, and Locke saw a knowing smile on the woman's lips.

Locke then asked Sebastian if he owned the land that he farmed. The old man replied, "I was once a soldier and I served the current noble's father. It was he that granted me the land to farm. Part of what I grow I give back as rent. So far, the son has continued the arrangement."

By the end of the meal, Locke was struggling to keep his eyes open. Shortly following the meal he was curled up on the floor with some animal hides, with sleep tugging at his consciousness. In his last moment of lucidity, he asked how he would be able to wake up in time to get to Callanco for the race. Sebastian assured him that he and his wife would be up quite early and they would wake him.

Locke awakened slowly at first to the voice of the farmer. Within moments, though, he remembered the importance of this day. Isa offered some bread, baked the day before, and cold meat, which the young man's stomach received reluctantly, agitated as it was in anticipation of the race. When he was finished, the woman bound the blisters of both his hands with clean linen cloths. With a kindly smile and a pat on the back, the farmer's wife sent Locke out to the barn where Sebastian was already feeding Arawae. The mare was happily munching on hay, blissfully unaware of what the day held in store for them. Neither man spoke as the horse was saddled and had each leg and hoof carefully checked. Locke thanked the older man for his help and promised to return after the race to repay his debt, regardless of

The Winds of Wharhalen

the outcome. The farmer nodded and said, "Be careful. I've watched the race, and riders get hurt. And not just because of accidents."

The sun had just appeared above the horizon as Locke rode away from the house toward Callanco. Locke thought about Sebastian's parting words, and then thought about fleeing the deadly raiders that had killed Jocar. But, this was only a race. Putting his fears aside for the moment, he dismissed the warning and let his thoughts drift back to Eylese, a subject that had occupied his mind every waking moment since he'd met her. Arawae was serene, perhaps anticipating another day hauling rocks.

When Locke arrived, a small crowd from the village had already gathered at the starting point of the race. The mood was festive, but, at the same time, the atmosphere was taut with anticipation. Magnificent horses, sensing the excitement, snorted and pranced and pawed the earth. Wealthy nobles stood about with entourages of armed guards. However, the majority of the onlookers were peasants who barely had enough money to even consider placing a wager on the race. For them, it was simply a holiday from the drudgery of their everyday lives. Locke remained on the fringe of this scene for a while, unnoticed by the others but all the while observing his opponents, both equine and human. Arawae stood quietly, and like her rider, took in all the details that surrounded her.

The sun had risen a full hand's width into the sky by the time the starter called for the horses. He announced that the race would consist of two circuits of the course and finish back in the center of the village. The only rules were that no weapons were allowed to be carried and that a rider must complete the course mounted on the same horse he'd started on. When he took his place among the starters, Locke felt the eyes of the other riders. He knew he was an unknown entity to them with his powerfully built mountain horse and unproven riding skills. To him, the whole group of them comprised just one

8 - The Race

faceless opponent to be defeated. His focus was down the course, which was to be ridden as fast as Arawae could take him.

As Locke took up slightly on the reins and leaned forward in the saddle, Arawae sensed the tension mounting. She shifted her feet in anticipation of the signal, and when it came, the mare's powerful flanks propelled horse and rider forward with the force and speed of a flash flood. Within five strides, she was half a length ahead of the others. The explosive start was much as Locke had expected from his horse. He knew, though, that those horses bred for more speed on the flats would eventually gain ground on them. His hope therefore was that he could ride his horse harder into and out of the turns and thereby neutralize their speed advantage. Not being very large, the village of Callanco was quickly left behind. Spectators still lined the course at intervals until the race route took the competitors around a wooded area where they would make a broad turn before heading back to town. By the time they reached the woods, a sleek black stallion had drawn slightly ahead of Arawae and several other horses were bunched just behind her. Going into the turn, Locke urged Arawae up on the leader's flank, and at the far side of the woods, the two were matching stride for stride. Drawing slightly ahead, the rider of the black suddenly drew a leather strap from inside his cloak. Before Locke could pull away from his rival, the other rider struck Arawae across the forehead. Stung and confused by this attack, the mare threw her head up and veered sharply to the right. When this happened, the knot of horses behind her raced by in pursuit of the black. Furious, Locke urged his mount on and as the course headed back toward Callanco, he was able to re-establish contact with the group.

In the tight turn inside the town, Arawae regained her advantage and began to thread her way through the pack. One by one, she moved past each tiring horse and by the time they were on the straight, headed back toward the woods, only the black was ahead of

The Winds of Wharhalen

her. The mare, now relishing the chase, quickly narrowed the gap between them. Locke was no longer urging his mount on—he knew she was now at top speed. However, the black was determined to keep his pursuer on his flank, and his ground-devouring stride matched his determination. Locke decided he could only be patient and wait. As the course began to turn to the right to skirt the woods, the opening he was waiting for finally materialized. The black, not negotiating the turn as well as his more agile rival, swung wide as Locke cut to the inside and regained the lead. Coming out of the turn, he gave Arawae her head and listened closely for the pursuit that was sure to come. As expected, the black came up fast on the straight and quickly drew abreast. In his periphery, Locke saw the strap come out again. This time though he was ready. Just as the rider raised his arm to strike, Locke grabbed his adversary's wrist with both hands. Using only his legs to guide his mount, and still holding fast to his opponent's arm, he began to veer away from the black. Locke's surprised victim struggled mightily to extricate himself, but the boy's grip was like a vise. As the two horses parted, the black's rider was dragged from the back of his mount. Only then did Locke relax his hold, watching as his hapless rival crashed heavily to the ground.

However, the brief struggle had allowed a cluster of horses to shrink Arawae's lead. Locke tried to urge her on, but he could tell she was beginning to tire. Her stride was still fluid, but the former speed was not there. Hopefully, Locke thought, the other horses were also tired. As they approached the edge of Callanco, a chestnut horse crept up on them until he was finally eye to eye with Arawae. Locke knew he couldn't ask any more from his horse as side by side the two combatants raced down the corridor lined with cheering people. Less than fifty yards from the finish, it looked like the chestnut would be able to get his nose in front of the faltering bay. But with Locke's hands moving in unison with the courageous animal's rhythmic stride, Arawae

8 - The Race

summoned one last burst of effort and surged ahead of the chestnut as they crossed the finish line.

Locke's exhilaration over winning the race was unmatched by anything he had ever experienced before. He paused momentarily to soak in the cheers of the people who crowded around his horse before he trotted back to receive his prize. Although the villagers seemed genuinely happy about this outsider's victory, Locke sensed, from the looks of some of the nobles, a cloud of resentment hanging over the proceedings. But when he held the winner's purse in his hand that was all that mattered. Once the tumult quieted down, Locke turned his attentions to the mare that had performed so courageously. It was then that he was approached by the man who had attempted to buy Arawae the day before the race.

"Congratulations. How did your mare come through the race?"

Locke, who was wiping down the glistening horse and feeling for any swelling in her legs answered, "She seems to be fine."

"It appears you made a good business decision by refusing my offer to buy her."

Locke tried to conceal his pleasure and simply nodded.

"I will give you twenty in gold for her right now. With the hundred that you already have, you will then be a very rich man."

Locke thought of Eylese. "It's a tempting offer, but I think I will probably need a fast horse to outrun the thieves who are going to want this gold."

The man shook his head and gave a disgusted sigh. "I think you are allowing sentiment to interfere with good business sense. But, I wish you luck."

Claiming the gold for winning the race was one thing; keeping it was another. He was a stranger in this region, he was alone, and he

The Winds of Wharhalen

was carrying a large amount of gold. It was as if he were wearing a huge target on his back. Therefore, Locke knew he needed a plan if he was to make it back to Eylese with the fifty gold coins necessary to buy her freedom. He felt that so long as he was in Callanco he was fairly safe. Thieves would likely prefer to wait until he was alone in the countryside before making an attempt to rob him. Traveling alone in Killarassee was always risky and especially so if you had something worth stealing.

With this in mind, Locke purchased a sword of fine-tempered steel. He needed it to let thieves know that taking the gold would not be easy. Next, he obtained two more coin pouches. In the first, he placed thirty of the gold coins. He then counted out the fifty coins necessary to buy Eylese's freedom and placed them in the second pouch. Using a portion of the remaining gold, he arranged for a two-night stay in the stable for Arawae, telling the proprietor that he would also spend the nights in the barn to ensure the mare's safekeeping. During the first night, he loaded the bottom of the original pouch with small pieces of iron from the blacksmith's work area, and then filled the remainder of the pouch with gold coins. In the early hours after midnight, Locke quietly slipped out of the stable with Arawae and rode the short distance to Sebastian's house. He was able to reach it without incident, but remained camped just outside the clearing where the house stood, opting to wait until daylight before making his arrival known to Sebastian and Isa.

When light began to show on the horizon and he could detect activity inside the house, Locke led Arawae into the clearing and knocked at the door. The farmer, a broad smile creasing his weathered and wrinkled face, welcomed the boy without question and offered him breakfast, which Locke gratefully accepted. The young man waited patiently for a question about the race, which never came. Finally, he could stand it no longer and said, "Aren't you going to ask me about the race?"

8 - The Race

Sebastian and Isa smiled in amusement. The farmer said, "We figured you would tell us when you were ready."

"We won!" The exclamation burst forth. With the dam now breached, the details came pouring out. When the story ended, Locke handed Sebastian the purse that contained thirty gold pieces. "Will you keep this for me? I fear that bandits will try to rob me on the road back."

Sebastian stared in disbelief. "You would trust me with this amount of gold?"

"Why not? You trusted me to return after the race. Take what I owe you and keep the rest for me until I come back with Eylese."

The older man nodded. "It will be here for you when you return."

"I had better leave now. The longer I stay, the more danger I put you in. Carrying this much gold makes me uneasy. I will be glad to rid myself of some of it." Locke then left the farm fully expecting to return in a short time. Beyond buying Eylese's freedom from Toulon, he had no other plan. Although now his prospects had certainly improved with the gold in his possession. Back on the road once more, he felt as nervous as a hunted animal. The miles passed slowly, both because he was anxious to see Eylese, and perhaps even more so because he kept expecting to be ambushed. The morning passed without seeing many other people on the road. Close to noon, he stopped to rest Arawae under a cluster of trees by a creek. The cool water was refreshing for both horse and man, and Locke felt he should have been able to relax and enjoy the peaceful moment. He had money in his pocket, a fast horse, and a beautiful girl waiting for him. But the boy had learned to be wary of good times, for in his experience, they were always a harbinger for the bad.

The Winds of Wharhalen

In another seven to eight hours he figured he would be back on Toulon's land and safe from the threat of bandits, ironic as it seemed. The nobles were able to keep their own fiefs relatively secure by their ability to pay for professional soldiers. As it happened, however, he was less than an hour into resuming his journey when out from a woods to his right came the first assault. It was sudden and swift, and he'd barely had time to draw his sword and ward off the blows of his assailant. The first man was soon joined by three others, and Locke was quickly surrounded. He fought so savagely though that he was at least able to clear some space between himself and his attackers.

"Give us the gold and we will let you live!" shouted one of the men.

Locke hesitated for a moment, not wishing to seem too eager to comply. "How do I know you will let me pass once you have the purse?"

"You are of no value to us. We only want the gold."

Locke let his shoulders slump to project an image of dejection. Slowly, with his left hand, he produced a leather pouch from his pack. Surveying the greedy faces of the thieves, he tossed the bulging pouch to the man who had spoken. This man then sheathed his sword and opened the pouch. Peering into it, he seemed satisfied, and drew the string at the top. "Now dismount. We also want your fine horse."

Locke sheathed his own sword and leaned forward as if to dismount. Lying low against Arawae's neck, he picked up the reins, squeezed his legs together and shouted, "Haah!" Arawae bolted between two horses so fast that she was twenty yards down the road before any of the thieves could even get their mounts turned. Locke had guessed that the men would be reluctant to leave the purse of gold in the possession of just one of their members, and sure enough, they

8 - The Race

all hesitated just long enough to make pursuit of the exceptionally fast mare pointless. Although Locke and Arawae were soon far from the thieves, the boy continued to keep up a torrid pace, wondering how long it would be until the brigands discovered that the purse contained mostly worthless pieces of iron concealed beneath a few gold coins.

By the time Locke arrived back on Toulon's lands it was nearly dark and he decided to camp at the site by the creek as he had done before. He realized that under the current circumstances he had no way of contacting Eylese other than by meeting her in the large grove as he had done every other time before. He was so anxious to see her again and so excited about now possessing the means to buy her freedom that waiting another twelve hours seemed interminable. Luckily, sleep came easily to the young man once darkness precluded any further activity. He had left Callanco in the middle of the night and traveled hard all day. He was tired but happy, the direction of his life having taken a dramatic, positive upturn.

Locke rose early the next morning and went to the grove to await the anticipated arrival of Eylese. The hours passed slowly for him, but by late morning his patience was rewarded by the sight of the graceful form of the young girl making her way into the grove by way of the usual path. When she looked up and saw him, he could see a joyous smile light up her face despite the great distance between them. She lifted up the heavy skirt of her dress to free her legs for running, and the long brown curls of her hair bounced on her shoulders as she hurried to him. When she got to where Locke was standing, she threw her arms around his neck and the much taller boy lifted her off her feet in a tight embrace. The feeling of the girl's body against his, the fragrance of her hair, and the softness of her cheek next to his filled Locke with such deep passion he thought there would never be anything to equal it. Soon his face was wet with her tears, and he asked if she was all right. "Yes," her wavering voice answered, "I am just so happy that you came back."

The Winds of Wharhalen

"Did you doubt it?"

Overwhelmed with emotion Eylese just shook her head.

"Look, Arawae won!" Locke produced the purse that contained the fifty gold coins.

The girl's eyes widened at first, and then another round of tears burst forth. Now her entire torso convulsed with sobs, and Locke enfolded her in his arms until they subsided. Amid her smiles, her laughter, and her tears, he described the race in infinite detail, relishing the opportunity to tell it again. When he was finished he said, "Shall we go and find your former master and unload some of this gold?"

Eylese smiled at the premature reference to her "former" master, and then nodded.

Holding hands, they started walking back in the direction from which Eylese always came to the grove with Locke leading Arawae. They left the grove and soon were on a path through an open meadow when the castle of Toulon came into view. Locke had never seen a castle before and was somewhat awestruck at first. He stopped walking and stood still for a few minutes studying the elaborate fortifications. Even from this distance, which was still over a half mile away, he could make out that there was an outer wall encompassing a large open space and beyond that a second wall closer to the castle. From behind the second wall, a circular keep rose skyward and was surrounded by battlements and towering watch turrets.

"This Toulon must have a lot of enemies if he needs to protect his house like that."

"I think this castle has been around a lot longer than he has," answered the girl.

8 - The Race

The gate through the outer wall was open and a bridge leading to it crossed a dry moat. When they got to the gate, a guard stopped them. "What is your business here?" he inquired of Locke.

"We are here to see Lord Toulon," said Locke, courteously.

"The Baron doesn't see peasants."

"This girl wishes to leave his service and I have brought enough gold to buy out the remainder of her debt."

The guard looked at Eylese. "I've seen you at the castle. What's your name?"

"Eylese."

"So is this true, Eylese?"

The girl nodded sheepishly.

"I will pass along your message." The man then signaled a young page who immediately came over to them. They conferred briefly and the page headed toward the castle.

While they waited, the guard said to Locke, "How did a peasant get such a fine horse?"

Locke bristled a bit at the man's tone, but remained civil. "I raised her from a foal back home in the Karpoans."

The guard sneered. "You stole her most likely. Only nobles have horses like that."

"Take this horse to the stable until we can find its rightful owner," he said to the other guard, who up to this point had remained silent.

Locke quickly turned and clapped his hands. With this signal, Arawae wheeled around and ran off in the direction from which they had come and eventually disappeared into the forest. To Arawae, this

The Winds of Wharhalen

was a game they played, but for Locke it was a proven method of getting his horse out of danger.

The guard's irritation at this turn of events became apparent by his expression. "We'll get that horse. More than likely, you probably took the gold from the same person you stole the horse from."

Locke was seething, but restrained himself for the sake of Eylese. After a while, the page returned and conferred with the guard. The self-important soldier looked at Locke and then at Eylese and said, "Lord Toulon will see you now."

Locke was troubled by the way he was being treated, but he tried to tell himself that once they got to see the nobleman face-to-face everything would be cleared up. Lord Toulon would see that he had the gold to buy the girl's freedom, and then he and Eylese would soon be on their way. The two were led through the bailey by the guard that had questioned them. To Locke, the area had the feeling of a village. There were stables, a blacksmith shop, an armorer, even a bakery. As they entered the courtyard on the other side, the huge gate through the inner wall seemed to swallow them. The boy from the Karpoans had never seen anything to match the extravagance he now encountered inside the castle. The two teenagers were brought directly before Lord Toulon in a hall so large that even the massive tapestries hanging from the walls couldn't keep their footsteps from echoing.

Toulon was a large, middle-aged man who apparently ate well. His thinning brown hair was tinged slightly with gray, and his face had a slightly bloated, reddish look. His eyes, dark and piercing even under the bushy brow, examined Locke closely, and then glanced at the young Eylese. The Baron addressed the girl first. "You are…"

"Eylese, sir." she answered with a bow.

"Ah, yes. What is the meaning of this?"

Locke then tried to speak. "Lord Toulon…"

8 - The Race

However, the noble raised his hand quickly to silence the young man. "Well, Eylese?"

All of a sudden Eylese couldn't find her voice.

Toulon then turned his attention to Locke. "You are a trespasser on my land, and you carry a sword. How do I know that you are not an assassin or a spy? Or perhaps even a thief?"

"I am none of those things. Eylese has told me that her service here was the result of the unfortunate circumstances of her father, and that her freedom could be bought for fifty gold coins. I have the money in my possession and wish to buy out the remainder of her service if you will allow me to."

The Baron arched a bushy eyebrow at this statement. "You have fifty gold coins?"

Locke produced the bulging purse. Toulon took it from him, opened it and dumped part of the contents into his hand. "Guard, this man is obviously a thief as you suspected. Dispose of him as we would any other criminal. As for you, young woman, for conspiring with this thief your punishment will be severe. And you will also remain in my service for an additional five years for your ingratitude."

Instantly, Locke was seized from behind by two guards, and before he could fight them off, he had a sword point at his throat. At the same time, Eylese was roughly dragged away from him, and as he was pushed out the door, the last thing he heard was her voice crying out, "No, no!"

The Winds of Wharhalen

CHAPTER NINE

Joal

Engrid was walking along the colonnade on her way to meet Myleia in the gardens. She had attempted to befriend the young woman ever since the wife of Kaine had come to Attalia but it hadn't been easy thus far. Myleia was shy, almost reclusive, retreating to her quarters whenever her presence wasn't required at an official function. This trait had worsened since Kaine had left for Ritola, and she was deprived of her husband's support. She was deferential enough to the Queen, but Engrid had hoped that in time they would become friends. There was precious little female presence at the castle, and although she would be loath to admit it, Engrid longed for feminine companionship. During the rebellion, she had lived almost like a man. Sharing their camps, listening to their bawdy stories, even dressing like a man. Since assuming the throne, she had shed the rough exterior of the rebel fighter, and had begun to dress in a manner more fitting for a Queen, opting for soft, flowing gowns that expressed her femininity. Indeed, her beauty was riveting, particularly the long lines of her slender body. The very statues that alternated with the columns on the corridor which she now tread, as beautiful as a sculptor could craft

The Winds of Wharhalen

them, were shamed by her loveliness. The exquisite features of her face, the flawless white skin, and the long, loose curls of blonde hair made her the perfect icon for the Killarasseans who considered her Queen of the Empire. However, the reality was that her power extended little beyond Attalia, as the trouble in Ritola indicated.

As Engrid entered the gardens, which were in the midst of summer splendor, the fragrances of the many and varied blossoms filled the air. The sweet, heavy perfume of the flowers mingled with the essence of mint and other intoxicating aromas. The red, yellow, and purple hues of the flowers formed a brilliant display as they were caressed by the low morning sun. Engrid loved the gardens. They, along with the colonnade, were built during the classic period in Killarassee and were located in the oldest part of the castle. Unfortunately, the gardens had been neglected during the many years that the barbarian Zironon had occupied Attalia, but like the Killarassean people, the plants were rugged and hardy and survived his reign to flourish again under the benevolence of their new caretakers.

The Queen saw Myleia at the far end of the gardens, just off the main path, sitting serenely on a bench. Her head was slightly bowed as she studied a dark green bush with large red-orange flowers. She was wearing a pale purple dress which, draping the young girl's delicate form, made her blend harmoniously with the setting. Indeed, Myleia's natural beauty clearly rivaled that of the flowers. In sharp contrast to the fair Queen, the other woman in the garden that morning had dark hair and eyes, with skin of vanilla cream, rather than milk. Engrid felt a tinge of envy, as all women do, when, in spite of their own beauty, they covet a lovely countenance that differs from theirs. But there was another reason for her envy, one which she felt deep inside, and that was because Myleia was in love and was loved in return. The Queen quickly shook off these feelings as she walked up to the bench where the girl was seated. Myleia, however, was so deep in contemplation that she was unaware of anyone else's presence in the garden.

9 - Joal

"Good morning, Myleia," said the Queen softly.

Myleia started, "Oh! Your Highness," she replied and rose quickly.

"Sit, sit," said Engrid, still not completely comfortable with her elevated status. "Unless you would prefer to walk."

"Yes, I would like to walk, if it pleases Your Majesty."

"When it's just the two of us, I wish you would simply call me Engrid."

"All right."

The two young women, both still in their early twenties, began to walk slowly along the paths of the gardens. "You seemed deep in meditation back there."

"Yes," replied Myleia, without volunteering any more information. "Has there been any more word from Ritola?"

"No. But I assure you, I will inform you as soon as I hear anything."

A long silence ensued. Finally, Myleia said, "It's so hard being apart from him again. It seems that we are destined never to be together very long."

"It is also your destiny to love each other intensely whenever you are together. You are most fortunate to have that."

"I'm sorry. I didn't mean to complain."

"It's all right. You have every reason to complain about a fate that has so far allowed you so few happy moments in your young life."

"I just don't know what I would do if I lost him now."

"Don't think about that. There is no use worrying about something that probably won't happen."

The Winds of Wharhalen

There was another long silence. Then Myleia shattered it by asking, "Have you ever been in love?"

Engrid's look of surprise must have frightened her companion, and, immediately, Myleia wished she could have taken the question back. "I'm sorry. I didn't mean to be impertinent."

"It's not impertinent, just personal." Engrid smiled. After a moment for reflection, she said, "I don't think so…" Then she hesitated. "There was one, but I think he was in love with someone else. Anyway, I was too busy at the time fighting a war and then learning to be a Queen. I never really gave him a chance."

"What happened?"

"He left. I doubt that I will ever see him again."

Myleia detected a note of melancholy in Engrid's voice and, discreetly avoiding eye contact, sought to chart a less perilous route. "Are we always going to be fighting wars?"

A slight, ironic smile seemed to cross the Queen's face this time. "I'm afraid so. The warlords in the outer reaches of the Empire regard the Monarchy as vulnerable. Some of them, like Vartan, for example, are attempting to take advantage of the situation to grab power for themselves. Luckily so far, most of the tribes are too busy fighting one another to mount much of a threat. However, if they ever became united, I doubt that we could stop them. And here in the central region, the nobles are always squabbling. About the only thing they can agree on is that I should never have become Queen in the first place."

"Why?"

"My father gave up the throne when he elected to stay in Tairellia. Many of the nobles think that the line of succession therefore was broken, and they should be the ones who decide who rules."

9 - Joal

"But while Zironon was in power they did nothing. It was you who helped lead the rebellion that finally got rid of him."

"I can tell you have been listening to Kaine. Regardless, I really don't think the nobles are much of a threat. I would like to be able to count on their support if we are invaded by the northern tribes, though. To be honest, there are actually more serious threats right here in Attalia."

"What are they?"

"Greedy men that resent the fact that I control the vast wealth accumulated by Zironon. They continually try to stir up the people against me. But we can't just give the money back. We need it to pay the professional soldiers that keep Attalia and the surrounding villages safe from attack. Horses, weapons, and armor all cost money."

"You carry a heavy burden. You wanted this life for yourself?"

"I think so. After all the years of fighting, I'm finally in a position to make decisions that can improve things here. Nearly everyone suffered under Zironon."

"What are you doing then about these traitors in your midst?"

"Joal, who is my eyes and ears in Attalia, keeps me informed of any individuals or groups that grow too strong or too vocal in their opposition. I also try to deal with legitimate complaints as quickly as possible. But if my enemies prefer not to confront me directly, then we have to seek them out."

The walk concluded after about an hour, and Engrid was encouraged that she had finally been able to start a dialogue with Myleia. She so desperately needed a companion of the same age and gender to talk to. After all, being a Queen didn't preclude her from being a woman. When she got back to her quarters in the palace, Joal was waiting for an audience. The look on his face revealed a sense of

The Winds of Wharhalen

urgency. When they were alone in the large room where she met with her closest advisors, she turned to her trusted aide and said, "You have news for me?"

"Yes. As you know, we have been watching a man named Haczlok, whom we consider to be the most dangerous of your enemies. Our spies have infiltrated some of his meetings, which are growing larger. He uses his rhetoric to inflame the serfs and lately he is getting bolder in his criticism of you. We have also discovered that he is secretly building up a large cache of weapons near the city."

"He must be preparing to equip an army. I want you to confiscate the weapons immediately. Use whatever force is necessary. Then I want to speak to Haczlok. Arrest him and bring him to me."

Joal nodded his approval. Left on his own to implement the details of its execution, there was no more to be said. He bowed and strode quickly out of the Queen's apartments.

Joal went immediately to his top officer, Xotar, and ordered him to assemble the knights for a raid the following morning. When Xotar asked the target of the raid, Joal replied that he could not divulge the location until they were underway the next day. It was not that he didn't trust Xotar; on the contrary, the man had been with Joal and Kaine since the early days and was a fine soldier. But Joal had his own network of spies that provided him with information, and he shared that information only with the Queen. If their intentions to raid the weapons cache were to leak out, Haczlok's followers could move everything in a single night and not leave a trace.

Very early the next morning, Joal and Xotar rode out of the city with a hundred men. If the raid was able to keep its element of surprise, they would meet with little resistance. However, if Haczlok suspected that the location of the cache was known, he might be capable of defending it with twice that number. At the rear of Joal's

9 - Joal

heavy cavalry came wagons on which to load the weapons when they were seized. As it quietly made its way through the streets and out of the gates, few were fully awake yet to witness the procession. It crossed the river at the shallows and was out of sight of the city walls before Attalia began to stir at the start of a new day. The cache was reported to be located near the small village of Goran, in a wooded area, far from the main road. The clearing where the weapons were being accumulated was accessible only by means of a narrow, rutted wagon path. Joal knew that the dense woods on both sides of the path would provide perfect cover for an ambush, so he sent two groups of riders out on his flanks before taking the main force onto the path. These "wings" fanned out among the tall trees on either side of the path to get behind anyone who might try to attack the caravan and then flee to safety into the woods.

Joal's instincts proved themselves accurate. The barrage of arrows that came from the trees once Joal's army appeared on the path took their initial toll as a number of the Queen's soldiers were hit and fell. But as the attackers began their planned retreat, they were quickly cut down by the flanking horsemen. Trapped in a vise by the pursuing troops from the trail, many were killed instantly while the rest vanished in panicked disarray. The remainder of the traitors, left to defend the cache, also fled and were only able to take with them their own weapons. At once, the army set about the task of loading the large quantity of arms onto the wagons for the trip back to Attalia. Although he had suffered four fatalities and six more of his numbers were wounded, Joal nevertheless considered the raid a success. They had struck a decisive blow against Haczlok's forces and perhaps discouraged a significant portion of his followers from continuing with their endeavors. He knew Haczlok would remain elusive, but for now, the Queen had asserted her ability to crush small uprisings.

The army may have left the city quietly that morning, but their return later that same day was anything but quiet. Joal had timed their

The Winds of Wharhalen

return strategically so that when the troops made their triumphant entry, everyone was able to see how decisively they had accomplished the raid. The Queen's fledgling regime still lacked credibility in some quarters, and so Joal realized that regardless of how fairly or efficiently Engrid dispensed justice, force was the only thing some people would ever understand.

Following the march into the city, Joal left it to Xotar to oversee the tasks of taking the captured weapons to the armory, making arrangements for the dead and wounded soldiers, and dismissing the knights. Meanwhile, the Officer-at-Arms went immediately to the Queen, who was waiting anxiously for a report on the raid. They met in the same room where she had given the order for the raid on the morning of the previous day. Engrid acknowledged the quick bow Joal made as he entered without speaking. There was little need for formality between the two friends, who had spent so many days together fighting Zironon. The chasm that now separated them in rank had no real substance. Engrid knew that she owed her position to men like Joal, and her tenuous hold on the crown was one that could slip away at any moment. As such, if she managed to survive such a turn of events, her friends, as in another time, would be all she had.

"The operation was a complete success. Resistance was light, and we were able to capture a large amount of weaponry."

"How many men did we lose?"

"Four dead, six wounded; most of the wounded should recover."

Engrid shook her head sadly. "I'll never get used to the casualty reports." Her face registered no joy at the news of the raid. Grimly, she asked, "Do we have Haczlok?"

"Not yet. It may take a few days to find him."

9 - Joal

The Queen nodded and then turned away toward the window. After a moment, as Joal waited to be dismissed, she said over her shoulder, "Good work, old friend. Thank you."

After leaving the Queen, Joal went to visit Cecel, who had been confined to his quarters in the castle since being returned to Attalia from the siege of Ritola. The injuries he'd received leading the attack to capture the city had been severe. His leg was broken, and he had lost a great amount of blood when a sword cut had nearly severed his right arm. He had also suffered a concussion and several fractured ribs. Only the quick work of his men in immediately removing him from the battle had prevented him from dying there. Never in all of the veteran soldier's many previous campaigns had Cecel been unable to leave the field under his own power. Thus, he had taken the defeat hard, and his mood was not helped by having to be relieved of command and the ensuing long convalescence.

By contrast, Joal was in a cheerful mood, having successfully carried out the raid on Haczlok's weapons cache and re-entered the city at the head of the triumphant troops. His friend no longer appeared to be in danger of dying from his injuries; therefore, Joal's primary mission was to cajole Cecel into a better mood. The Gruenlander was being well-cared for in the castle, but Cecel was a man of action and not used to being looked after like a child. When Joal entered his quarters he passed a young girl, her face showing obvious distress, hurrying from the room.

"Greetings, Cecel. Are you the cause of the unhappiness I detected in your fair attendant?"

"I suppose I was rude to her. My temper is short these days."

"Perhaps you could spare her your unpleasant nature and let her come to work for me. She is certainly better looking than any of my servants."

The Winds of Wharhalen

"I will keep her for no other reason than to prevent her from falling into your hands. I know well what work you have in mind for her."

Joal shrugged. He had a reputation, not undeserved, for his roguish ways. Women, drinking, and gambling, were well-known components of his past, and still a part of his present, even now that he had assumed the role of the Queen's top Officer-at Arms. The two friends, therefore, made an interesting contrast, with the big Gruenlander never having completely shed his simple country nature, despite having risen to great power in his own land. Even though his fall was as swift as his assent, he was destined to rise again in Killarassee.

"It appears that you are at least eating well, Cecel. You look like a bear putting on a layer of fat for the winter."

Cecel patted his ample stomach. "Do you think so?" he replied, as if he had taken it as a compliment.

"I do. How is the leg healing?"

"The cursed thing still won't hold me. I tried to take a few steps this morning."

"What about the ribs?"

"Not much better. It even hurts to breathe. I heard that you went on a mission and returned with a lot of weapons."

"It went well. Resistance was light, and they didn't have much warning. The cache was fairly large though, which makes me believe that Haczlok is trying to raise an army."

"What would be his purpose?

"He wants Attalia, and, of course the treasury which comes with it."

9 - Joal

"How could he accomplish that?"

"With allies on the inside to let his army in when the time is right."

Cecel let this thought sink in before he changed subjects. "What do you think Kaine's chances are at Ritola?"

"You know how hard that place is to attack. Kaine is most likely in for a long siege."

"Sometimes I think it was easier being a thief. At least then you always knew who your enemies were."

"Easier, yes. Who knows? Perhaps some day we will be thieves again. In any case, this has been a long day, and it's getting late. I will see you tomorrow, Cecel."

"Take care, Joal, I don't need to tell you that you have enemies out there."

Joal shrugged. It was true that, as the one who stood between the Queen and all who would seek to overthrow her, he was an obvious target. When he left Cecel's quarters, he went to have dinner in the lower town. He could have eaten at the castle but, true to his nature, he preferred the rowdy atmosphere among the peasants. That's where most of his friends were, and Joal also knew it was where he could find women.

In the early hours of the morning, as he started back through the deserted streets toward the castle, Joal, in spite of his ale-clouded reverie, suspected that he was being followed. He was in an area that was formerly a part of the lists. The village of Attalia itself had spread out from an ancient castle as more and more villages seeking protection sprung up outside its walls. At the moment, Joal was still far from the outer castle wall and the bailey where an attack would be less likely. When he ducked down a narrow path between two houses where

The Winds of Wharhalen

it was dark and cluttered, Joal really felt no fear because he was in his element. After all, he had gotten out of so many tight spots as a thief. However, as he came back into the open on the other side, two knights with swords drawn confronted him. Their armor bore no insignia and their helmets concealed their faces. Joal drew his sword and attacked furiously. In the frenzy of ringing steel that followed, he managed to kill one of his assailants. But the remaining knight was soon joined by two more who'd come up the path behind Joal, and, in the end, the vicious deed was accomplished. On the dark streets of Attalia, the Queen's top Officer-at Arms lay dead in a pool of blood.

CHAPTER TEN

The Quarry

L ocke raised the huge iron hammer and brought it crashing down on the rock, breaking off a chunk which was then picked up and carried away to the cutters. The hammer rose and fell again and again until the muscles in his arms and back cried out for relief. He knew he had only a brief moment to rest, though, before the overseer would notice the inactivity. Then the whip would bite into the flesh on his bare back or legs if he didn't resume his labors.

The unrelenting sun bore down on the laborers in the quarry. The rainy season was over, and the temperatures seemed to rise daily. The work went on from dawn until dusk, with no relief and no hope for escape. The rocks were broken from the solid walls, then cut into rough blocks and hauled away on horse-drawn carts to be used in building projects. The crews of whip-wielding overseers rotated in and out of the miserable hole, but the only escape for the condemned slaves was death. A line of archers on the rim of the quarry prevented anyone with thoughts of attempting an early exit.

Locke was told by one of the other workers on his arrival that the average prisoner lived six months after starting in the quarry. Locke

The Winds of Wharhalen

figured he was somewhere in his fifth month now, even though he lost track of time, for every day was the same. Even during the winter months the same routine prevailed. He remembered there had been one day off though. It was a day when rain had fallen heavily for twelve hours one night, nearly flooding the quarry and making the trails in and out impassable for the carts. Work had to be suspended for the day so as not to endanger the horses.

At night the slaves huddled under a canopy that extended out from a rocky overhang, shackles clamped securely around their ankles. The slaves' sleeping area was ringed with guards armed with swords and spears. Not one among the prisoners could ever recall any successful escape attempts.

As he worked, Locke thought back to the day Toulon's treachery had made him a slave. As he was taken from the great hall by the guards, he could hear the pitiful voice of Eylese crying out to him. Struggling desperately, he broke free from his captors momentarily, but the dull impact of a blow to the back of his head quickly sent him staggering. The resulting din that resonated inside his skull was like the roar of the ocean rushing into a cavern. When he began to regain his senses, he found himself on his hands and knees. As he tried to get to his feet, more blows fell upon his shoulders and head. The pain caused him to cry out, and his limbs lost their strength. Then as he lay face down on the ground, neither hearing nor seeing, the pounding inside his head finally gave way to unconsciousness.

At one point, Locke remembered waking up briefly only to discover himself inside a cart that jostled his body and made him acutely aware of his injuries. In addition, his hands and feet were tied and each bump caused excruciating pain behind his eyes. He had difficulty focusing at the time but thought that the cart had bars on the door and window. Eventually, the pain forced him to close his eyes, and he passed out again.

10 - The Quarry

When he next remembered regaining consciousness, Locke recalled being dragged into a sales ring with about two dozen other men and women. He was too weak to resist and his clouded thoughts were only able to comprehend fragments of the proceedings. After the sale, he was loaded onto an open wagon with five or six men whose ragged clothes were a reflection of their low social status. The journey to the quarry had taken two days, during which time these unfortunates were given one meal and two water-breaks each day. On their arrival, they were put to work immediately, even while Locke was still experiencing severe headaches and occasional blackouts. During these spells, he would sometimes fall, only to be whipped by the overseer until he would regain his feet and start working again.

The overseer's whip returned Locke's mind back into the present. The workers were now being told to line up to be examined. He noticed a man on horseback with mounted guards riding down the steep, narrow path into the pit. He was accompanied by the superintendent and two guards bearing crossbows. Once he got to the bottom of the pit, the man dismounted and walked among the slaves, inspecting them as one would horses entering a sales ring. Three times he stopped and pointed, and each time he did, one of the slaves would be taken off the line and herded up the path to the rim. Although Locke wasn't aware of it, the man must have pointed to him, because suddenly the youth was roughly pulled from his position and walked up the path to join the others.

When those that had been separated reached the top, the superintendent said to the four, "You have been chosen to work for Lord Tarbaukis. It is a privilege that you must continually show that you are worthy of. The slightest transgression will ensure that you will be returned here to spend the rest of your days in the pit."

With this new master and the mounted guards, the four slaves, joined by a single chain shackled to their wrists, started walking to the north, seemingly exchanging one life of bondage for a new one. After traveling the rest of the day, they eventually began to pass grain fields, orchards and pastures that radiated out from the palisade of a great castle. Locke thought to himself, when he saw the edifice that stood in the distance, that it was undoubtedly built from blocks that had come from the same quarry that had claimed so many lives. It also brought back the memory of Toulon's castle and the pain that was eternally seared into his consciousness by the treacherous acts of the noble. In spite of the intense hatred of these men of power that burned inside him, the sight of all these living, growing things in the midst of this agricultural landscape somehow revived faint embers of life within Locke. The very air of the place seemed cool and sweet to lungs previously choked for months by rock dust in the quarry. Their arrival at the castle was late in the day, and with darkness closing in quickly, the group of new slaves was kept chained together and slept under armed supervision inside the palisade on a wide stretch of open ground until the next day. For Locke and the others, accustomed to sleeping under uncomfortable conditions, this was no worse than the shelter at the quarry. In fact, the refreshing breeze and pleasant fragrances of the orchards nearby was a considerable improvement over filthy bodies crowded together, with the stench of sweat, disease, and inescapable death.

In the morning they were taken to a creek that flowed through pastures where animals were grazing. The chains were removed, and these wretched creatures from the quarry, their bodies scarred and dirty, were told to wash. Their clothes were then taken from them and burned. While they were in the creek, a young woman passed by them on horseback. She was cantering a magnificent black stallion and rode with great command and a haughty bearing. She barely gave the group a passing glance as she rode into the nearby woods. These slaves were of no more consequence to this privileged girl than the cattle that grazed in the fields.

10 - The Quarry

However, the sight of the girl caused Locke to think of Eylese. She'd never really been out of his mind. As painful as it was to recall what he had lost, he still couldn't keep himself from memories of the times when they were together. He remembered her soft brown hair, her expressive eyes, and the sweet smell of her skin when his face was near her cheek. Sometimes he imagined their kisses and could almost feel her lips on his mouth. There were times, however, when he tried to recall her image and couldn't. When this happened, it would frighten and frustrate him, because her memory was a needed escape that would take him away from the misery of his present life as a slave. Always, though, his thoughts of those pleasant days spent with Eylese ended with a renewed feeling of anger and hatred he felt for Toulon, who'd taken it all away from him.

Locke and the others were then given new clothes and taken to quarters just within the outer wall and fed. After eating, the men were put to work in a hayfield, cutting the long blades of grasses. It seemed early in the season for a cutting, but Locke reminded himself that he was now much farther south than he was accustomed to. He was given a long-handled cutting tool for this purpose, its long, curved steel blade well-suited to the task, but it also brought to Locke's mind other uses.

There was no whip-wielding overseer here, and the men were allowed to work at a pace that surely would have incurred the wrath of their previous masters in the quarry. However, they still did have to wear chains which shackled their legs together, and a guard on horseback was always assigned to watch over them. Females, a sight non-existent in the quarries, would bring casks of water around to them at intervals. These breaks were certainly welcome as the sun in the open fields was unrelenting, but the water and the rest were actually no more refreshing to these wretched souls than the mere presence of the women themselves.

The Winds of Wharhalen

Days and then weeks went by without much change in routine. The location and the type of labor varied, however. Sometimes the slaves would be used to clear rocks and stumps; sometimes to cut and haul trees from the forested areas; and sometimes to plow fields where they were permitted to use horses. It was in this latter area that Locke quickly distinguished himself from the other men. Because he understood horses, he was usually able to get even the most recalcitrant of the animals to do their jobs efficiently. Gradually, he was given more and more responsibilities near the stables, working around the large number of horses kept there. Of course, the horses that Locke worked with were not fine riding horses like the one that he'd seen being ridden by the young mistress of the castle. Instead, he worked in the barn with the large and rugged plow and wagon horses, which were used to pull the supply wagons, plow the fields, pull stumps, and haul logs from the woods. In an adjacent barn, there were powerfully built war horses bred to carry fully-armored knights.

Another barn, not far away, was the one Locke found most interesting. It was there that he often saw the girl working with the light-legged riding horses. These were horses bred for speed and conformation like the ones he'd seen in Callanco. But what especially commanded the boy's attention was the young mistress herself. It was highly unusual to see a woman even riding horses, let alone training them. Although there were always men at hand to assist her, it was obvious that the girl was in charge. Furthermore, whenever Locke saw her in the paddock areas she was always wearing pants, something else very much out of the ordinary. He couldn't recall ever having seen a woman in pants before, but he admitted to himself that the way they revealed the shape of her legs and hips was actually quite pleasing. Apparently, Locke wasn't the only one whose attention was diverted by the girl. For whenever she walked around the stable area, her chin held high, shoulders back, and long, dark hair bouncing with every step, it seemed like all work would come to a stop.

10 - The Quarry

There were times when Locke's anger at his enslavement threatened to boil to the surface, and if it weren't for the vast difference between conditions in the fief as opposed to those of the quarry, it probably would have. He hated himself for the way he had so readily submitted to his subservience here, but when he recalled the pain and suffering and slow death of those condemned to the quarry, he rationalized that this was just a form of survival. He decided he would wait, and eventually the opportunity to escape would present itself. Certainly, there was more potential for escape here than in the quarry. In the meantime, he liked working with the horses, and he was gradually regaining his health by eating better food and living in more sanitary conditions. And, not insignificantly, in his new position at the horse barns, the leg chains had come off.

One day, as Locke was carrying a basket of manure out of the workhorse barn, he heard a commotion coming from the adjacent barn and was nearly run down by a frightened horse that had a saddle, but no rider. He looked back in the direction from which it was fleeing to see the young mistress slowly getting to her feet. Men rushed over quickly to assist her, but Locke could tell from her demeanor that she was in no mood to be helped. She stomped her foot, shook her head, and uttered some curses he could barely make out. The horse, in the meantime, had stopped by a paddock where Locke's horses had been turned out while their stalls were being cleaned. Locke started for the runaway, then heard the girl yell, "Stop!" as she stormed past him. As she angrily approached the horse, the animal shied away, doubling the distance between himself and his pursuer.

With a gesture, the girl indicated that she was now willing to have help, and two men in her service immidiately began to pursue the wayward steed. This, of course, prompted the stallion to frolic and kick and further widen the gap of freedom. As the chase wore on, much to the apparent delight of the horse, and to the consternation of the humans, the reins fell down around the horse's legs, causing him to trip several times, once even going down to his knees. The girl, fearing for the horse's safety, called off the effort to capture him and turned in disgust to return to the residence. At this point, Grizzel, the stable master in the workhorse barn, approached the girl and said, "Pardon me mistress, but would you like me to have this man retrieve the stallion for you?"

Locke, standing nearby, realized that Grizzel was referring to him, and stood waiting for the girl's response. "What? A slave? Are you joking, Grizzel?"

"No mistress, he has…a way with horses."

The girl, now seeing that Grizzel was serious, said, "All right, but if Tarano is injured in any way, this slave shall be flogged."

Grizzel nodded in Locke's direction.

Locke indeed had a way with horses. As a young boy he had spent most of his time around horses, studying their behavior and learning what caused them to react the way they did to specific influences in their environment. He had even taken the time to learn new ways to maneuver around these intelligent animals, rejecting the excessively harsh, traditional breaking and training methods that men seemed to have passed down from one generation to another. He had, in effect, learned to behave like a horse, and in doing so, was able to gain their trust.

As he separated himself from the others, Locke began to move around the stallion without ever approaching it in a direct line. He'd observed how, when the others had done that, they had only managed to drive the horse farther away. Locke never faced the animal, always keeping the axis of his shoulders at right angles. When he would pause, Tarano would watch him carefully, waiting for the sudden, threatening posture that never came. Locke kept his gaze turned slightly away,

10 - *The Quarry*

appearing indifferent, and after a few minutes, the stallion took a few tentative steps toward him. Locke then moved off in a slightly different direction, always making sure to keep about the same distance between them. Again, Tarano moved closer, head down, close to the grass in a submissive posture. This intricate dance continued in unhurried fashion until eventually the two participants were less than a foot apart. When Locke slowly extended his hand and touched the great stallion on the shoulder in a reassuring way, the bond was complete. Tarano then allowed Locke to take the reins and followed passively while being led back to the astounded group of onlookers. Locke approached the girl and offered her the reins. He wasn't sure what kind of a reaction to expect from this spoiled child and bowed his head slightly in mock deference. Locke observed that the young mistress was about sixteen years old and had black hair and dark flashing eyes. Also, her features were handsomely shaped, and her skin had the fresh luster of youth. The young man had to admit to himself that, in spite of her arrogant demeanor, she was exquisitely beautiful. A smile from those sensuous lips would have been thanks enough for the service he had rendered, but even that was not forthcoming. The girl's eyes found Locke's gaze and reveled in a moment of satisfaction that this boy found her as attractive as she was unattainable. Then, she simply took the reins in her delicate hand, turned without a word, and walked the stallion back to the barn.

The next day Locke was reassigned to the barn where the riding horses were kept. Grizzel wasn't happy to lose his best horse handler, but it was obvious that the order had come from a higher authority. Locke's new assignment brought him in daily contact with the girl and he soon realized that her passion for horses was genuine, for she spent much of each day training, riding, even grooming her large stable of finely-bred equines. Most of the time, Locke would receive his orders from Otillion, the large, dark-skinned horse master. Once in a while, when she would require something, the girl would merely address

The Winds of Wharhalen

the boy as "slave"; but the rest of the time they would simply move about in the barn in an intricate choreography of awareness and avoidance. Locke did observe though that the young girl's shoddy treatment of people did not transfer over to her treatment of animals. She was quite knowledgeable and showed a gentle nature when handling all her horses, and they responded to her in kind.

One afternoon, as the day's activities were winding down in the barn, the girl abruptly addressed Locke. The way the words erupted from her lips, it seemed as though they'd been pent-up for days. "Slave, I want you to teach me how to catch a horse that has run away."

Locke, who was not facing the young woman at the time, smiled in satisfaction. He managed to suppress the smile, however, before turning to face her. "I didn't realize that there were any horses unaccounted for, Mistress."

"No, no there aren't. I mean *when* a horse has run away, how do you catch it like you did the other day?"

Locke studied her face. It was a contradiction of frustration at having to ask a slave for advice and an earnest desire to learn something new. "Horses never really run away. Oh, they like to express their independence every once in a while by separating from us, but they are herd animals, and, by nature, they always seek the company of other horses. And, if we treat them with kindness, they will also seek ours as well."

"But why then, when you go to catch them, do they run farther away?"

"When you aggressively try to catch them, they think you are driving them away. And to a horse, the worst punishment is to be driven away from the herd."

"So, to catch them you..." The girl, now captivated, drew closer.

10 - The Quarry

"You must assume a posture of welcoming that lets them know that it's all right to come back."

The girl thought about this for a minute. "Are you teasing me? Because if you are…" Her dark eyes flashed.

"Risk a flogging to play a joke on the young mistress? That would be foolish indeed."

"I want you to teach me how to do it."

Locke bowed slightly.

"We'll start tomorrow morning," she said, resuming her haughty air once again. With that, she turned and strode out of the barn leaving the boy to finish his cleaning.

The next day, Locke was brought to the barn by the guards in the usual manner—each slave taken to his place of work and put in the custody of an overseer. In Locke's case, it was Otillion. The large, powerfully-built black man was then immediately relieved of this duty by the slender, teenage girl whom Locke had since learned was named Kira. Although Otillion retired to the background, he was never out of sight of the young mistress. The girl was dressed in her customary riding attire, with boots that came up to her knees, tight-fitting leggings that defined the comely shape of her lower body, and a loose shirt that was tied with a sash around her slim waist. Locke hadn't realized that a girl could dress in men's clothing and still look so emphatically feminine.

"Let's get started," said Kira, in her characteristically impatient manner.

"All right, which horse do you think is the most difficult to work with?"

"Tarano," she replied, without hesitation.

The Winds of Wharhalen

Locke went to the stallion's stall and led the great animal out using a coil of rope threaded through the halter. As the horse was led out into an empty paddock, the girl followed. Locke suddenly stopped and said to her, "If I show you how to do this, will you call me by my name?"

Kira looked stunned by this insolence.

"I have a name," pursued Locke.

"You are in no position to bargain. You are a slave and I could have you sent back to the quarries."

"So you know about the quarries then. Do you also know that men sent there usually die within six months?"

A look of discomfort came over Kira's face, which she quickly tried to conceal by hardening the line of her mouth and narrowing her eyes. "Proceed with the demonstration or you will wish you were never born, name or no name."

Locke let Tarano go in the paddock and uncoiled the rope. He cast the end of the rope toward the horse and started the animal running. He next pursued the surprised beast by continuing to snake the line out over the ground. Each time the horse would try to stop running, Locke would drive him on, circling the paddock.

"Why do you keep driving him away, when he wishes to stop?" inquired Kira.

"He has to be ready to return to me."

"How do you know he isn't ready?"

"Watch his head. His ears, his mouth, the position of his head will tell me."

After about five minutes of this dance between man and horse, even the girl could see a difference in the animal's behavior. Finally,

10 - The Quarry

Locke ended the chase. He stood with his shoulders turned away from Tarano, and looked away indifferently. Slowly, the horse began to approach. As he grew nearer, Locke moved off in a slightly different direction, always keeping the axis of his shoulders at a position ninety degrees to the horse. Tarano continued moving closer. When only a foot separated the two, Locke stretched his arm out to touch the animal's side. Tarano flinched. Locke immediately snaked the rope out again and drove the horse away. When Tarano showed what Locke had determined was the proper degree of contrition, the boy let him approach again. This time when Locke reached out to touch him on the shoulder, Tarano didn't move a muscle. Locke then gently stroked the animal on its sides, its legs, its neck, and finally took hold of the halter and rubbed the appreciative equine between the eyes.

The rapt girl stood in amazement, but only for a moment before she asked, "Can I try it now?"

"Not with this horse. He's done. You won't have any trouble with him again unless he is mistreated and begins to fear people. Let's get out another horse."

Kira proved herself to be an observant pupil. With the next horse, a filly named Cloud, the girl followed Locke's procedures step by step. There were times when she would show impatience, letting the horse stop too soon or trying to approach too quickly, but each time Locke would gently instruct her as to what to do next with a few well-chosen words. When Cloud ultimately stood quietly and let Kira take the halter, the young mistress could not contain her smile. "Let's do another one."

So it went the rest of the day, until half of the horses in the barn had been "gentled" by Locke and the girl. The horses were not the only ones changed by this experience, though, as Locke noticed a gradual softening of Kira's haughty demeanor as well. The more she became engrossed in working with the horses, the more it seemed that

The Winds of Wharhalen

the barrier between the two teenagers crumbled as well. In time, the previously stern features of her pretty face began to brighten, and the tone of her voice lost its air of arrogance. When the last horse had been put away and the barn had been swept, the girl turned to Locke and said, "I'll expect you here tomorrow morning to show me more of what you know—by the way, what *is* your name?"

The boy tried not to let his satisfaction at this question show. "Locke," he answered, with a slight bow of his head.

"I'll see you in the morning then, Locke."

"As you wish, Mistress."

CHAPTER ELEVEN

Kira

As the days passed, anyone watching the relationship which was forming between Locke and Kira, would have scarcely guessed that it was one between mistress and slave. Locke was always careful to avoid comments or actions that would hint of familiarity. The girl, on the other hand, appeared to grow less guarded, her behavior sometimes becoming almost flirtatious. The physical attraction was understandable, but beyond that, there was the common bond of a mutual interest in horses. Under Locke's tutelage, the girl's understanding of the nature of the animals grew to match her already strong love for them. The transformation that took place in Kira during this time had the effect of enhancing her already great beauty by softening the features of her face and allowing a previously hidden warmth to be exuded.

Locke, who had at their first meeting, held nothing but disdain for the pretentious daughter of his owner, suddenly found himself looking forward to their time together. Each interlude afforded him an opportunity to escape into a world that seemed like play to him: the beautiful riding horses that curbed their wild and powerful natures

The Winds of Wharhalen

under his skillful hand combined with the equally beautiful young girl who valued his knowledge. Deep in the recesses of his mind, it had occurred to him that Kira was perhaps becoming attached to him in a way that had little to do with his expertise as a trainer of horses. It flattered him as a man but scared him as a slave, a position over which the girl still maintained tremendous leverage. Fear of the escalating relationship mixed with his growing attraction to the young woman to create an intoxicating air of excitement.

One afternoon at the close of a training session, Kira asked Locke, "How did a slave learn so much about horses?"

"I haven't always been a slave."

The answer seemed to surprise the girl, as if slavery was an inescapable caste into which one was born. "Then how did you become a slave?"

"I had only been enslaved for about five months when I was brought here. Before that, I was a trader in the Karpoans. When my partner was killed by bandits last summer, I left the Karpoans to come south. I won a great deal of money racing my horse, but it was stolen from me, and to conceal the crime, the thief sold me to the slavers."

"Who was the person who did this to you?"

"His name is Toulon. He is Lord of a fief much like this one."

"A nobleman did this to you?"

Locke nodded. "Why are you surprised? Your father owns slaves. Why do you think that is? Why doesn't he just have peasants do the work here?"

"There aren't enough of them. So many of the young men have either been killed or are off fighting in a war somewhere. Father needs to use slaves to make a profit from the land."

"Have you ever thought about how people become slaves?"

11 - Kira

Kira looked perplexed. "Surely your case is unusual. I assume the others don't know anything else."

"That's not true. Every day people are sold into slavery, many of them women and children. The path of their lives is thus very often determined by forces beyond their control. Like the girl whose freedom I was trying to buy from Toulon."

A cloud passed over Kira's expression. Locke worried that he may have revealed too much.

"The girl?" asked Kira, eyes now cast toward the ground. "Were you in love with her?"

Locke stumbled over his answer. "I... I don't know for sure."

The composure of the young mistress seemed to be slipping away. She then muttered something about having to get ready for dinner and turned to leave.

"Should I be here to work with the horses tomorrow?" asked Locke, temporarily arresting the girl's flight.

Kira hesitated for a moment, then turned her head back toward the boy. "Yes, yes, of course." She then continued on.

The next day, Locke had expected a change in Kira's attitude due to the things that he had told her the day before, but, quite the contrary, the girl seemed even friendlier than usual. Conversation, however, was limited only to that which pertained to training the horses. The work proceeded as it had every other day prior to this, and once again they found themselves alone together in the barn at day's end. With the horses put away for the night, and no more work to be done, Kira seemed to be intentionally lingering. In the air there was a slight nuance of tension, and Locke waited expectantly while busying himself with cleaning.

The Winds of Wharhalen

"If what you told me yesterday is true," Kira started, "then it is not right for you to remain a slave any longer."

A feeling of elation began to swell within Locke. Perhaps he finally had an advocate who could speak on his behalf in higher places. He turned to face the girl but didn't say anything, lest his voice betray his eagerness.

"I could bring the matter before my father, but it will still be difficult to pursue the case and prove your innocence. Even if we confronted this Toulon, it would be your word against his. And noble against peasant, at that."

Locke remained silent but studied the girl's eyes intently, waiting for the next line of reasoning.

"My father might free you as a favor to me if I plead with him, but I really don't want to lose you as a horse trainer."

Locke made a slight gesture with his head to indicate that he was still listening.

"So, would you agree to stay and continue to work here with the horses if you were no longer a slave?"

Locke stifled his inclination to answer quickly and paused to ponder his response. If he agreed to the girl's deal and became a free man, wouldn't he be free to leave whenever he chose? But if he left before Kira was ready for him to leave, couldn't she then have him hunted down and sent back to the quarry? He didn't want to lose this ally, but if he agreed to stay, wasn't he then just becoming her personal slave? How was that much different than his present situation?

"Mistress, your sympathy for my case is extremely kind. However, if I were ever to find myself a free man, I would still have a matter to settle with Toulon. I couldn't do that from here."

11 - Kira

Kira cast her eyes downward. She started to say something else, but her jaw clamped down on the words before they could come out. She shrugged as if to indicate that it didn't matter to her, and simply said as she walked out of the barn, "I'll see you in the morning."

The next day, things were much as they were before the conversation had taken place. If Kira held any resentment at Locke's response to her offer, she concealed it well. A little past mid-afternoon, the girl suddenly announced to Locke, "I want to take a ride. Saddle Southwind for me. Saddle Tarano too; I want you to go with me."

Although he had ridden a little in the ring to demonstrate technique to Kira, Locke had never been allowed away from the barn area before. Since being transferred from the fields to the stable areas, Locke's status had improved considerably. But he was still a slave nonetheless. As he saddled his horse, a feeling of trepidation rose in him. He was entering perilous territory in his relationship with Kira. To ride away from the castle with the Lord's daughter would undoubtedly attract a lot of attention, but at the same time he could hardly refuse an order from her.

Kira led the way through the woods when the trail was narrow and slowed to allow Locke to come abreast when it widened. Part of the time they rode in silence, but occasionally the girl would chat amiably and point things out that she had seen on other rides. After a while Locke, in spite of his apprehension, found the riding pleasurable, as well as the company of the pretty young woman. The wood was cool and the light dim and this caused Locke to think of the grove where he'd met Eylese.

As they emerged from the wood into a broad meadow with waving blades of grass, Kira looked over at him and said, "I'll race you to the other side," and, without waiting for a reply, put her heels to Southwind, who responded explosively and was quickly away by five lengths. Tarano didn't need much urging by his rider though and soon

The Winds of Wharhalen

made up the lost ground. Locke knew that his horse could easily overtake Southwind, but he didn't think the mistress would appreciate being passed, so he stayed at her flank until they neared the boundary of the meadow, when he pulled up alongside her, creating a virtually even finish.

They slowed to a walk through another stretch of woods, and then came to another opening that ended on a bluff with a breathtaking view of the valley below. "Let's rest the horses here before starting back," said Kira, dismounting. They grounded their reins and left the horses to graze in the clearing. After the girl walked to the edge of the cliff, she motioned for Locke to join her. As they stood gazing at the peaceful scene before them, Kira slipped her arm around Locke's and leaned her head on his shoulder. Alone as they were, the show of familiarity seemed almost natural to the boy, but he still feared the wrath of the girl if she were to feel spurned.

"Locke, would it be so terrible staying here with me? We have such fun together. As a free man, you would be able to advance in station and accumulate wealth, and I would be a powerful ally." As she was saying this, she turned to face him and placed her hands on his chest.

"I *do* enjoy being with you, Kira," using her name for the first time. "But what you propose does not really make me a free man. It only makes me your lap dog."

"But you must admit it would be a very comfortable lap," she said mockingly, and put her arms around his waist. Her body was now pressed against his, and her head lay against his chest.

Locke felt a weakening of his resolve as the girl's body was now doing what her words could not. "But, we would still always be slave and mistress. When you grow tired of me, that is what would remain," he protested.

11 - Kira

"Sometimes I wonder which of us is the slave." Kira looked up with her head slightly tilted and gazed into his eyes. Her beautiful eyes were pleading her case and her full, parted lips awaited a reply.

Locke then kissed her tenderly, and the tender kiss quickly swelled into a passionate one as the girl's emotions were at last released. Locke tried to tell himself that he was only yielding to the girl's seduction out of self-preservation, but, in reality, her soft mouth, sweet fragrance, and supple body were filling him with excitement.

On the way back to the stables, Locke and Kira were each absorbed in their own thoughts. The boy, still intoxicated with feelings that he'd never before imagined having under the circumstances, was trying to sort things out in his mind. His relationship with the girl had escalated far beyond his control. Somehow he had allowed himself to be swept along with Kira's emotional attachment for him and her plans for their future. But he knew he couldn't go along with a deal that would bind him to her in exchange for his freedom, for no assurance existed that could protect him from her vengeance if the relationship were to sour. He had, on the other hand, now put her in a vulnerable position in which she would feel hurt and betrayed if he tried to back out. It was this burden he carried with him as the two rode back through the woods.

The next day, Locke was working with Cloud in the ring while Kira watched from the perimeter. Lord Tarbaukis, Kira's father whom Locke rarely saw, came out to the stables with a man clad in partial armor, whose appearance gave evidence of many battles fought. His hair and beard were shaggy; his clothes, while of fine quality, looked as though they had been worn for a long time without a change. He bore the scars of fighting, and his demeanor was one of strength and dominance. His eyes were piercing in their gaze, as if they could look into one's soul to determine friend or foe. This soldier and the noble stood for a time watching Locke work, and the contrast between the

The Winds of Wharhalen

two was stark. Unlike his fellow observer, Kira's father was slightly built and dressed neatly in the clothing of a nobleman. He wasn't old, but it was evident that his reddish hair was receding from his forehead. The two men then moved on in the direction of the barns. When he saw them, Locke looked over at Kira, who seemed as perplexed at the presence of this rare visitor as he was. She shrugged to indicate that she didn't know what was going on. He smiled at her and continued with the filly's schooling.

Later that day, when Locke was finishing up in the barn and Kira was pretending to be busy in order to stay with him, Otillion walked in. He bowed slightly to acknowledge the girl, and then addressed Locke. "You'll be leaving the fief tomorrow."

Locke could only think that this had something to do with Kira, and that he was being sent back to the quarry. "What have I done to displease my owner?" Locke knew that he could do nothing to influence such a decision, but he hoped to find out how much was known of his relationship with the girl.

"Nothing. You have been sold. The Royal Army has purchased remounts from us, and they need a handler. The soldier making the purchase saw you working with the horses this morning and wants you to accompany the herd to Ritola. Lord Tarbaukis made you part of the deal."

"Ritola? Why are they taking horses to Ritola?"

"The army is laying siege to the city there; it has been going on for months. Enough questions; you now belong to the Queen. Be ready to leave with the horses at sunrise."

Kira had remained quiet and out of sight during this conversation. However, as soon as Otillion left she said, "I must talk to my father immediately. I can't let you leave."

"What will you say to him?"

11 - Kira

"I'll tell him how valuable you are in the stables. How much you have improved the horses."

"But if he thinks your interest goes beyond that, it will make it even more certain that he will want me gone."

"I'll be discreet." The girl rose on her toes and placed a loving kiss on Locke's mouth, then hurried away.

Kira found her father in the castle with her mother. Although she feared that her mother would see through her motives more clearly than her father, she thought it would be even more suspicious if she asked her to leave.

"I have heard that you sold a number of horses to the army."

Tarbaukis looked up and examined the girl's expression. "Yes, just common stock. None of your fine horses."

"I also heard that the slave that has been working with my horses is to go with them."

"Where did you hear that?"

Kira hesitated slightly. "Otillion."

"Well, that is true also."

"Father, he has a gift for working with horses. He has taught them so much. Does it have to be him?"

"A slave from the quarry who is a gifted horse trainer? Really, Kira," said her father, shaking his head.

"He has only been a slave for five months. He was cheated out of his fortune and then sold to the slavers."

Now both parents were scrutinizing the girl as this revelation came pouring out.

"He told you this?"

The Winds of Wharhalen

Kira nodded, realizing that she had let too much emotion slip into her voice.

"And you believed him?"

"Yes."

Her mother then entered the conversation for the first time. "It would appear that you know far more about this slave than you should," she said disapprovingly.

"It doesn't matter now," said Tarbaukis, "the deal is made. He leaves tomorrow with the horses."

"Please! You must send someone else in his place."

"Enough! We'll have no more discussion about it. In the future, Kira, you must remember who you are. We don't become familiar with slaves. If I hadn't just sold him, he'd be flogged and sent back to the quarry just for talking to you."

Kira knew she had lost. She turned quickly and left the room, tears beginning to well up in her eyes.

After she had left, her mother turned to her husband and said, "Have someone watch her; I don't want her leaving the residence tonight."

"Do you think she is...emotionally attached to this boy?"

The woman said, "I am certain of it."

Kira returned to the barn in hopes that Locke was still there. She found only Otillion.

"Where is the boy who trains the horses?"

The stable master appeared surprised by the question. "He's locked up in his quarters for the night, Mistress."

"Get him for me."

11 - Kira

"I don't understand."

"I want to talk to him."

"I think it would be better to wait until morning."

"I need to talk to him *now*."

"I don't have the authority to retrieve a slave that has been locked up for the night."

"I'm giving you the authority!" said the girl, her voice beginning to rise.

Just at that moment, one of the Lord's Men-at-Arms came into the barn. "Mistress, your father has sent me to bring you back to the castle."

"I suppose he told you to drag me back if necessary."

"If necessary."

Kira regained her composure. Assuming the haughty demeanor that Locke had seen when he first came to the farm, she wheeled around and strode defiantly back to the castle.

The next morning, Locke was released from his quarters as always, but instead of eating with the other slaves, he was given part of a loaf of bread and a flask of water. He was then taken to the paddock where the fifteen horses to be transferred had been kept the night before. The soldier was already there with his own mount, and a saddle had been placed on one of the sale horses for Locke to ride. Locke looked around, hoping to see Kira. He knew she would try to say goodbye if she could, but suspected that, having tried to plead his case, she was now being confined by her father until he was gone. Although deep inside he knew that what the girl had wanted for them would never have worked out, there still existed a longing to see her again. She had somehow managed to rekindle the fire of life within him at a time when months in the quarry had nearly extinguished it.

The Winds of Wharhalen

CHAPTER TWELVE

Braslon

Engrid, aside from her personal guards, was the last to leave the cemetery after the interment of Joal. Cecel was too ill to attend the funeral and Kaine was hundreds of miles away at Ritola. The effect of Joal's death on the Queen was profound. Not only was he one of her few close friends, he was the shield that protected her from the dangers of her precarious position on the throne. She now felt naked, vulnerable, and utterly alone. Never had the burden of ruling the Empire been so overwhelming. Once she had recovered from the initial shock of the assassination, her first thought was to recall Kaine from Ritola. He was the leader that held the respect of all the soldiers, both present and past. Haczlok wouldn't challenge her authority if Kaine were in Attalia. But, she thought, "How firm is my hold on the crown if I always need Kaine to help me maintain it? Wouldn't my position as ruler be diminished even in the eyes of Kaine himself if I had to recall him from an important campaign just to put down a minor disturbance in my own capital? Besides, if the army is unable to secure Ritola, the whole region could collapse. Our inability to extend our control beyond Attalia would further encourage uprisings all over the Empire. No, I will have to somehow figure out how to manage the situation here without Kaine."

Thus, Engrid immediately went about the task of finding someone to take over military command in Attalia. Cecel was still physically unable to lead an army and, in any case, lacked the ruthless cunning necessary for political intrigue. Xotar and Skauld, men she knew from the days of the rebellion, were common soldiers that would be ineffective as leaders. Attuis, Captain of her personal guard, was smart, but young and inexperienced in ancillary matters of the Empire. Among the nobles, there was one that name stood out. Lord Braslon's family had lived for centuries in the region occupied by Attalia. When Kaine had led the rebellion against Zironon's son, Sharnov, in the chaotic days following the death of the warlord, Braslon was the first of the Lords to offer his knights in service. Since then, he had helped ease the transition from the rule of the warlord Zironon to that of Engrid. He was popular with the people in and around Attalia; in fact, even more popular than the new Queen herself, who was still regarded by many as a foreigner, having come to Killarassee after having grown up in Tairellia. Engrid desperately needed someone who had the people's trust so that she would learn of conspiracies before they grew beyond her ability to contain them. Furthermore, Braslon was also a proven leader on the battlefield, who had earned the respect of his Men-at-Arms by fighting courageously alongside them. After carefully considering all these and other pertinent factors, and delaying her decision for a day to make sure that her thinking was clear, she summoned Braslon to the castle.

The fief of this nobleman was the nearest of several in a patchwork radiating out from the great walled city. The nobles, with families dating back to the time of the Old Kings, were enjoying relative prosperity under Engrid. In return for their service in helping to overthrow Zironon, the Queen had relaxed payment of the heavy

12 - Braslon

tributes demanded of them in the past. Braslon's father was Lord of the fief when Zironon had defeated King Jonas and the nobles thirty years ago. The elder Braslon had died shortly after that, and his son had grown up with a reluctant allegiance to the hated warlord. Like the other nobles, however, he awaited the day in which the great families of Killarassee would once again rise in influence. They had reached their zenith in the era following the breakup of the Empire of the Old Kings. The ascent of Jonas signaled the end of that era, and the reign of Zironon further relegated the nobles to their secondary position in the hierarchy of power. Lord Braslon was now approaching middle age and had far more hair in the full beard on his face than he did on his head. Engrid had met Braslon on a number of occasions, and he had often supported her in discussions with the nobles. They seemed to listen to him and she felt he would be valuable to her if help from the nobles was ever needed in repelling an invasion from the tribes to the north. Perhaps the appointment of one of their own to an important post would go far toward integrating them into a regime that had, so far, only included those close to her and Kaine during the rebellion.

Lord Braslon walked briskly into the chamber and bowed respectfully.

"Thank you for coming, Lord Braslon. The matter I need to discuss with you is one that cannot be delayed. The Empire has lost a great leader. And I have lost a friend."

"I had heard that one of your Officers-at-Arms had been murdered, Your Majesty. I am sorry."

"Thank you. Joal's importance went beyond his command of the First Legion. He was also my eyes and ears in and around Attalia. Without knowing who my enemies are, it will be difficult to maintain order. Therefore, I need someone I can trust to take Joal's place. You are one of the most prominent nobles. The others listen to you and respect you. Also, you are familiar with the region and have great influence. It would be a serious oversight on my part not to ask for your help."

"You may be overestimating my influence with the other nobles, but I admit I do have some knowledge of the area, having lived here all my life."

"Then I will get to the point. I would like you to move here to Attalia for a time. Take command of the First Legion and use its strengths to crush any resistance that develops while the rest of the army is away fighting at Ritola. Use the people that you know to discover who is stirring up dissent. Have you heard the name Haczlok?"

"Yes, Your Majesty."

"What do you know about him?"

"It is said that he previously worked as a spy for Zironon and his reports led to many executions. He is a shadowy figure, capable of disappearing for long periods, such as he did right after the warlord died. He emerged sometime later, but his movements are still difficult to track. Regardless, it has been reported that he has many followers and seems to be gaining more all the time."

"Can you find him?"

"It might take some time. But I think so."

"Are you willing to help me then? For this service, you will rise above all the other nobles, and you will be well-rewarded."

"My father was loyal to your grandfather. I think he would want to ensure that the Monarchy survives."

"Then we have an agreement?"

Braslon bowed.

After the nobleman had left the room, Engrid felt a sense of relief. It was done. She had acted swiftly to fill the void left by Joal's

12 - Braslon

death, and Kaine didn't have to be involved. Furthermore, Braslon had a shrewd mind and was a proven, capable leader. So why then was she still feeling a little uneasy about asking one of the nobles for help?

In the ensuing weeks, Braslon brought a number of his knights to Attalia and immediately took charge of the existing forces that had been left to defend the city. From time to time he led strikes against Haczlok's followers, usually finding them in the countryside around Attalia, in encampments by the river, sometimes even in the heart of the city itself. For the most part, these were small operations, generally involving only a few dozen men. Some weapons were captured, several prisoners taken, and there'd been few casualties. Although Haczlok still remained at large, Braslon seemed to be keeping him on the defensive in the meantime. Several weeks of relative quiet soon followed this flurry of activity with no major disturbances in or around Attalia. But then one day Braslon came to the Queen looking very concerned. Bowing quickly, the commander wasted no time in getting to the point. "I think Haczlok is planning an attack on Attalia. All these little disturbances over the past few months were just diversions. He now has an army encamped less than fifty miles to the north."

"How did that happen? An army isn't easy to hide."

"The area is sparsely populated and heavily forested."

"How big is this army?"

"It is estimated to be around four thousand. Mostly infantry."

"Where did he get four thousand men?"

"The exile Sharnov has been recruiting in Karkesso for about a year now. Men have been trickling in slowly so as not to attract a lot of attention. Haczlok has followers around Attalia, too. Some of them have also joined this army."

Engrid remained silent while she tried to absorb everything the noble was telling her.

The Winds of Wharhalen

"There's more."

"All right, tell me."

"Ej Tauk-Zar is moving down from the Karpoans to join them."

"How many men does he have?"

"When Ej Tauk-Zar reaches them, their number will double, as well as adding some of the swiftest mounted warriors in the Empire to their forces. I also have information that they are building war machinery—catapults and siege towers."

"I see." Engrid tried not to show the panic that was swelling within her. "Do you have a plan?"

"Your Majesty should send the First Legion out to crush Haczlok before Ej Tauk-Zar arrives."

"How close is he?"

"My sources tell me that he is still about a week away. Not more than two. Therefore, we must not delay."

Engrid thought about this for a minute. "But with the First Legion fifty miles from Attalia, it would leave the city undefended."

"True, but as long as we keep them between the city and Haczlok's army, there is no direct threat."

"Is there no chance that our army could be flanked?"

"In addition to the infantry, we have two units of heavy cavalry. We would keep them on our flanks to ensure that no army could get by us."

"It seems risky. Wouldn't we be better able to defend the city if we keep the Legion back?"

12 - Braslon

"The longer we wait, the stronger Haczlok becomes. His army grows by the day. With what we have now, we couldn't defend the entire perimeter of the city. We would be spread too thin. The Legion's effectiveness is in the open field of battle. Plus, there is the possibility that when the attack on the city comes, Haczlok could get help from within. Of course, if in the meantime Kaine returns from Ritola…"

"You know that's impossible. Even if Kaine could withdraw from Ritola, it would be weeks before he could move his army back to Attalia. Are you sure you can defeat Haczlok's army if you engage them in the hills?"

"With the cavalry, I am certain we would overwhelm them. If we wait though, we will lose that advantage. The First Legion is your best-trained and best-armed fighting force. They move swiftly, have good discipline, and they are loyal. I think we can remove the threat of Haczlok once and for all. A crushing defeat will also discourage the other warlords from further action."

"How soon can you be ready to move?"

"Three days should be enough."

"All right, ready the Legion. But don't move on Haczlok until I give the final word."

Braslon nodded his agreement.

After the noble left, Engrid sent for Skauld. Since taking command, Braslon had been replacing Joal's men with his own in key positions. This was understandable, but it had made the Queen feel more and more detached from control as men she was familiar with were having less to do with the strategic decisions. Skauld had been with her since the early days of the rebellion, even before Kaine had joined them. He was a rough-edged peasant, but possessed good skills as a soldier and, above all, was unfailingly loyal. When he arrived in the chamber, Engrid gave him these instructions: "I want you to ride as fast

The Winds of Wharhalen

as you can to this location, *(indicating on a map the spot where Braslon had said Haczlok's army was forming)* and gather as much information as you can about the enemy force that is gathering there. Be careful not to be discovered and return with your report to me as soon as possible. Don't spend any more time there than is absolutely necessary. Report only to me, and don't let anyone know you're going. Do you understand? *No one* is to know you are doing this."

"Yes, Your Majesty. Should I leave immediately?"

"Wait until dark. Return at night as well."

Skauld bowed and left the Queen alone with her thoughts. The results of Skauld's reconnaissance could possibly delay any operation by Braslon. And, until now, she had had no reason to question Braslon's performance in his new position. However, letting the last of her army leave Attalia was risky, and her general uneasiness about the nobles still gnawed at her.

Three days later Braslon had the army ready to move, but when he sought the Queen's permission to take the field, he was told to wait. "Why delay, Your Majesty? Haczlok grows stronger by the day. We will soon lose our advantage."

"Not yet," was Engrid's only reply.

Braslon relented, but was back the next day with the same request. Again he was denied. The fifth day came and went, but there was still no sign of Skauld. When Braslon's request was again denied on the sixth day, his frustration became readily apparent. Outwardly, Engrid appeared calm and steadfast, while inwardly she was in turmoil. What if Skauld had been discovered and was killed or taken captive? She was certain that Braslon was beginning to suspect that she didn't fully trust him. And, what if the delay in sending out her army really did cost them the victory? Braslon would then surely brand her as timid and indecisive. It might even encourage a revolt by the nobles.

12 - Braslon

Sometime during a restless sixth night, Engrid's attendant came to her and said that Skauld had returned to Attalia. The Queen had left explicit instructions that she was to be awakened at any hour when her agent came to the castle.

Engrid put on a robe and received Skauld in the room adjacent to her sleeping quarters. The pretenses of royalty were quickly put aside between the two old comrades. During the days of the revolution, Engrid had dressed in the manner of a warrior and lived and fought beside Skauld and the other rebels. "I was beginning to worry about you, Skauld. Did you have trouble?"

"I got a little closer to the fringe of their encampment than I intended and couldn't move for a long time without being seen. The area is densely wooded and difficult to observe from a distance."

"I am glad you were able to get out. Can you make a good estimate of their strength?"

Skauld nodded. "I would put their numbers at between four and five thousand, mostly infantry. Of those, perhaps eight hundred are archers. There are about two hundred horses. They are also building war machines: two large battering rams, four siege towers, three catapults and a mangonel. They also have about twenty-five mantlets."

"None of those things would help them though if we were to strike first. Did you see any sign of a large army joining them from the north?"

"No, but the forest is so thick there that even from the highest elevation it's hard to see what's beneath the canopy. That's why I had to get so close."

"Then let me ask you this. If the First Legion were to engage this army in the hills, how would you judge the outcome?"

"We would defeat them."

The Winds of Wharhalen

"Thank you, Skauld; you have performed a great service to me."

Skauld bowed and left the room. Engrid had what she needed. The next morning, she summoned Braslon and gave him permission to attack Haczlok's army.

The First Legion, much of which had already been assembled outside the city by Braslon in anticipation of the orders to march, left Attalia the next day. Accompanied by two units of fully armored knights, they made a grand spectacle as they crossed the river and disappeared over the rise.

Three days later, it was quite a different sight that presented itself at the city gates. Xotar had returned with a few of the knights. The frothy horses indicated that they had been ridden hard with no rest and were nearly ready to drop from beneath their riders. As soon as Xotar arrived at the castle, he entered the great hall where the Queen awaited, dropped to one knee in exhaustion, and uttered the words, "We were betrayed!"

"Betrayed? How?"

"Braslon led us straight into a trap."

The words crushed Engrid like an anvil. She felt a sudden wave of nausea rise up in her stomach. "All right, Xotar," she tried to keep her voice calm, "tell me what happened."

"We thought that we would engage the enemy in about five or six days. On the third day, Braslon ordered the knights in from the flanks. I thought at the time that it was a strange order, but we assumed he was going to put them in front of the infantry when we attacked. We had only gone about another two miles after that when we were surrounded by the enemy."

12 - Braslon

"Wait; why didn't the forward scouts warn you?" Engrid interrupted.

"They were Braslon's men, Your Majesty."

Engrid shook her head in despair. She was having difficulty breathing and couldn't make herself look Xotar in the eye. "Continue."

"Braslon ordered an immediate surrender. We were told to give up our weapons, and we would be spared. We tried to fight, but they had archers positioned on a hill above us. We were completely surrounded and Braslon's knights were in our midst. And Haczlok has already been joined by a huge army of warriors from the north. They had twice our number. I decided to take my knights and try to break through the lines that were still forming behind us. Although we lost quite a few men, we were able to cut a swath through their lines and get free. We were pursued for a distance, but they eventually gave up. We rode hard all the way back here."

"How many men did you bring back?"

"Twenty-eight."

"I greatly appreciate your courage, Xotar. Tend to your wounds, get something to eat and return here in four hours. At that time we will meet with Attuis and formulate a plan to defend the city."

Xotar bowed and left the chamber without another word.

Engrid wondered what was going through his mind. Did he place the blame on her for trusting Braslon? Surely he realized how hopeless their present situation was. Without the First Legion, Attalia was now defenseless. She knew Haczlok was probably also aware of this and could overrun the city within days if he decided to press his advantage.

"How could I have been so stupid?" Engrid berated herself. "I have jeopardized the stability of the whole Empire. If Attalia falls to

The Winds of Wharhalen

Haczlok and Ej Tauk-Zar, then nothing will stop more warlords from seizing land all across Killarassee."

Later that day, Engrid, Xotar, and Attuis, Captain of the castle guards, met in Cecel's chambers to plan the defense of Attalia. The wounded Gruenlander still couldn't walk any great distance, so they took the meeting to him. Their most pressing need, of course, was the large deficit in the number of men they would need to slow down what would be a massive attacking force. Recruitment would not be a simple matter. Most of the serfs had either been sent with the army to Ritola or were in the captured First Legion. There was also the matter of Haczlok's followers that might still be in the city. Attuis suggested that the loyal castle guard be divided into units and assigned to each defense point to keep an eye on the recruits at those positions. Their orders would be to kill anyone that refused to follow orders or abandoned their post. It was a distasteful expediency, but all at the meeting agreed that, under the circumstances, it was necessary.

The process of arming what was left of the serfs would also begin right away. The next morning, before dawn, the mood of the defenders got a slight lift when a second group of horsemen straggled back through the city gates. In addition, this one was slightly larger than the one Xotar had brought in. Some had wounds, but they were all well-trained knights. Most likely their horses would be of little use in the upcoming siege, but at the moment, Attalia could use all the professional Men-at Arms that it could get.

The process of moving a large army and its war machinery is time-consuming, so it wasn't until nearly two weeks later that the horde of Haczlok and Ej Tauk-Zar appeared on the horizon. During that time the defenders had worked feverishly to arm and organize every able-bodied man in Attalia and to prepare for defense of the walls. The plan was to hold the outer wall of the city for as long as possible, then eventually fall back to the palisade, thereby abandoning the lower town.

12 - Braslon

Next would come a retreat to a position behind the inner curtain wall and, finally, to the battlements of the castle itself.

When the first attack came, Haczlok attempted to breach the gate of the outermost wall with battering rams. As soon as Haczlok's forces reached the gates, the archers rained down arrows on the attackers from atop the walls and eventually forced them to fall back out of range. The small victory buoyed the spirits of those defending the city for the moment, but Engrid knew it would be fleeting. The next time, several assaults came at different locations, stretching the corps of archers along several points on the wall. When the gate was finally breached, Haczlok's troops started to pour through. Fortunately, Xotar had anticipated this and rushed his men, whom he'd kept in reserve, to meet the onslaught. In fierce fighting, the attackers were eventually driven back, and the gate secured. This success came at a terrible cost, however, for not only were the defenders' losses high, but Xotar himself was among the casualties. When informed of this, Engrid's mood reached the point of almost total despair. Without experienced commanders, she knew organization would quickly crumble. At present, Attuis had his hands full trying to stay in command of his scattered castle guards. And she knew Cecel could give counsel, but was unable to stand long enough to lead troops in battle.

Nighttime brought a welcome respite for the occupants of the city, but the next day Haczlok's numbers proved to be too much and the outer wall gate was breached again. This time the defenders were forced to fall back to the palisade. The lower town now lost, the Queen's forces could only watch as Haczlok's army was able to move their siege equipment closer to the castle. Engrid called a meeting with the few Officers-at-Arms she had left. The situation was dire. It was no longer a matter of *if* the castle would fall, but simply when and under what circumstances. Haczlok was a cohort of Zironon, Braslon was a traitor, and Ej Tauk-Zar was a butcher. To seek terms with this dishonorable trio was unthinkable. The Queen, therefore, solicited opinions.

Attuis began, "When Attalia is in the hands of Haczlok and his allies, there will be many executions and Your Majesty…" His voice trailed off.

"Go on," said Engrid.

"Your treatment will be the harshest. Haczlok will show no mercy. I'm sorry, but death by your own hand would be preferable."

"I see. Cecel?"

The once robust warrior, now diminished by his injuries and long convalescence, thought long before answering. "I do not differ in opinion from Attuis. But there can be no surrender. We must fight to the last."

Engrid now spoke. Her voice was firm and steady. "Since seeking terms is considered unacceptable, and it is likely that their machines will breech the palisade within the next few days, I suggest that we formulate a plan to ensure our survival after we are no longer in possession of Attalia."

The Queen's last statement drew bewildered expressions from the three soldiers. Engrid continued, "You have probably heard rumors of the tunnels than run under the city. Well, I can assure you they do exist. Joal was familiar with them and he once showed me the entrances. Haczlok won't take retribution against the people of Attalia. He will prefer to make an example of its leaders and claim the treasury. If we can disappear and take the treasure with us, he gains only a hollow victory. In turn, we can continue to harass them from our hiding places, demoralizing and weakening them in the process until Kaine returns from Ritola." The Queen watched as the expressions of confusion changed to those of approval of her plan.

12 - Braslon

"It's a desperate plan, but what else do we have?" said Skauld, entering the discussion for the first time. "As for myself, I would rather keep fighting the enemy any way I can."

Each of the others then nodded his assent. Thus, it was decided. The four leaders would divide their forces into two groups, one commanded by Attuis, the other by the Queen. Skauld would assist Engrid while Cecel would continue his recuperation in hiding until he could be of use to Attuis.

The meeting ended with the sad resignation that Attalia would fall but with a determination that the fight would nevertheless go on. As the Queen watched the last of her comrades depart, she sat pondering how it had come to this. She was no longer the young idealist that had led the fight against Zironon. That girl didn't exist any longer. And the reign of Queen Engrid that had started with so much promise was suddenly on the brink of total collapse and threatened to vanish, unremembered, into history.

The Winds of Wharhalen

CHAPTER THIRTEEN

Ritola

L ocke returned to the campsite after checking on the herd of horses in his care. Having secured the end of the tether, the last few remnants of light were evaporating from the evening sky as he approached the faint glow of the fire that Cobal was nurturing. So far the soldier had treated Locke fairly, and while the boy wouldn't describe their relationship as friendly, during the past six days, much of the tension between them had worn away. As always with Locke, riding and the forest helped dull the jagged edge of knowing that he was still a prisoner.

The long days of riding had given him plenty of time to think about the events of the past year—the death of Jocar, the race with Arawae, his enslavement at the hands of the treacherous Toulon, and now, in another complete change of fate, he was heading toward a military engagement of which he knew little, if anything, about the dynamics of the conflict. Of course, his thoughts never strayed too far from Eylese, although now even those, so uncluttered before, had become blurred with the memory of Kira. The beautiful, headstrong girl with her passion for horses had ignited a fire within Locke that

The Winds of Wharhalen

threatened to force everything else from his mind. The flames of this inferno seemed to start in his stomach and travel upward, consuming everything in their path until the resulting smoke entered his brain. In spite of the young man's helplessness to combat these feelings, he didn't try too hard to rid his thoughts of them, for somehow they made him feel inexplicably happy. Perhaps it was because the heights to which they'd lifted him were in such stark contrast to the depths of despair he'd felt after Jocar's death and during his own virtual death sentence in the quarry.

When Locke sat down by the fire, he did not even elicit a glance from the grizzled warrior. Cobal probably wasn't as old as he looked to the young man. But his long hair, only partially held in a braid and the thick beard that obscured his face and neck left only a pair of keen gray eyes as windows into the man. He had a wide scar on one cheek that spilled over onto his nose, and the nose itself took on an unnatural shape, undoubtedly having been broken at least once.

"Will we reach Ritola tomorrow?"

Cobal still didn't look up from the fire. "We will. We actually could have gone the rest of the way tonight, but it would have been risky coming up on the encampment in the dark. With this many horses, we could have easily been mistaken for Vartan's men. They sometimes sneak out of the city at night for raids."

"What's the fight about?"

The soldier looked up and studied the young man's face with probing eyes.

"I know I don't have a choice in this," continued Locke, "but if I'm going to take part in a war, I'd at least like to know who's in the fight and why."

Cobal looked down into the fire again as if searching for the answer. "Vartan is a local warlord whose family had control of this

13 - Ritola

region for years. His father was defeated by Zironon, who was in turn defeated by the Queen, and for thirty years he has waited for his chance to seize control again. He is challenging the Queen's authority to rule the south from Attalia."

"What gives her that authority?"

Cobal glanced up at the young man and then suppressed a smile beneath his beard at the naïve audacity of the horse trainer. "The Queen's grandfather, Jonas, was ruler over the whole Empire before Zironon overthrew him. Engrid was born in Tairellia where her father was in exile. When she came of age, she returned and with Kaine's help, killed Zironon and drove out his sons."

"But then Vartan's father and Engrid's grandfather would have been in power at the same time. How could that be?"

"Jonas was powerful, but he was also smart. He knew that he couldn't rule the entire Empire if he had to fight every warlord. He allowed some of the warlords to remain in control of their regions as long as they pledged their loyalty to him. For their part, warlords like Vartan's father were content to rule unchallenged in their own regions, knowing that Jonas would prevent any other warlords from getting too strong and threatening them. You don't know any of this?"

"I've heard some of it. But I never really paid much attention to it. I couldn't do anything about it anyway. Are we on the right side?"

Cobal sighed. "Who decides which side is right? Sometimes your side is picked for you. All that really matters is who wins." As he said this, he clamped the shackle on Locke's ankle that would keep him chained to a tree for the night.

Late the next morning, Cobal and Locke arrived on the ridge overlooking the walled city of Ritola. It sat nearly a mile in the distance, with the castle built on a rocky crag. Pine forest grew part of the way up the slope on two sides, but the trees had been cut down by the defenders out to a distance of about two hundred yards in both directions. Thus, the forward approach to the walls was a long, sloping plain uninterrupted by any prominent features.

Looking down, Kaine's camp spread out before them at the bottom of the ridge. All preparations seemed to have been made for a long siege. Earthen ramparts had been constructed both front and rear, and a company of archers defended each side. The horses were sequestered near the rear of the encampment where feeding and waste removal was expedited. Mounted patrols guarded the routes in and out as convoys kept the camp supplied from local sources. Locke and Cobal were met by one of these patrols almost as soon as they appeared over the ridge. When Cobal was recognized, the herd was immediately escorted down the hillside.

Inside the encampment, Locke drew little attention since the men were so used to the constant flow of suppliers and recruits. He observed the mix of ethnic groups and the span of ages of the men. They appeared well-fed and well-equipped and the camp was, in general, orderly, with good discipline. That is, there was a notable absence of brawling and prostitutes. He was put under the command of a soldier named Broecker, who looked over the new mounts approvingly. Broecker was an impressive man — tall and straight, with light hair and blue eyes. His craggy features were handsome in a stark sort of way, and his body looked to be sculpted from stone. This was not a warrior you would want to face in battle, thought Locke.

"Are these animals ready to be put into service immediately, boy?" said the Sergeant to Locke.

"They are all broke to ride, but none have seen combat before."

"I suppose I could say the same about most of the human recruits that have come in here during the past two months. I'll assign

13 - Ritola

five men to help you get the horses as ready as you can in the next week. Then, they'll have to be put into the rotation."

Locke nodded, and within the hour, five men, ranging in age from their late teens to early twenties, approached him. He found the five to be good horsemen, as he observed them take the group of mounts through a series of difficult training exercises. These involved riding the horses through a course of obstacles, shooting arrows while guiding the horse with only their legs, and sparring with swords while mounted. The well-trained horses of Locke responded well, in some cases even better than their riders. The most difficult task for the animals was getting used to the presence of menacing blades swinging about their heads and the clanging of steel. Locke and the five young soldiers only got through half of the horses that first day, but as the week wore on and the animals became more accustomed to the training, the time that it took to work the whole herd of remounts lessened. Because of his natural affinity for horses and riding, Locke found the training routine to be invigorating. To speed the process along, Locke was allowed to participate as a rider and quickly gained the respect of the others for his excellent horsemanship. His skill with a sword improved rapidly too; soon, he was nearly the equal of many of the young knights.

Since his arrival at the encampment, Locke had witnessed no hostilities. The walls of Ritola loomed in the distance, silent and foreboding, the people within confined like prisoners. The privations of such an existence could only be imagined. However, starvation, disease, and filth would obviously be the inevitable by-products of a long siege. It had gone on nearly eight months now and with the approach of summer, Vartan could expect renewed attacks on his tired defenders.

It hadn't been easy for the Royal Army either. The winter months, although not especially harsh this year, brought cool, damp,

The Winds of Wharhalen

muddy conditions that had caused widespread illness among the troops. Desertions had also taken a huge toll. Many recruits took the gold they got for signing on and then simply slipped away in the night. Some were pursued and captured, and their summary executions were used to serve notice to others that might have similar ideas. But Kaine lacked the manpower to track down all deserters in the vast countryside, so many did get away. Recruiting lagged, and so Kaine was able to successfully replace only about two of every three men that left. So, although large, the force that contained Vartan had not grown to the proportions necessary to overwhelm Ritola.

At the dawn of the fifth day following Locke's arrival, an event occurred that would take the boy's fate in still another direction. Out of the mists of the first morning light, a surprise attack came on the horse compound. It was a large force, several hundred strong, and the mounted warriors cut through the sleepy camp with murderous efficiency. Many of the royal soldiers were slain even before they could reach their horses. The speed of the assault and the element of surprise plunged the affected part of the encampment into chaos. Locke, already on the verge of wakefulness, since he was accustomed to rising early to feed the horses, stayed low and carefully surveyed the situation around him.

Fear gripped the young man as he saw men being slaughtered just a few yards away; their lives abruptly ended by this merciless horde. Although he was familiar with sudden violence, having lived most of his life in the Karpoans, he had never seen killing on this scale before. The number of men that went down during the first few minutes of the attack unnerved Locke. Part of him wanted to cling to the ground and pretend to be dead in the hope of being overlooked. But there was that other part—the part that contained a smoldering rage that had been building for the past year. Rage from Jocar's brutal death. Rage at having his life and his love torn from him by Toulon. The embers of

13 - Ritola

that rage, stoked by his cruel treatment in the quarry, were about to erupt into an inferno.

Once standing, he knew he would quickly become an easy target, so he had to be certain as to what action he would take next. He had no weapon, the sword that he practiced with having been returned to the weapons cache at the end of each day. Looking around him, he spotted the iron shackles that he'd worn until coming to the encampment. In one agile movement, Locke grabbed one end of the chain, stood up and swung at a horseman galloping past. The heavy iron clamp caught the rider flush in the face, and he fell to the ground. Locke instantly seized the man's sword and mounted the now riderless horse. Now on an even plane with the attackers, he rode directly across the flow of the onslaught, engaging each of the invaders as they came. One by one they all fell before Locke's flashing blade. Fueled by his anger and heedless of danger, he was able to overwhelm his adversaries with his powerful arm. He may have been new to swordsmanship, but as a horseman he was without peer. Again and again, his skillful maneuvers on horseback allowed him to gain an advantage in the attacks that came against him. He circled back to where some of the Queen's Men-at-Arms had finally been successful in gaining mounts and were now fighting furiously against superior numbers. Locke fought his way through to them and then back out again to avoid being surrounded. In his wake, a group of knights suddenly began to rally behind this whirlwind of death. Soon, they had formed a wedge, with Locke at the point, and drove it deep into the enemy force.

So strong was this counterattack that Vartan's men quickly lost the momentum that the element of surprise had given them, thereby allowing more of the soldiers of the Royal Army time to regroup and join the fight. Archers next rushed to the fighting and began to pick off enemy riders. Realizing that the battle was turning against them, the leader of the attack tried to order a retreat but found that the perimeter

The Winds of Wharhalen

was rapidly closing in. Now in disarray, fragments of the strike force started to break free and ride for the safety of the surrounding hills. However, as the circle continued to tighten around what was left of the main force, Vartan's men realized the hopelessness of their situation and surrendered. By the time the fighting within the encampment drew to a close, nearly a third of the attackers were dead and another third were prisoners.

The rest of Vartan's men were left scattered among the hills to straggle back to Ritola. Broecker's unit, severely crippled by the attack, was ordered not to pursue these small groups. Some of the warlord's men, now outside of Ritola, might simply choose to desert. Others could hide out in the vast countryside for weeks before attempting to return. The results of the raid were inconclusive. The element of surprise had caused heavy casualties among the royal forces, but the swiftness of the response had prevented Vartan from achieving a victory.

When the fighting was over, Locke's weary sword arm dropped to his side, the blade foul with blood and pieces of flesh. His energy spent, the horror that surrounded him caused him to gag as he fought back the sickness in his stomach. The field was strewn with the dead, and the cries of the wounded rung in his ears. He saw men, many of whom were apparently hardened to the aftermath of battle, already starting to work on caring for the wounded. He shook himself free from the stupor that had rendered him motionless for a time and started rounding up horses. It was preferable to the task that fell to many others—collecting the dead. Some of the horses had injuries, and Locke began taking care of those after he had herded them all back together again. The job was immense, and it was late into the afternoon when he was approached by Broecker.

"I saw what you did this morning."

"Sir?"

13 - Ritola

"You fought well."

"I was just trying to survive."

"It was more than that. Your courage helped turn the battle." With that, the Sergeant shook his head. "A slave who shows us how to fight," he muttered.

Locke stiffened at the label. "I haven't always been a slave."

"So, you were a soldier?" said Broecker, brightening.

"No, I have never been a soldier. I just haven't always been a slave."

"Well, you're a soldier now. We need warriors if we are to win this fight. If you survive, you'll never be a slave again."

"What do you want me to do?"

"Finish training those remounts. Then we'll find some armor for you. Looks like you already have a sword. And here," he said, tossing a small bag toward Locke. "It's the gold that we have been giving the recruits for joining us. You've more than earned it today."

The Winds of Wharhalen

CHAPTER FOURTEEN

Attalia

Now inside the outer wall of Attalia, Haczlok's army awaited the signal to advance. The machines of war — the battering rams, the siege towers, the mangonel for hurling huge stones at the walls — were all in place. The ambitious conspirators Haczlok, Sharnov, Ej Tauk-Zar, and Braslon were getting closer to achieving their vision for the Empire. The first thing Haczlok, the shrewd broker of power, intended to do was allow the exiled Sharnov to return to Killarassee and become Regent in Attalia. Next, they would divide and share half of the vast treasury amassed by Sharnov's father, Zironon. Ej Tauk-Zar, would take a fourth of the treasury and have free reign to overrun the northern half of Killarassee. The noble Braslon, who didn't really like the other three, would be given the remaining fourth of the treasury and assume the title of Prince. He would, at last, have supremacy over all the other nobles and his realm would extend from his present lands south all the way to the great sea.

Meanwhile, inside the outer castle wall, the defenders were preparing to hold the palisade for as long as possible. Archers lined the top of the wall and wooden scaffolds were hung over the edge to

The Winds of Wharhalen

facilitate dropping stones and boiling oil on the attackers once they reached the base of the wall. Troops massed in the bailey, ready to resist the assaults that were sure to come through breaches. Weapons had also been placed in the hands of refugees from the lower town who had sought the protection of the castle after the fall of the outer city wall. Unfortunately, though, many had to be turned away since the town population had long ago outstripped the capacity of the castle grounds. Therefore, the ones who were let in were mainly those men who could help defend the castle.

Haczlok began the assault by pounding the wall with stones from the mangonel. He did this all of the first day. The wall was almost twelve feet thick, but there was nothing that the defenders could do to prevent it from gradually crumbling. Once night fell, the defenders worked in the dark to push stones and debris back into the gash and build barriers that could slow the inevitable onslaught to come. They probably only gained a few hours at most, though, since the pounding of the mangonel began again shortly after dawn. Once the wall was again breached, Haczlok sent his infantry into the opening. Arrows immediately rained down on the attackers and the initial resistance from the troops in the bailey was strong. While this fight was continuing, Haczlok moved his battering rams into position near the main gate. They, too, drew heavy arrow fire and stones dropped from the top of the wall. Eventually, the gate was smashed and more troops came pouring through, where these were met by more defenders from the bailey, whose numbers were shrinking. Haczlok then brought up his siege towers loaded with more soldiers. The archers on the walls began to lob flaming arrows into the towers, most of which were either extinguished or thrown out immediately. One tower, however, did start to burn from below the top platform and soon became a raging inferno. The cries of the doomed men, who were unable to get down the crowded ramp past their comrades, could be heard above the din of battle. Nevertheless, three of the towers successfully made it to the wall and quickly began depositing their human cargo. The defenders of the castle, now overwhelmed by an enemy with vastly superior numbers, began to fall back toward the inner curtain wall. As the light began to fade, the carnage that could be seen in the bailey was horrific. Cries of agony from the wounded hung on air that was thick and heavy with dust from the rubble and smoke from the burning towers. Piles of bodies clogged the passages where the attackers had broken through, and the field was strewn with those cut down during the retreat. However, a few defenders made it to temporary safety within the inner wall and courtyard of the castle, and prepared themselves to make their last stand from its battlements.

In the castle it was decided that the Queen's plan would go into effect as soon as the gate to the courtyard was breached. After that, there would no longer be any way to prevent the enemy from overrunning the rest of the castle. About twenty-five yards behind the gate a straw barrier was erected across the courtyard. Once it was ignited to provide a cover for the last of the Queen's Officers-at-Arms to escape, the white flag would be run up and the soldiers manning the battlements and turrets would surrender.

When the palisade could no longer hold back the hordes of Haczlok, Engrid and Myleia left the castle in the middle of the night by way of secret passages that had existed for centuries, passages which could only be reached through a series of mazes that wound through the bowels of the castle. As she moved closer to the passages, Engrid wondered how many other rulers in countless other castles had made a similar journey. She'd learned during her studies that when castles fall, monarchs flee. Sometimes they would go to other castles, sometimes to other countries. But in this instance Engrid did not go far. A well-concealed entrance to a tunnel swallowed up the two young women and allowed them the chance for survival amidst a vast network of caverns that ran under the city.

The Winds of Wharhalen

The caverns had been built hundreds of years before by an army of slaves at the command of King Atton in the era of the Old Kings. The King had feared so much for his own safety and that of his family that in order to keep the project a secret, those slaves that didn't die during the construction were slain upon its completion.

Just prior to the attack on Attalia, Engrid ordered the entire treasury transferred to the caverns so that it wouldn't fall into the hands of Haczlok and his allies. Then, as the end of the battle drew nearer, one by one, the Queen's Officers-at-Arms and a few of their most trusted men slipped away and entered their subterranean refuge. Finally, Skauld stood alone behind the gate to the courtyard, left to command the brave remnants of the Royal Army. Still, Haczlok was made to pay dearly for his victory. Since the inner walls were inaccessible to the siege towers, the attackers would have to use scaling ladders if they were to go over them. Arrows and boiling oil took a terrible toll on the poor souls that were given this task. Getting a battering ram close enough to the main gate to do its damage also proved costly. The gritty defenders held onto the castle for another whole day before the gate was finally breached. On that final, fateful day of battle, Skauld gave the order to run up the flag of surrender, as he torched the straw bales, and in the smoke and chaos that ensued, vanished into the maze of the caverns.

Since Haczlok's victory had come so late in the day, it wasn't until the morning of the next day that he realized that the Queen and all of her Officers-at-Arms had escaped. Realizing that the search for the treasure might take weeks and fearing what his troops might do to Attalia in the meantime, he ordered Ej Tauk-Zar to take his warriors outside the city wall to prevent uncontrolled pillaging. This angered the warlord at first, but Haczlok eventually convinced him to be patient and wait for the treasure to be found. At the same time, Sharnov's men were told to make camp in the lower town, where they would be kept busy disposing of the dead, caring for the wounded and repairing the

14 - Attalia

damage done to the walls. Haczlok knew that eventually Kaine would return from Ritola, and when he did, defense of Attalia would become the responsibility of the new occupants.

The Winds of Wharhalen

CHAPTER FIFTEEN

Cecel

The siege of Ritola was in its eighteenth month, and Kaine was in the process of tightening the vise in which he held the walled city. The devices that his troops had built since arriving were in place now, and for the past week catapults had been lobbing fireballs into the city. The resulting fires within the walls were straining Ritola's resources, especially water, and demoralizing its citizens. Kaine hoped that Vartan would finally see no other recourse than to send his army out to resolve the conflict in open battle. It was difficult and expensive to continue to hold his own army together, but Kaine knew that the toll in lives an all-out assault on the walls would take would be terrible. As each day went by, he hated this campaign more and longed to be back in Attalia with Myleia. Duty, however, dictated that he finish what he started here, but the conflict that raged within him matched that of any battle on the field. Nevertheless, Kaine knew that the only way this war could end was with the death of Vartan, and he hoped that Vartan's own men might come to this same conclusion and one day turn on him and do the job themselves. That result would save countless lives. Kaine had no desire to spill more Killarassean blood if

The Winds of Wharhalen

Vartan's horde would simply bring it upon themselves to disband and go home.

Vartan's hope of help from the east had died with Patrov. Without a leader, the loose coalition of tribes that had been assembled by Vartan's brother quickly began to disintegrate. Ritola was now totally isolated. The warlord's only hope was that the deprivations of life in Kaine's encampment would eventually erode the resolve of the Royal Army. And if large-scale desertions started to take place, Kaine might grow impatient and attack prematurely, or better yet, give up the siege and pull back to Attalia.

The days dragged on in Kaine's camp. The approach of spring had improved the overall mood of the men, but for the commander, one lonely day was just like any other. The boredom of camp made it impossible for Kaine to hold back the flood of memories.

After Kaine and Joal joined forces to steal from Zironon, their first targets were necessarily small. After all, they were just two against the ruler of the entire Empire. Their first acquisition was a couple of horses taken from two of Zironon's soldiers who were breaking up a fight inside a tavern, a fight started, of course, by Joal. During the melee, Kaine rode off with the two fine horses, and the partners met later in a wooded glen across the Veral River. From there they quickly put many miles between themselves and Attalia. Their initial plan was to make their strikes at great distances from one another so that, at first, Zironon's men wouldn't even suspect it was the same bandits. They would be a minor annoyance to the warlord at first, and they hoped it would be a long time before they would be taken seriously.

Weapons were the next item on their procurement list and the best of these were in the hands of Zironon's soldiers. Hunting bows were easily obtainable, however, and Kaine and Joal bought two, plus

15 - Cecel

arrows with steel points designed for killing deer. Choosing a location for an ambush on the main road with great care, they were rewarded two days later with a small patrol of Zironon's men. The spot was isolated, far from any post in either direction and was bordered on both sides with dense forest. Joal, who had no qualms about killing one of Zironon's soldiers from ambush, picked off one of the six men with his first shot. It wasn't a long shot though, and the rest of the soldiers turned and pursued Joal into the woods. Meanwhile Kaine, waiting behind a tree some distance into the woods, took down the second man at such close range and with such great force that the arrow penetrated the chain mail of his torso and exited the soldier's back after entering the front of his chest. Maneuvering in the thick forest was so difficult for the horses that a third man went down before the soldiers could even ascertain how many men they were pursuing. The remaining three then fled the woods, leaving the dead behind to be stripped of their weapons and equipment.

    Kaine and Joal were now well-equipped with weapons and armor and had a growing string of horses. They next established a base camp far from the spot of the ambush to keep their remounts. It was situated in a secluded wood just inside the area of Killarassee known as the frontier. It bordered a low, grassy area that was surrounded on all sides by trees and a creek split the meadow in half. They labored for several weeks constructing a rail fence around the meadow, and when they were finished, the horses were able to fend for themselves whenever the two thieves were away, often for days at a time. They felt it was good to remain out of sight during that time anyway, since the closer together their raids came, the more urgency Zironon would feel to pursue them. It was shortly after this period that they met Cecel. The large, bear-like man with the massive torso and the dark, penetrating eyes had most recently fled his native Gruenland after being involved in the ill-fated regime of Jauryl. He had once been a hero there, having helped overthrow the tyrant, Olhoufin. But when a revolt rose up

The Winds of Wharhalen

against Jauryl, Cecel became a scapegoat and was fortunate to have escaped with his life. Coming to Killarassee with no money and no friends, he had used his resourcefulness to start a new life. When he located a river crossing that seemed in need of a ferry, he constructed a crude barge that could be pulled across the stream by means of a rope which stretched from one side to the other. During the summer, the water level, coming only to a man's knees, was low enough to wade across; but during other parts of the year, the level would rise to dangerous levels to cross. During these times, herdsmen and farmers were forced to take a lengthy detour to get their livestock to the markets, having to travel nearly twenty miles to the south before coming to a bridge. Cecel's barge operation quickly became an attractive alternative. He charged a small toll to ferry the herds of sheep and pigs across safely, and before long, had established a modest but profitable business.

    Kaine and Joal had stopped to talk with the big Gruenlander a few times and had even availed themselves of his services once when the river was running particularly high. However, one day as they approached the crossing, they observed four of Zironon's men in a heated confrontation with Cecel. Although they couldn't make out what was being said, suddenly the ferry operator was defending himself from the heavily-armed soldiers. His only weapon was the long pole he used to push the barge out from the bank. In the hands of an ordinary man, it would have been a feeble defense against the steel swords of the soldiers, but, wielded by the huge warrior, the fight was, at least momentarily, a standoff. That didn't last for long, for Kaine and Joal swept down on horseback and dropped two of the soldiers with arrows as the distance narrowed to about sixty feet. Pulling the horses up, they drew two more arrows and the fight was over. Four bodies lay on the road, while Cecel stared in amazement at the men who had come to his aid. Recovering, he said, "Look at the mess you have made of my river

15 - Cecel

crossing. How is a man supposed to conduct his business in the midst of this clutter of dead bodies?"

Kaine replied, "I don't think you'll be conducting anything here anymore. Zironon won't be happy when he learns you have killed four of his men."

"But I didn't kill any of them."

"Perhaps not. But he doesn't know that. They were sent by Zironon to put you out of business, am I right?"

Cecel nodded. "They said that only the warlord has the right to make money on river crossings. How is a man supposed to make a living?"

"Well, as for us, we make our living stealing from Zironon. Since you apparently no longer have a ferry business, would you like to join us?"

"I don't appear to have a lot of options at this time. Do you eat well?"

"I can assure you, if nothing else, we will see that you are well-fed."

"I haven't had a better offer today."

With that, the three new comrades collected up the weapons of the dead soldiers, took all four horses, and rode off to further adventures.

Kaine smiled a little at the memory. Joal and Cecel's friendship had helped ease the loneliness and torment of that time, and he wished that they were here with him at Ritola. This had been a long and expensive campaign. The cost of maintaining an army this size in the field was staggering, but, fortunately, so far the loss in lives was small.

The Winds of Wharhalen

Kaine wasn't about to let his impatience to end this extended ordeal tempt him to foolishly launch an assault on the walls.

As it turned out he didn't have to. Dissension within the city was forcing Vartan's hand. The people of Ritola had turned against him and his hungry troops were growing more restless by the day. Kaine had proven to be a stubborn and worthy foe, and the only way to keep this rebellion from crumbling into insignificance would be to unleash his warriors with all their pent-up fury and drive the Royal Army out of the region.

However, as Vartan's army prepared to leave the security of the walls, Kaine was not unaware of the coming change in the standoff. The signal fires from the lookouts that he had placed in the rocks above Ritola, warned him of the warlord's shift to the offensive. So, on the morning that the gates of the city swung open, the entire might of Kaine's army stood poised for battle on the plain.

The two armies that faced each other that day were in marked contrast from each other. The ragged dress of Vartan's infantry reflected its disdain for organization. Their armaments lacked uniformity as well, with the foot soldiers as likely to be carrying axes and spears as swords. The warlord's bowmen took up their position behind his infantry, intending to launch their arrows over the heads of their own men. The massive bows they carried had pull-weights that would have frustrated an average man, but their range was nearly twice that of the bows the royal archers carried. Kaine knew that this would take a terrible toll on his infantry if the archers were allowed to fire unmolested at his forces until the two armies were fully engaged. In addition, Vartan had deployed a large number of swift horsemen poised to strike from the left flank.

On the other end of the field, the Royal Army, flying the banner of the Queen, was resplendent by comparison. They were uniformly attired in blue and gold and held ranks like the well-drilled

15 - Cecel

force that they were. Indeed, drilling was one of the few things they were able to do to relieve boredom during the long months of the siege. However, their bright uniforms and well-organized precision belied their inexperience. Aside from the core legion that Kaine had brought from Attalia, the remainder of his troops had been locally recruited for this campaign and consisted primarily of men who had never been in battle before.

In numbers, the two sides were about equal. Because of desertions during the winter months, Kaine's infantry total was barely 7,000; and, in spite of extensive intense recruiting inside Ritola, disease had capped Vartan's scruffy force at a little over 6,000. Kaine felt confident, though, that if he could neutralize Vartan's bowmen, his foot soldiers could handle the main brunt of the fighting on the plain. To this purpose, he planned to use his mounted archers who had proved their worth in the raids on Patrov.

In the other half of his cavalry sat a lanky young man, dressed in full armor, astride a powerful warhorse, preparing for his first major battle. Locke Thomason had quickly become a horseman without peer in the ranks of Kaine's army. In addition to his elevation from slave to soldier (not a huge leap), he had been made Officer of horses. He had also been given a nearly complete set of armor and was allowed to train with a group of young, aspiring knights. In spite of all this, the young man's stomach was queasy on the eve of the battle, and he'd slept fitfully the previous night. During the raid in which he had acquitted himself so bravely, he knew he had simply reacted to a life-threatening situation. He had had no time to contemplate the peril before acting. The scope of this coming battle, however, was overwhelming, and the thought of so many men dying on this field that lay in front of Ritola filled him with revulsion. In spite of this, he knew his fortunes had changed dramatically for the better. In a short period of time, he had gone from his darkest hours as a slave in the quarry, perhaps just a few weeks from an anonymous death, to a role in this battle that might help determine the destiny of the whole Empire. He was a warrior now, but his anger over the cruel blows that life had struck him had not yet diminished. In his rage he could fight back at those that sought to destroy him, and those enemies would feel his wrath.

During the long months of the siege, when he wasn't tending to the horses or honing his skills with a sword, there were many quiet moments; during these times, he would often think about Eylese — innocent Eylese, whose fate had been determined by her family's poverty. Locke struggled to remember the details of her face, the touch of her hand, the words that she spoke, the warmth of her body. He soon realized that his memories of Eylese provided him with a serene corner separate from the turbulence of his life. It was a sanctuary tied to the memory of the brief interlude they'd shared in the grove, where time and trouble were suspended. The passing days were eroding these once vivid images, however, and he feared that soon they would vanish altogether. He felt a deep sense of guilt that he had not been able to free her from bondage and that she still suffered at the hands of the cruel Toulon. His deeper feelings for her, which he did not fully understand, remained buried under the layers of events that had occurred since he had been torn from her embrace.

And if Locke allowed himself to reflect on the recent past long enough, his thoughts would invariably also include Kira. Although his memories of the young, spoiled, headstrong girl were different from those of Eylese, in some ways they were more intense. Her dark beauty still haunted his dreams, and his thoughts of her while he was awake could not easily be dismissed. The enchanting eyes, the sensuous mouth, and the firm curves of her body were disturbing reminders that clung to him like burrs to a horse's mane. In some respects, he was grateful that circumstances had pulled them apart, for surely the path they were on would have led to disaster for him. Still, deep inside, he couldn't be sure if he were ever again free to go wherever he pleased, he wouldn't be drawn back to that destructive flame. The days in which he was free to make his own choices were still a distant fantasy, however, and the looming battle might take away those choices forever.

Kaine sent his swift mounted archers out in a wide, flanking maneuver to the right. Their objective was to attack Vartan's bowmen at the rear of infantry. At the same time, the heavy cavalry of the Royal Army was sent to engage Vartan's horseman on the other side of the battlefield. This would prevent Vartan's cavalry from coming to the aid of the bowmen. Broecker led his knights into the attack, with Locke close behind. With lances lowered and riding at full speed, the collision between the two masses of horsemen created a cacophony that resonated across the entire valley. In the initial stages of the encounter, Locke killed one man with the point of his lance, but the impact had been so violent that the shaft splintered. Now well in the midst of the enemy force, he drew his sword to fight off the warriors that were on all sides.

Meanwhile, on the other side of the field, Vartan's bowmen proved to be no match for the fast-moving mounted archers that swept in, delivered their deadly shafts, and then rode away at full gallop. Again and again, they made their lethal passes, completely occupying the attention of the grounded bowmen. Vartan's men held their ground bravely, but unaccustomed to hitting targets moving on horseback, they were at a significant disadvantage. Realizing that his long bowmen had been taken out of the fight, Vartan gave the order for his infantry to advance. Kaine now had a chance to reveal his next tactic. He had concealed his own bowmen in the middle of his infantry. As Vartan's forces neared, the Royal Army's front lines parted, and Vartan's on-rushing men were met by a hail of arrows. And as soon as the first line of archers would loose their shafts, they would immediately kneel down while the next line would shoot over them. This constant barrage of arrows took a bloody toll, but the forces of Vartan continued forward in the face of it. Finally, the royal archers had to fall back and the infantry lines closed in behind them. In spite of suffering terrible

The Winds of Wharhalen

losses, the warriors from Ritola had momentum when the two armies met with a terrible collision of steel and bodies. In fierce fighting, many of the Royal Army's green recruits soon lost their courage and started to fall back onto their own men behind them. Subsequently, the center of Kaine's infantry began to collapse, and Vartan's savage fighters gained a new sense of confidence.

While the Royal Army's infantry was being pushed back, the battle was going better for the heavy cavalry. Superior armor was the biggest difference on that side of the field. In spite of the ferocity and courage of Vartan's warriors, their numbers were growing thinner as the well-equipped knights of the Queen fought with deadly precision. Eventually, their lines broken, the horsemen of Vartan began to scatter. However, rather than pursue the fragments of the rapidly disintegrating cavalry, Broecker rallied his knights around him for a charge into the midst of the infantry battle. Locke followed closely as the Sergeant rode at the point of the attack, which was directed at the right flank of the surging mass of foot soldiers. Now facing an opponent on two sides, Vartan's men began to lose some of their momentum, allowing the Royal Army's infantry an opportunity to regroup and mount a counterattack.

In the middle of this sea of combat, Locke suddenly found himself surrounded. His horse was terrified but still responded bravely in spite of the din and the crush of bodies. The animal received a horrific wound when a lance pierced his chest, but he managed to stay on his feet as Locke continued to deal out death from his flashing blade. Locke saw his comrades pulled down off their horses and chopped to pieces, and he saw the enemy being trampled under horses' hooves. Broecker, not far away, was an inspiration to his troops as he carved a wide swath through the mass of humanity. He was like a mighty fortress, repulsing repeated assaults. Suddenly, though, Broecker's mount received a mortal wound and went down. Vartan's savage fighters were quickly on the man, but, even on the ground, no single warrior was his equal, and he fought on. Locke tried to reach him but, at the same time, he was also desperately trying to avoid being dragged from his saddle. He wheeled his horse around to throw aside his attacker on one side while warding off the blows of another. Finally extricating himself for the moment, he looked for his Sergeant, but he discovered he could no longer be helped. Locke caught a fleeting glimpse of the crumpled body just before he was carried away on another wave of attacks.

Survival in any battle requires some degree of luck, and good fortune was with Locke this day. The counterattack of the Royal Army finally began to drive the enemy back toward the walls. Vartan's men, their numbers rapidly dwindling, started concentrating on trying to preserve their own lives rather than achieve victory. Soon it became a rout, with Locke and the other knights pursuing the retreating army toward the citadel. The gates of the city had been left open to receive the remnants of the infantry, and this presented an opportunity for Kaine's army to penetrate the outer wall. However, Vartan's cavalry had regrouped at this point and was covering the retreat. Kaine, watching from a rise on his army's right flank, didn't want his men to get trapped just inside the first wall where they could be picked off by archers; so he sounded the recall. This was another fortunate turn for Locke, because just moments later, his courageous horse, mortally wounded from the lance in his chest, collapsed and died.

Locke walked back through the awful carnage of the battle scene. The dead and dying stretched for nearly three-quarters of a mile across the valley. He came upon a great war horse struggling to get up in spite of a severed tendon in its leg and a spear protruding from his neck. Locke placed his hand on the animal's head, uttered a few comforting words, and then ended its suffering with his sword. He could have done the same for the countless men he walked past, whose condition was equally helpless, but men weren't allowed to render that same service to each other. After much searching, he finally found

The Winds of Wharhalen

Broecker. The memory of returning to Jocar's body on the plateau in the Karpoans came rushing back. For the second time in his life he had been powerless to prevent a friend's violent death. It was difficult picking up the once-powerful warrior's limp body, but he did, and carried it back to camp.

The Royal Army took a large number of prisoners from the battlefield, some from the corps of bowmen that eventually surrendered to the mounted archers, and many other wounded men who were unable to make it back to Ritola. They set up a camp for the captives at the rear of their lines and posted guards. Kaine disliked having to use his soldiers to guard prisoners, but so long as they were contained, these men were no longer a threat. Vartan's defenses were greatly weakened without them, and, in the balance, the battle would have to have been considered a victory. The warlord had failed to drive Kaine's army from the field, and his men were still confined to the pestilence-ridden city. Ironically, the lucky ones were those who'd been taken prisoner, for during their confinement they were treated well and ate better than they had in months. Best of all, they were out of the war.

CHAPTER SIXTEEN

The Resistance

E ngrid drew her bow and held the razor-sharp point of the arrow steady on her target. At the same moment, six more arrows were trained on the cluster of soldiers in the narrow lane. Just then, one of the soldiers realized their peril and shouted. The one that Engrid had in her sights turned just as she loosed the arrow. The shaft hit him in the left shoulder and lodged there. "Damn!" The Queen hissed as she slipped another arrow in the bow. Her shot had been the signal for the other archers, and when the deadly barrage ended, it left only two soldiers standing in addition to hers, with four more writhing on the ground. More arrows flew and the panicked men had no further chance to escape. Engrid's group then fell upon the wounded with their swords and in a flurry of steel blades, seven more of the invaders of Attalia were dead.

Without speaking, the raiders quickly melted into the environs of the vast city, eventually finding their way back into the caverns. Employing these tactics, the organized resistance to the occupation of Attalia was able to fight back against the forces of Haczlok and Braslon. The army of Ej Tauk-Zar was still being kept outside the city

The Winds of Wharhalen

walls, where they had begun to build their own settlement while Sharnov's men had made themselves at home in the lower town, in spite of growing resentment by the residents. The toll in dead soldiers and destroyed equipment was mounting by the day, but so far Haczlok had been unable to capture any of the resistance leaders. He had questioned many of the city's inhabitants; in fact, the castle dungeon was overflowing with suspects. Torture and even execution had also failed to reveal the hiding places of his tormentors and had actually turned out to be counterproductive, having caused new resistance groups to form. Fires were started, supplies disappeared or were ruined, and rock-throwing mobs were now confronting his soldiers in the streets on a regular basis.

Worst of all for Haczlok, the rich treasury that he had hoped to claim by capturing Attalia was gone and Ej Tauk-Zar was growing restless, having been promised a fourth of the missing prize. Furthermore, his men were disgruntled at having been denied the right to plunder the city, and there was widespread talk among them of going home. Haczlok tried as best he could to reassure the warlord that once the Queen and her men were located, the treasure would be theirs as well. Haczlok then turned his wrath on Braslon, blaming him for letting Engrid and the others slip through their fingers. Braslon, in turn, was behind most of the torture and executions that were used to extract information from captives and suspects. And so, in Attalia, where he had once commanded respect prior to the attack on the city, the very name Braslon was now synonymous with traitor.

Engrid, her long blond hair hidden under a cap and her willowy figure concealed by men's clothing, slipped almost invisibly through the back streets of the city. The longbows and deadly arrows employed by her raiding party had been collected and hidden by one of its members. The rest of the group dispersed to take separate routes back to the caverns. This was a new type of warfare from the kind she

16 - The Resistance

was used to. In the days when she rode with Kaine, Cecel, and Joal against Zironon, they would make lightning raids on horseback, and then cover long distances to return to their hidden camps. Fighting within the confines of Attalia, she and the others had learned to adapt to tight quarters and had created new tactics specifically for that purpose. However, it was a grim business, staging ambushes in which there could be no survivors and she hated the killing, but her hatred of Haczlok and Braslon was greater still. At the moment, though, all her small band could do was harass and disrupt the occupiers. But if they could substantially weaken Haczlok's grip on the city, it would make it easier for Kaine to defeat him when he returned from Ritola. And he *must* return from Ritola. She would not even let herself consider the alternative. In the meantime, she and her companions would hold out as long as necessary and continue to fight back any way they could.

Into the bowels of Attalia she crept, through one of the many hidden entrances to the caverns. This one was concealed under the floor of a hovel tucked away in a crowded section of the middle town. Joal had originally shown her the way into the caverns, although the entrances were changed from time to time. Those who knew their location guarded the secret carefully, for they were the most secure hiding places in Attalia. The labyrinth of tunnels, although fairly extensive, was dwarfed by the enormity of the walled city itself. Braslon could search for years and not find it. Once inside the dark, damp tunnel, Engrid felt her anxiety diminishing. As courageous as the Queen was, and even though she had successfully endured many tough fights, the thought of capture by these ruthless enemies still caused her blood to run cold. She immediately tried to banish any thoughts of what her fate at their hands would be. For her, there was only this moment, this day, with the faint glimmer of hope stored deep in the recesses of her mind that the future held the possibility of a victory for Kaine's army.

The Winds of Wharhalen

Soon her solitary thoughts were pushed away as she began to encounter other members of the resistance. She passed through one small chamber where two guards were posted and then into a larger one where work on weapons went on busily. The light was dim, as always, and a thin cloud of smoke clung to the ceiling from the lanterns that burned there to chase away the constant night. After a few greetings and questions as to which of the raiders had returned, Engrid proceeded to the room that she shared with Myleia. As the only two women who had gone underground when Attalia fell, they had further cemented their friendship. When the Queen entered the room, the diminutive Myleia was busy practicing with a sword, as Engrid had caught her doing many times before, and thus was no longer alarmed to see it. In addition, the young, dark-haired girl had, during their exodus, left her pretty gowns in the world above and now dressed in the manner of the warrior Queen herself; that is, like a man.

"If your husband could only see you now, he would be shocked to see what a ruffian you have become," chided Engrid, good-naturedly.

Myleia didn't smile. "I would hope instead that he would be happy I was still alive and ready to defend myself."

The Queen nodded. "At least that you are still alive. And I definitely plan to keep you that way."

Myleia understood the comment as an effort to deflect another attempt by Myleia to assume a more active role in the resistance. Ignoring it for the moment, Myleia pressed on. "Please let me go with you on the next raid."

"Absolutely not. We have already had this discussion too many times. I will not let you endanger your life or risk getting you captured. Kaine would never forgive me if anything happened to you."

"And yet you willingly take risks everyday, and you are the most valuable person here. I am nothing."

"To Kaine, you are everything. He loves you so much that he would trade away the entire army for you without a moment's hesitation."

Myleia bristled, her beautiful, dark eyes flashing. "You make him sound weak."

"Not at all; Kaine is passionate. We're talking about a man who slit the throat of his own father to rid the Empire of a cruel tyrant. But you, Myleia, are his passion of passions. The only reason he isn't here now is because he thinks you are safe."

"You are saying that he would abandon Ritola to Vartan if he thought I was in danger?"

"I am sure of it. And I am just as sure that he would kill me if I was somehow responsible for your death."

"So you are never going to let me go on a raid then?"

"Don't you see that I can't take that risk? I have to decide what is best for you as well as for the Empire."

Myleia seethed. "Like you did when you handed the army over to Braslon?"

The hurt showed in Engrid's face. "Just because I made one mistake doesn't mean I have to be forced into another one."

The two women didn't speak again for the rest of that day. The chilly atmosphere remained until they went to sleep that night. However, the next morning when Engrid awoke, Myleia wasn't there. The Queen immediately went out into the large chamber and asked the men there if anyone had seen the young girl. They all replied that they had not. Knowing Myleia could not walk around without being noticed

The Winds of Wharhalen

by the men, Engrid felt a sudden wave of terror wash over her. She rushed back into the room they shared and started looking among Myleia's things and discovered that the short sword was gone as well as the bow she practiced with almost daily. Engrid immediately sent men to scour the tunnels in case the girl was simply out practicing somewhere. Hours went by and the search turned up nothing. The Queen grew frantic. By now, she was certain that Myleia had snuck out of the caverns on some foolish mission in an attempt to try to prove her worth to the cause. She considered sending search parties out into the city to look for her, but Attalia was so vast that the chance of finding her was miniscule. Add to that the risk of her raiders randomly searching the city without a definite objective and she realized that such an undertaking could put the entire resistance effort in jeopardy. Their raids up to now had been carefully planned and executed with surgical precision—the attack groups always knew where their target was, how they were going to get to their objective and how they were going to get back. No, the foolhardy girl was on her own. Engrid was just going to have to wait and hope for Myleia's return.

The hours passed slowly and afternoon eventually faded into evening. Of course, in the caverns it was always night so it was easy to get confused. The resistance fighters might as well have been blind moles burrowing in the ground, their forays above ground their only way of keeping track of the passing days. Engrid didn't even know which of the entrances Myleia had used to exit the tunnels; therefore, she had no way of knowing where to look for her return.

As evening fell on the world above, Engrid felt that she could wait no more. And so she decided to use the cover of night to go out and survey a wide circle around the entrance she had used the day before. The risks above ground were great for the Queen. Although Engrid had maintained some trustworthy contacts within Attalia, Braslon's spies were everywhere. And the price on the Queen's head

16 - The Resistance

would be more than enough to shift nearly anyone's loyalties. Concealing her appearance and arming herself, she made her way through the tunnels and eventually emerged into the bare hovel that housed the entrance. While in the caverns, Engrid thought she'd detected small footprints going in the opposite direction from the ones she had made coming back the previous day. But in the dim flickering light of her torch it'd been difficult to discern one mark from another on the damp, stone floor that had seen so many feet in the past few months. But when she checked the floor in the shabby building more closely, she was certain that there were recent prints made by boots leading away from the hole. A damp boot makes a distinct print on a dry dusty floor, and these were definitely smaller than the ones she had made.

Encouraged that she had at least chosen the correct entrance, Engrid carefully ventured forth into the dark back street; distant voices from one of the surrounding houses were the only sounds breaking the nighttime silence. She had only gone about a hundred yards when she noticed a bright glimmer of light in the distance. The Queen had been out in that area at night many times before and had never seen a light so bright in that direction. As she moved toward it, she realized that it was farther away than she had originally thought. Then it came to her. Fire! There was a huge fire in the direction of the lower town where Sharnov's men were camped. Such a large fire would draw a lot of men to extinguish it, so she decided to turn back. She circled to her left and started back up the hill, when a voice came from the shadows. "Engrid!" someone had hissed in a loud whisper.

It startled her to know that someone was watching her when she'd thought she was alone. To hear her name added to her fright. Instinctively, her hand went to the sword at her belt just as a diminutive figure appeared from out of the dark. "I thought that was you when I started following you a ways back, but I wanted to be sure."

The Winds of Wharhalen

Engrid relaxed her grip on the sword. "You were *following* me?" she asked incredulously.

"Yes, I saw you coming from the direction of the house as I was returning and was curious. After I had a chance to get a closer look, I knew it had to be you."

"Why?"

Myleia smiled condescendingly. "I have seen you put on those same clothes so many times before, and, besides, you have a distinctive walk."

Engrid brushed aside the comment. "So, what have you been *doing* all day?"

"Most of the day I spent searching for a suitable target."

"Suitable for what?"

"My raid."

"Your what?"

"My raid. You wouldn't let me go on your raids, so I decided to stage one of my own."

Engrid sighed. "So what did you find?"

Myleia pointed in the direction of the fire, which had now grown even brighter against the night sky.

"Sharnov's men have set up a compound near the outer wall in the lower town."

Engrid nodded.

"They have taken all the houses for their own use. They have barracks, a bakery, stables, an armory…I set fire to the armory."

Her voice had a child-like excitement to it as she smiled sweetly

16 - The Resistance

from under the hood that covered her raven tresses and partially concealed her pretty features. Engrid shook her head resignedly, "Let's get back to the house before someone sees us talking here and gets suspicious."

Once back inside the tunnels, Engrid spoke once more. "You know, I could place you under guard to keep you from leaving again."

"Yes, you could and further my status as your prisoner. Engrid, do you realize what it's like to stay underground day after day and never see the sun? To be treated like an object to be guarded and not a person who has some worth? Please, let me help."

"I guess if you are with me at least then I can watch out for you."

"We can watch out for each other."

The two were silent for the rest of the walk back to their chamber. When they were getting ready for bed, Myleia said, "I'm sorry that I made the comment about Braslon yesterday. That was unfair. I just lost my temper."

A tear started down Engrid's cheek, which she quickly whisked away.

The Winds of Wharhalen

CHAPTER SEVENTEEN

Zironon

In the days following the battle around Ritola there was a period of relative quiet while the Royal Army buried its dead and tended to its wounded. The confrontation had been somewhat indecisive, with both sides suffering heavy casualties. Vartan had failed to drive Kaine's army from the field, but what was left of his forces was still firmly entrenched within the city. The Royal Army was similarly depleted, and if it had previously been undersized to succeed in an all-out assault on the walls, that fact was even more apparent now.

Kaine's patience, already severely tested, was growing thin. As he contemplated what course of action to take next, his thoughts drifted back to another time when he had to make a decision that would similarly have a dramatic impact on the future of the Empire.

Kaine and Joal's alliance that had initially started out merely as a way to steal from Zironon had grown into a gang of about forty men. Accordingly, their raids had grown much bolder, and their notoriety had gained near folk hero status among the populace. After they'd met

The Winds of Wharhalen

the exiled princess from Tairellia who would someday become Queen, Engrid eventually convinced them to join forces with her rebel group in an effort to consolidate power against the warlord.

Unfortunately, the newly formed alliance met a crushing defeat at the Temple of the Old Kings after one of Kaine's own band betrayed them. Kaine had managed to escape with part of his raiders still intact but feared that as a result of the betrayal Zironon now knew too much about his activities. Kaine next recalled the discussion that he'd had with his trusted partners, Joal and Cecel: "Zironon won't rest until he has hunted us all down and killed us. And none of our hideouts should be considered safe any longer now that we have been betrayed."

"More than likely, he already knows the location of all of them," offered Cecel.

"We should disband so that we are harder to find, maybe even try to leave the country for a while," suggested Joal.

"Or we could just kill him," said Kaine, with a cold, calm voice.

Cecel's features remained frozen in an expression of amazement for several moments. Joal, on the other hand, recovered quickly. "After we kill him, then what?"

"If suddenly there is no Zironon, there will be a temporary power void. We then step into that void and start an all-out rebellion."

"What if the people won't follow us?"

"The only thing that prevents the people from rising up against Zironon is fear. I think they will grow bolder if he is removed."

"What about his sons?"

"Neither son is respected by the old warlord's soldiers. The peasants have no use for them either and the nobles certainly won't

17 - Zironon

support them. They don't even like each other. Therefore, it will be difficult for them to assume power, especially if they have to deal with widespread rebellion."

Joal and Cecel nodded slowly, as if only partially convinced. Cecel finally broke the silence. "I have been through two revolutions in Gruenland. Long-held discontent can often cause a revolt to spread quickly. But seldom are these things quickly resolved. Much blood will be spilled first."

"It might be worth it if the Empire can be rid of Zironon. Unless, of course, the blood spilled is mine," said Joal. "Or yours, Cecel," he quickly added.

"So then how are we going to bring about this assassination?" inquired Cecel.

"First, we need to know how Zironon spends his days and nights. Where he goes, what he does, how many guards are with him, every detail. Joal, that's your job. Report back in a week and then we'll decide on a plan."

A week later to the day Joal was back with the information on Zironon's activities. "Probably the time when he would be most vulnerable would be on one of his visits to the baths. His guard detail is lightest at those times, and the baths would be much easier to seal off than his quarters in the castle."

"And you can predict which days he is going to be there?"

"Not with absolute certainty, but he goes every few days, and when he does, he spends the whole afternoon there. The old lecher also has young girls sent to him. They are taken away from their families and kept for his amusement until he has grown tired of them."

At these words the pain and anger grew quickly inside Kaine. He thought of another young girl from the village of Galen.

The Winds of Wharhalen

The baths were located about five miles from Attalia at the site of natural warm springs of volcanic origin. The site had been used for centuries by a succession of rulers, and its opulence was unequaled anywhere else in Killarassee. The exterior suggested a temple from the era of the Old Kings, graceful in form and built to last a millennium and beyond. Kaine and his men had been there for two days before Zironon arrived. They'd anticipated his arrival when a young peasant girl, no more than sixteen years old, had been brought there that morning. Once Zironon went into the baths, the two men who had brought the girl earlier came out and joined the four that had accompanied the old warlord. Soon the six guards were circling the building in pairs, a complete circuit taking about ten minutes.

Kaine stationed his men around the building, the forest surrounding the baths providing adequate cover for them to get within range of their arrows. Three men were strategically positioned opposite a point that the sentries would have to pass. The third archer in each group was there in case one of the first two arrows missed their intended targets. The strike had to be quick and noiseless so that there wouldn't be time for Zironon to be warned. Kaine's whistle signaled the shots, and in less than a minute, it was over. The guards that didn't die immediately by being stuck by arrows were dispatched as Kaine's men fell upon them with swords. With Zironon's sentries gone, Kaine and Cecel slipped quietly into the building.

Visibility inside the structure was limited by the billows of steam rising from the hot spring. The walls and floor were polished marble and the large circular spa occupied the center of the room. Kaine indicated with a gesture of his hand for Cecel to stay by the door. Then, he started circling slowly to the right. In just seconds, his eye caught a slight movement in the mist. As he raised his sword, he saw that it was the young girl, cowering against the wall. Kaine's eyes flitted from right to left, his fingers tightly gripping the sword. Not

17 - Zironon

detecting any other movement, he glanced back at the girl. The short tunic that she wore was soaked through and clung to her slender body. Her long, brown hair hung in wet ringlets on her bare shoulders and her frightened eyes were red from crying.

Suddenly, another figure charged at them from out of the fog, and this one had a sword. Kaine barely avoided the attack, parrying the blade just before its point reached him. Soon the sound of steel striking steel was reverberating loudly against the marble walls as the two fought savagely without either combatant gaining an advantage at first. There was a momentary pause when the two combatants stepped back from each other. For the first time in his life, Kaine was face to face with his father. The old man was wrinkled and scarred, and his haggard face reflected the many years of debauchery. Still, his back was straight and his muscles powerful as he stood there naked except for a wet loincloth. He hadn't held the Empire in his grasp for over thirty years by being a weakling. Kaine felt neither fear of, nor sympathy for, this stranger though. His only emotion was unrelenting hatred.

"Who are you and why are you here?" asked the old warlord.

"I am Kaine, and I have come to kill you."

"Do I know you?"

"You might know me as the leader of a gang of bandits that have been stealing from you and killing your soldiers for the past year."

The old man frowned and cocked his head to one side. "But that isn't all of it, is it? A thief doesn't suddenly become an assassin."

"There is also the matter of a girl from the village of Galen, twenty-six years ago. You raped her."

"There were lots of girls. There have always been girls."

"This one was my mother. And to spare you any more guessing games, I am your son."

The Winds of Wharhalen

"Ha! Another bastard son! Most of them just want money. What makes you so different?"

"Because someone has to end your miserable existence and no one has a better reason than me!"

With that, Kaine began his attack anew. The old warrior fended it off skillfully and in the furious fighting, the warlord's blade tore through the younger man's shoulder. Kaine spun away but Zironon pressed on. In his unrelenting attack, he made a careless error, and Kaine slashed the back of his leg. His hamstring severed, the leg could no longer support his weight. As the warlord staggered forward, the two adversaries locked blades. Swiftly, Kaine drew a knife with his other hand and before Zironon could extricate himself, the razor sharp blade slid across his throat. There was no sound, no further struggle. The warlord simply crumpled to the floor, then lay there in an ever-widening pool of blood.

Kaine stood over the body for a few moments and tried to assess his feelings. He wanted to feel something. Elation, remorse, satisfaction, sorrow, anything but the terrible anger that had held him captive all these years. But he realized he didn't feel any different. Zironon was a monster, but he wasn't the only monster. There was still more to do.

Kaine then turned to the girl and stretched out his hand to her. She whimpered and pulled farther away. He spoke softly to her. "We won't hurt you. We won't let anyone else hurt you. We're going to take you back to your home now." Slowly, cautiously, she let him take her arm. They walked to the door where Cecel was still waiting. "Zironon is dead," he said to the big Gruenlander. "It's our time now."

CHAPTER EIGHTEEN

The Mission

Kaine called a meeting with his Officers-at-Arms. The number of experienced leaders had dwindled during the Ritola campaign, so most of those assembled had recently received their promotions in the field. Among them was the tall, blonde-haired youth, Locke Thomason. Even the people from his village in the Karpoans might not have recognized him even though it had only been two years since his days there. In the time between, he had felt the lash as a slave, toiled in the quarry, killed countless men in battle, seen friends die, and been wounded several times himself. Although his lanky frame had filled out with harder, sinewy muscle, the greatest change could be seen in his face. Gone was much of the soft, youthful innocence and carefree bravado. It had been replaced by features that, while still handsome, made him look much older than his actual years and appeared to be chiseled from stone. The boyish smile was gone. In its place was a firm-set jaw and slightly sunken cheeks that emphasized the prominent bones below his ice-blue eyes, eyes that never seemed to rest. They were steady, unwavering, and their mistrust pierced the very soul of anyone who dared to meet his gaze.

The Winds of Wharhalen

After distinguishing himself in the most recent battle, Locke was knighted. This was a largely symbolic gesture on the part of Kaine, since anyone in the Empire could call themselves a knight if they had the means to purchase a horse, armor, and weapons. Some knights stayed in the service of a particular noble and usually received money or land for their service; others were nothing more than mercenaries, fighting for whoever paid them and switching allegiance frequently. Being a knight of the Queen, though, had certain unique advantages. The royal treasury made it possible for the crown to provide its knights with the finest armor and weapons. There was also the strength of numbers—very seldom did a knight have to go into battle without plenty of support from infantry, archers, and other knights. In addition, royal knights were provided living quarters in Attalia. And finally, the Queen's knights were generally given land after returning from a campaign. In reality, Locke had already been performing the function of a knight. But this confirmation of his status could be of tremendous value to him if he managed to live long enough to return to Attalia.

Among the older soldiers, there was still Drobek and Sauric. The other Officers-at-Arms present included Locke, Andros, and a young Grausak named Ivo. When he was first brought to Ritola, Locke had struggled with the presence of so many native Wharhalens in the ranks. His previous exposure to Grausaks in the Karpoans had not been favorable. For the most part, he considered them to be thieves and murderers. But he had found that, while they weren't the most congenial of people, they were courageous in battle and no more likely to steal things than any of the other soldiers there. Regardless, he had always admired their superb horsemanship, and he now had several excellent riders serving alongside him in his unit.

Kaine opened the meeting by addressing the men. "We need to bring this campaign to a close. Many of our enlistments are up soon,

18 - The Mission

and it's going to be difficult to keep the men here much longer. The supply of new recruits in the area has dried up. Vartan might be able to hold on through the summer and if we have to spend another winter here, we won't have an army. I want to send a small group of men around the perimeter of Ritola to find a way in. Vartan's army is so depleted right now that he can't adequately patrol the whole wall any more, so our chances are better now than they were earlier. Once inside, the group will try to make their way to the front gate during the night. When they give us the signal that they are in place and ready to open the gates, we'll have an attack prepared that will overwhelm any defense they can mount. If we can keep the element of surprise and do this while most of Vartan's men are sleeping, we should be able to minimize our casualties."

There was a brief period when no one said anything, although the expressions on the men's faces seemed to indicate approval of the plan. Locke was the first to speak. "I'll go."

When no other voice was heard, Kaine replied, "Do you have five men in your command that you would trust to take with you?"

"Yes."

"All right, stay and we'll discuss the details. Everyone else is dismissed."

When all the other soldiers had left the tent, Kaine studied the young man carefully. It was the first time he had spoken privately with Locke, but he was not unaware of the young soldier's exploits in the campaign. His officers had reported that this former slave and horse trainer was not only courageous and resourceful, but he was rapidly developing an almost fanatical sense of loyalty from the men he led. His ferocity in battle had subsequently created an aura of invincibility around him, even while seeming reckless to the point of suicidal. Kaine, therefore, needed to find out if this new hero in his army was

The Winds of Wharhalen

stable enough to lead such an important mission as this one. "Why did you volunteer?" he finally asked.

Locke's cold stare never wavered. "I came here as a slave. I was told that when this campaign was over, I will have earned my freedom. Most of the other men here are fighting for money. I'm fighting to regain control over my life. If I can somehow help to end this campaign quickly, then it suits my purpose."

"I have been told that from the way you fight, you might not live to see the end of this campaign."

Locke shrugged. "Men who fight timidly don't survive long either."

"What is it that you will do with your life once it is yours again to control?"

"I made a promise to someone that I have been unable to keep thus far. If it is still possible to fulfill it after this war, I intend to do so."

"Do you mind telling me what this promise was?"

Locke hesitated slightly for the first time. Then he began in a steady voice. "There is a girl who is bound in servitude to a cruel nobleman. I once made a promise to her that I would buy her freedom. When I went to this Lord to pay him for her release, he took my money, extended the length of her servitude and sold me to the slave traders. If I am fortunate enough to somehow survive Ritola, I intend to go back and finish the business that I started with this man."

Kaine could see by the resolute expression on the boy's face that he was serious. In the cold, focused eyes, the firm set jaw, he saw someone who could only be stopped by death. It made Kaine think of Myleia. Her father had imprisoned him because he'd sought the girl's hand. Then he profited financially by forcing his daughter to marry a foreign prince. "You are no longer a slave," he continued. "You are a

18 - The Mission

knight of the Queen. I would say that your future looks a lot brighter now than when you came here. And if you live to see the end of this war, you will have gold, a fine horse, and excellent weapons."

"I had gold and a fine horse. A nobleman took them from me."

Kaine sighed resignedly. "I would like to be able to tell you that we can right the wrong that has been done to you. But proving that a noble has committed a crime is difficult. If you go after this man to seek vengeance, I doubt if I can help you. But if you can help me win this war, I will make sure you have everything that a great Knight of the Realm deserves. Go now. Pick your men, equip them with whatever they will need, and be ready to leave tomorrow night. Ride out of camp to the north, and then circle back to where the pine forest starts on the west side of the city. Leave one man with the horses and then, with the others, climb the rocks to an elevation from which you can reach the wall. Be sure to avoid the sentries but move across quickly. Once you're inside, make your way to the front gate at the outermost city wall. When you are sure you can get it open, send two flaming arrows into the sky. I will give you until the second night to make it to the gate. When we see the arrows, we will be prepared to attack. If you don't make it happen by the third night, we'll assume you didn't make it to the gate."

Locke nodded that he understood, turned and left the tent. Kaine disliked being at the head of an army. He knew that he himself should be the one going into Ritola, not some twenty-year-old boy. He had spent a large part of his life sneaking in and out of places, but since the revolution, he was the leader that had held the Royal Army together. And it was the Royal Army that kept Engrid on the throne. Like it or not, he would have to continue to try and find men that were an extension of himself to send out on missions like this one.

The Winds of Wharhalen

Locke spent the rest of the day talking to some of the men he had come to know in his unit. He didn't address the whole group concerning the mission for fear there could be a spy in their midst. Instead, he went individually to the men he trusted the most and talked with them privately. There were Jarre and Borke, Killarasseans like himself, and Edle, a Gruenlander. He also talked to Marchek, a fierce Grausak, and to a local, Zarmir, who, unlike the others, had actually been inside Ritola. All agreed to go, figuring it was no more dangerous than storming the walls and might actually have a greater chance of succeeding.

Locke reported back to Kaine that he had his men, and the six spent the next day securing the equipment they would need. Just before dusk, they rode out of camp heading in the opposite direction from the city. After about two miles, they started a long loop back toward the forested part of the crag Ritola was built on. It was almost midnight when they reached the point where they would leave their horses. Borke, a short, square-built southerner, was assigned to stay with their horses.

From that point Locke and the other four men began their climb on foot up the steep face of rock in the pitch black of night. Not even so much as a candle could be used, because it would be seen from the walls. The climb would have been difficult in daylight, but at night it seemed impossible. As such, their progress was measured in inches rather than feet and the sky was brightening before they finally crept to an elevation that would allow them to reach the walls that surrounded the city. In a recess hidden among the rocks, the five men could finally rest. They wouldn't be able to move during daylight without risking being spotted; so, precarious as their perch might have seemed, they all maneuvered into the most comfortable positions they could find for sleep. When darkness came to the valley again, they moved from their alcove into a position where they could observe the activity atop the

18 - The Mission

walls. For an hour they observed the circuit of the sentries. Once they had an idea of the interval between guards, they used one of these intervals to reach the wall. Locke threw a large grappling hook attached to a scaling rope over the top. He scrambled up the side and on reaching the ledge on the other side, he crouched low so that his shape wouldn't show against the night sky. Silently, he notched an arrow in his bow and waited for the approach of the next guard. The unlucky soldier fell with a dull thud, then four more raiders quickly joined Locke on the wall.

The location where they climbed down into Ritola was between the outside curtain wall of the castle and the less heavily-guarded perimeter wall of the city. It was patrolled by a number of sentries that kept a watch on the plain below the town. Moving between the rows of dwellings that crowded the winding streets on the mountainside, the dark of the night became their ally. Zarmir led the way, with the other four following in pairs spaced at intervals so as not to attract attention. Before starting out from camp, Locke's band of invaders had exchanged their bright blue and gold uniforms for the drab garments taken from dead enemy soldiers. Things were going smoothly so far, Locke thought, but he knew the difficult part was yet to come when they reached the gate, which would be more heavily guarded.

Locke and Jarre, bringing up the rear, had just reached the end of a row of low buildings on their right when voices came from up ahead of them. Locke thought he heard Zarmir's voice speaking one of the local dialects. Before they could be seen, Locke quickly pushed open a door in one of the houses, and he and Jarre slipped into the building. Inside, the room was pitch-black, but Locke could detect the faint odor of cooked food. As he was trying to make out his surroundings, he noticed the dim glow of embers. Suddenly, a candle was lit, and the room emerged from darkness. Locke and Jarre wheeled around as one and found themselves looking into the frightened eyes of a young woman sitting up in bed holding a candle. As she started to speak, Locke rushed over to her and stifled her voice by placing his hand over her mouth. As she struggled, the candle fell from her hand and landed on the floor where it was picked up and quickly extinguished by Jarre. Using more force than he wanted to, Locke ended up with nearly all of his weight pressed down on the squirming body.

"We're not here to harm you," Locke whispered when the struggle finally subsided. "We're here to take back Ritola from Vartan and bring an end to the war. If I take my hand from your mouth, will you promise not to scream?"

When the woman nodded, Locke carefully slipped his hand away from her lips, and she remained quiet. Gradually, he removed his weight from her trembling body. "I'm sorry we frightened you, but we couldn't risk being discovered. Our friends already may have been taken prisoner. But if we succeed in our mission, the war could be over soon."

"Soon?" repeated a soft, frightened voice. "It has been so long."

"Yes, and too many men have died."

"My husband is dead," came the voice somberly. "And my brother still defends the walls."

"I'm truly sorry. Vartan has made Ritola a battleground. But this is not Ritola's fight. It is Vartan's fight."

"I hate Vartan," came the voice again. "Because of him most of our men are dead, and our children are starving."

18 - The Mission

"Please just let us stay for a few minutes until we can leave without being seen, and then we will do what we can to bring peace back to your city," Locke whispered.

"Mother?" Came a small voice from the darkness. "Who is there?"

"Shhh," soothed the woman, "we have visitors, but they won't hurt us. Go back to sleep."

"Is it uncle?" the tiny voice persisted.

"No, but they are friends."

Locke felt a wave of relief as the room was once more quiet. No one spoke again for a time as Locke sat on the edge of the bed listening for sounds from the outside. After a while the voices had died away, and only the slight rustle of covers from across the room interrupted the silence. The woman's breathing, so close by, had lengthened and eventually slowed as the time passed. Finally, Locke whispered to Jarre, "Check outside the door."

Jarre, who was standing by the door all along, opened it slightly and listened. Locke then heard the door open wider, followed by a whisper, "It's clear."

Locke got up from the bed, and then turned to where the woman lay silent. "Stay out of sight when the attack comes, and keep the child close to you." He started toward the door, and then asked, "What is your name?"

"Tasha," came the reply.

"Thank you, Tasha. You may have played a part in ending this war. I hope so, at least."

"I do, too."

The Winds of Wharhalen

Jarre and Locke slipped quietly out into the street. Staying close to buildings when they could and crossing open spaces carefully, they gradually moved from the darker part of the city toward the outer wall gate that was lighted by torches all night. Finally, they reached a wide open grazing area that presented the last gulf for them to cross before they would reach the front gates. It would be impossible to cross it without being seen, and so they decided it would be best if they stayed close to the base of the wall and as much out of the view of the sentries as possible. Never had a walk seemed so long to Locke before. The long sweeping outer wall carved a semicircular arc that ran at least two miles long along the hillside below the citadel. At last they reached the gate and the platform where the mechanism for opening and closing the drawbridge was located. Knives drawn, the two men started up the steps. Before the two surprised guards stationed at the top could utter a cry, Jarre and Locke silenced them.

"Ready the two arrows," whispered Locke while he studied the mechanism that lowered the great bridge to the city. A cogwheel let out the ropes connected to the top of the drawbridge. He realized he didn't want to start lowering the huge wooden bridge too soon because once he started it down, it would immediately draw attention. Jarre then lit the two arrows from one of the torches atop the platform. Just as he drew his bow to send them over the wall, he was struck in the back by an arrow that had come from a sentry on the west wall. As he fell, the flaming arrows fell harmlessly to the floor of the platform. It would do no good to lower the bridge now since the sentry who had seen them had sounded the alarm. Soldiers were now running for the platform and one had even gained the steps. Suddenly, the man was felled by an arrow, and a familiar voice called out to Locke, "Send the signal!"

It was Marchek. Locke looked up long enough to see the Grausak, along with Edle and Zarmir, barricaded along the wall about sixty feet from the platform, sending a deadly barrage of arrows at

18 - The Mission

anyone who got close to the steps. Locke quickly gathered up the still-flaming shafts, notched them in his bow and sent them in a high arc over the wall and into the night sky. Just then, he felt a searing pain in his left arm. When he looked down he saw the bloody point of an arrow protruding from the front of his upper arm. There was no time to deal with it, though, as he had to get the bridge lowered before the Royal Army reached the walls. With only one good arm now, he couldn't turn the cogwheel, but he could still cut the ropes. That task, however, turned out to be far more difficult than Locke had originally thought it would be. The twisted rope was thick, nearly two inches across and his sword wasn't sharp enough to make much progress in cutting through it; so he began hacking.

As the turmoil around him grew more intense he could see that his three allies, fighting gallantly, were under heavy attack. When he was finally able to cut through the first rope, Locke could see the torches of Kaine's forces in the distance. The huge drawbridge groaned as one side was freed. One soldier, however, had managed to avoid the fusillade of arrows laid down by Marchek and the others and began to climb the steps. Locke met the man's sword with his own, and they fought fiercely for what seemed an eternity as the need to get the bridge down reached critical urgency. While Locke continued to deflect blow after blow, he suddenly felt a searing pain in his leg when his opponent's blade slashed his upper leg. Desperate to end this fight quickly, he attacked furiously. Somehow in the blur of flashing steel that followed, Locke's sword managed to find its way into the man's shoulder. The other's weapon fell from his hand and clattered to the platform. Locke tried to free his blade but could not, as the two became entangled and fell hard to the deck. As they continued to fight, they rolled close to the edge of the platform where they were exposed to a barrage of arrows. All of a sudden, the struggle ceased. Locke pushed the limp body away from him, and it tumbled over the side. Trying to crawl back to the ropes, he was hit with another arrow, this time in the

The Winds of Wharhalen

shoulder of his already crippled left side. Despite the excruciating pain, and struggling to remain conscious, Locke picked up the sword of his vanquished foe and returned to hacking at the second rope. He could now hear the sound of hoof beats coming across the plain. Working furiously, his sword arm aching with fatigue and growing weaker by the minute, the last few strands of the rope finally gave way, and the bridge came crashing down. Seconds later, the Queen's knights poured through the gate. Locke, his enemies now otherwise occupied, was no longer under attack. He then collapsed from pain and fatigue onto the platform and started to lose consciousness. He fought against it as long as he could, but the events swirling about him soon blurred and he passed out.

CHAPTER NINETEEN

Tasha

Locke had blacked out in the darkness of the pre-dawn hours, but he awoke in bright afternoon sunlight. And when he did, he heard no sounds of war, only the human agony of the wounded. Everywhere around him were injured men, some with wounds that would heal, others simply awaiting death. There were men from both sides of the conflict, lying side by side now in a makeshift infirmary in the bailey of the castle. One of the women working with the wounded happened to notice Locke as he was attempting to raise himself up. Her weather-worn face was wrinkled, and the hair visible beneath her head covering was flecked with gray. Her eyes were tired and sad, but there was kindness in them, too. She came over to him, knelt by his side and examined the bandages on his arm and leg. The arrow that had pierced his left arm had been removed, as had the one in the back of his shoulder. His wounds had been bound tightly, and the torn muscles ached even when he was motionless. The bandage wrapped around his leg had bloodstains, and the woman set about changing it.

The Winds of Wharhalen

Locke tried to speak, but his voice failed. When the woman cradled his head in her hand and helped him drink some water, he was finally able to say "Thank you."

She smiled grimly and nodded.

As Locke tried to clear his hazy recollection of what had happened, his thoughts raced back to the early morning hours. The last thing he could remember was the sight of the horsemen pouring through the open gate. But that would have only gotten them as far as the town below the citadel, he thought. How did he get inside the curtain wall? As she finished bandaging his leg he asked the woman, "Is Vartan still in control of the castle?"

"Vartan is dead. It's over."

Before Locke could pose his next question, the woman had moved on to care for another patient. He tried to recall more details but couldn't. Then he lapsed back into unconsciousness.

The next time Locke awoke, it was early evening, and he felt a chill. When he began to shake uncontrollably, the old woman covered him with a blanket. As the warmth returned to his body, he heard voices of men that sounded familiar, but they spoke in hushed tones, and he couldn't tell what they talked about. Eventually the voices faded away, and again, so too did his consciousness. He awoke several more times during the evening and into the night, usually when the pain in his shoulder and arm jarred him into awareness whenever he tried to change positions. He was vaguely aware of the old woman trying to feed him at times. He'd lost all track of time, but his periods of wakefulness eventually grew longer and he was becoming more lucid. Each time he woke up the number of bodies around him seemed to be smaller in number, and he wondered how many of them had died and how many had recovered. One time he imagined himself being thrown into a mass grave with the dead and was jolted out of a shallow sleep.

19 - Tasha

He awoke drenched in sweat and shaking, but it was fear, rather than fever, that had caused him to shake this time. The sweat seemed to break the fever that had gripped him for days, though, and he rested more comfortably after that. For the first time since before the battle, he thought of Eylese. He had to live. He wanted to see her again, and he also knew that without his help, she might never escape Toulon.

Over the next few days Locke grew strong enough to sit up for longer periods of time and soon began to eat on his own. His first visitor, at least the first one that he was aware of, was Marchek. The powerfully built Grausak with the reddish beard who stood before him seemed like a giant looking down on the pale and gaunt young man. "It looks like you're going to make it. For a long time, we weren't sure."

"I wouldn't still be here if it weren't for you and the others. Tell me, did Jarre…?"

The Grausak shook his shaggy head.

"What about Edle and Zarmir?"

"They survived. Vartan's men forgot about us once they were forced to fight the whole army coming through their gate."

"What happened to you when we got separated?"

"One of Vartan's patrols enlisted our help. It was dark in the street, our clothes fooled them, and Zarmir sounds like them. They put us to work. Luckily, we were able to slip away later. We got to the gate about the time you and Jarre made it up the platform."

"Have you seen Borke?"

"Yeah, he brought the horses back after the battle—missed out on the whole thing."

Locke smiled weakly. "I don't remember much. I think I passed out right after the drawbridge fell."

The Winds of Wharhalen

"It was pretty confusing for awhile. Vartan's men weren't able to put up much resistance in the city. A lot of them surrendered on the spot. Some kept on fighting, though, and fell back to the curtain wall. A few of them made it inside before the gate was closed. By the end of the day, we had control of the city. The next day Kaine started moving the catapults and battering rams into place."

"Wait. How many days has it been since I opened the gate?"

"I don't know. Over a week now I suppose."

"A week!" Locke tried to comprehend the passage of that much time with no recollection of it. "So then what happened?"

"The curtain wall fell quickly. They didn't have enough men to keep us away from it. We were just starting to attack the castle when they surrendered it."

"Vartan surrendered?"

"No. His own men killed him. Then they surrendered."

Locke shook his head in disbelief. "They could have saved a lot of lives if they had done that sooner."

The next day, Kaine came to see Locke. "How are you feeling?"

"Better than I did a few days ago."

"You and your men did a good job. Once we got inside the city wall, things went pretty fast after that. You probably saved a lot of lives."

"Will someone else just take Vartan's place?"

19 - Tasha

Kaine shook his head. "I don't think so. I think the rebellion died with Vartan. The south doesn't have the tribal rivalries that the north does. This area has had its fill of war for a while."

Locke thought of Tasha.

Kaine continued. "This was an important victory for the Queen, Locke. Unity will always be elusive, and there will always be small flare-ups, but a strong crown in Attalia helps deter major wars and makes the people feel more secure."

There was a long silence between the two men. Then Kaine spoke again. "As soon as you're strong enough, I'd like you to come to Attalia and receive the rewards that you deserve. But that's up to you. After all, you're a free man now and can do as you like."

Locke nodded slowly. In his own mind, he had always been free. But after all he had been through, it still sounded good to hear someone else say it.

"If you're still determined to go after that noble who cheated you, wait until you're stronger. You can recuperate in Attalia. But I still hope you'll change your mind. Personally, I could easily look the other way while you take your revenge. That is, if you could actually succeed. But, unfortunately, there are some people who won't."

Locke had to agree he was in no shape to confront Toulon. "When do you leave for Attalia?"

"It will be about another week until we can have the army ready to move. A lot of enlistments are up, and we've started letting some of them go. There has been a lot of work to do—burying the dead, breaking down our encampment, processing prisoners, collecting weapons—the men are exhausted, but at the same time, they're anxious to get back to Attalia."

The Winds of Wharhalen

"If I am ready to ride by the time you leave, I'll go with you. If not, I'll still come to Attalia when I'm able. I'll decide after that how to deal with the other business."

"Fair enough." With that, Kaine turned and walked away without another word.

Locke's recovery progressed quickly enough so that in a few more days he was able to stand for periods of time and shortly thereafter began to take short walks. The gash in his leg had closed, but some muscle had been cut and it hurt to walk on it. Gradually, though, his walks grew longer, and one day he made it to the house where he and Jarre had hidden the night of the crucial mission. It took a while to find it, but when he was reasonably certain he had, there were two children playing outside, a boy who looked to be about five and a girl about three. They paid little attention to him; just another soldier from the Royal Army now occupying the city. The door was open, and he could see a slender young woman working inside. She didn't notice him at first, and when he spoke, it momentarily startled her. "Excuse me, but are you Tasha?"

The woman, in her early twenties, had light brown hair and fair skin mottled with freckles. Her features were not unattractive, but she had a tired look, and her eyes were filled with sadness. "Yes," she answered cautiously.

"My name is Locke. You allowed me to hide in your house the night we opened the gate."

"I recognize your voice now. I am glad you are still alive."

"I might not have been if it hadn't been for your kindness."

"The other man, is he…?"

"He was killed."

"I'm sorry."

19 - Tasha

"Is your brother all right?"

"Yes, he was released two days ago."

"I'm glad. I want you to have this," said Locke, taking out the pouch of gold that had been given to him by Broecker.

The woman shook her head self-consciously.

"No, please don't refuse," said Locke, taking her hand and placing the pouch in it. "You could have revealed us, and then I would be dead now. I'm sorry that we frightened you that night." He gently squeezed her hand around the gold. "You have children to care for. Use this for them."

Locke could see tears welling up in the woman's sad eyes just before she cast them downward. He quickly turned and walked back out into the street where the children were still playing close to the door.

Later that day Locke found Borke, who had been put in charge of the horses when Locke was elevated in rank. The good-natured young horseman, only a little older than Locke, seemed genuinely happy to see the young Officer-at-Arms. "How are your injuries healing?"

"All right, I guess. I'm getting a little restless, though. I want to be able to leave Ritola with the rest of you and so I need to try riding. Can you help me find a horse? A nice gentle one."

Borke chuckled. He knew the irony of this question. Locke was the best horseman of them all. "Maybe we should just throw you across the back of one of the pack horses like a sack of grain."

The two young Killarasseans turned and walked toward the temporary stables that had been set up inside the city wall to accommodate the large number of cavalry horses. Although it was not mentioned between them, a different mood had come over them and all the other men as well. For the first time in nearly two years, the

The Winds of Wharhalen

specter of death wasn't hanging over them. Locke realized he was probably feeling what every other soldier that had ever survived a war before him must have felt—a great relief that they'd made it while so many others didn't. Surviving combat is always uncertain. But how many soldiers would actually be willing to fight if they didn't have the feeling that death was going to happen to someone else and not them? Also, Locke supposed that every soldier engaged in combat had something that kept him going. For him it was his mission of revenge against Toulon and thoughts of a possible reunion with Eylese.

When they reached the area where the horses had been moved after the city was secure, they walked among the quiet, oblivious animals, which were contently munching hay. Locke wondered to himself what lasting images of battle the horses carried with them. Many carried outward scars, and he felt a tinge of regret that men had forced these gentle creatures to become instruments of brutality and killing. "Pick one," said Borke, interrupting his friend's thoughts.

They stopped before one that Locke thought he recognized. It was one of the remounts that he'd brought with him from the fief where he had been a slave. The memories of Kira came flooding back to him. The time they had spent training horses and just being a boy and girl together now seemed like a peaceful island in a sea of turmoil. They were pleasant memories. Her kisses, her touch, the way her body felt when he held her in his arms; these things were still fresh in his mind. Fresher even than his thoughts of Eylese. He quickly shook himself free of those thoughts and started to examine the horse. The mare had obviously seen battle and bore the marks of it on her head and chest. But she had survived, unlike many of her companions, much as Locke had survived. He led her out and had a saddle placed on her back as she stood dutifully awaiting her rider.

As he got up on the mare, pain shot through Locke's left arm and shoulder. The gash in his leg, still not fully healed, felt like it was

19 - Tasha

being pulled apart as he straddled her broad back. In spite of the discomfort though, it felt good to be back in the saddle again. They walked at first, then broke into a trot, and finally into a slow gallop. Soon they were as one, these two battle-scarred veterans. As Locke pulled the mare up in front of Borke, he said, "It looks like I'll be returning to Attalia with you."

The Winds of Wharhalen

CHAPTER TWENTY

Ej Tauk-Zar

While Engrid lay on the hard cot that served as a bed, her mind jumped from one fragmented thought to another. She had never been completely able to adjust her sleep cycles to the underground world of the caverns. There had been another raid today, and Myleia had come along with her on it. Her young friend, so sweet and gentle before the war and subsequent occupation, had shown a different dimension in the months since. She had proven to be resourceful, clever, fearless, and had no aversion toward killing. Engrid had seen a dark side to Myleia's nature, and sometimes it chilled her to see the pent-up hatred in the girl manifest itself in these bloody forays into the city above.

The resistance had lost a man in the fighting this day. He was wounded during the raid and died later in the caverns. However, over the course of the occupation, their casualties had been relatively light when compared with those inflicted on the enemy. Recruiting larger numbers to compensate for their inevitable losses would certainly have been feasible in light of the hatred in the city toward Haczlok and

The Winds of Wharhalen

Braslon, but it would also have been dangerous. It would take only one traitor in their midst to destroy their entire operation. If their hiding places in the caverns were ever to be discovered, they could all be wiped out in a single day.

The Queen's mind sought a more soothing haven and so it drifted back to the days when she'd lived in Tairellia with her parents, Willander and Felixia. They'd set a living example for their daughter of honesty, integrity, and self-discipline, while at the same time encouraging young Engrid to form her own opinions and make choices. Willander had come to Tairellia while still quite young, and Killarassee did not hold good memories for him. His parents had died there, and the pain that he'd felt over their loss took a long time to fade. During his adolescence, he absorbed himself in intellectual pursuits, particularly philosophical studies. He'd also participated in the rigorous physical training that all Tairellian youths underwent, learning the fighting skills taught to boys and girls alike. But while many of the other boys seemed to thrive on fighting and conflict, violence was not in Willander's nature.

Engrid's mother, Felixia, on the other hand, was more fiery and passionate. Although also highly intelligent, she reveled in the athletic contests and competed fiercely. The long, graceful lines of her body and her animal-like strength and quickness caused her to be both admired and envied.

Engrid was more like her mother. She often pushed the limits of her physical skills beyond even those of the high Tairellian standards. There were no other girls in Tairellia who could match her skills, so she found her competitive level among the most highly-skilled boys. Threatened by her prowess and intensity, others of her age soon began to avoid Engrid. If that bothered her, though, she didn't let it show. Idealistic and equally as stubborn, she was also fixated on the

20 - Ej Tauk-Zar

Killarassean rebellion against Zironon, the murderer of her grandfather.

Engrid had always felt a little bit cheated that Kaine had been able to exact his revenge on the old warlord before the culmination of her quest. But, in spite of the occasional clash of their strong personalities, the Queen was indebted to Kaine for his help. In a lawless land ruled by violence, it was necessary to have strong allies. Engrid realized that it was better to have Kaine as a friend than an enemy.

Engrid was awakened with the news that Ej Tauk-Zar's forces were massed outside the city gates in full battle readiness demanding entrance. It had been rumored for weeks that the growing unrest of the warlord's men was about to boil over into armed conflict with the forces of Sharnov, who held the favored position of occupying the city. Ej Tauk-Zar, having negotiated with Haczlok during this period with little progress, had reached the end of his patience and decided on a full confrontation. Haczlok was nervous as he contemplated the barbarous horde overrunning the city, leaving little standing in its wake. He knew that eventually Kaine would return from Ritola, and without a strong, unified force to defend Attalia, his personal plans for the Empire would collapse. At present, he commanded a demoralized army. The attacks from the Queen's resistance had not only reduced his numbers, but he had still not found the treasury, which subsequently necessitated plundering an already hostile populace in order to pay his troops. Now loomed this threat of an all-out battle with his former allies.

Haczlok knew he would need to buy more time. He had hoped to keep Ej Tauk-Zar's army outside the walls to engage Kaine's legion when it returned from Ritola, but Attalia had fallen quickly, Ritola had resisted stubbornly, and the Royal Army was still absent. In the meantime, the treacherous Haczlok had been stalling by pretending to negotiate with Ej Tauk-Zar. The warlord was not fooled, though, and

The Winds of Wharhalen

now could not be found. He had turned command over to one of his ambitious, young warriors and a clash could no longer be headed off.

Hugely superior numbers favored the barbarians, but they had difficulty pressing this advantage once they reached the city gate. At first it appeared they would break through into the city, but after about a half-hour of brutal fighting, they were pushed back. Sharnov's troops, however, had suffered heavy losses, and now the city was under siege. Haczlok decided to send out a messenger to seek a meeting with Ej Tauk-Zar.

Now wielding considerable leverage, Ej Tauk-Zar reappeared and forced Haczlok to come to him for the meeting. The two leaders, whose deep distrust for each other was apparent despite the feigned cordiality, ultimately reached an agreement that granted concessions which reflected the warlord's now superior position. It was agreed that Sharnov's forces would fall back to positions behind the curtain wall, and leave the rest of Attalia to Ej Tauk-Zar's men. In addition, the search for the royal treasury would continue, and when it was found, it would be divided as originally planned.

As might have been expected, once inside the walls, the unrestrained horde swept through the city like a swarm of locusts, going from house to house, taking whatever they wanted. Attalia's citizens either resisted and died or hid waiting and hoping for the menace to subside. Women, who failed in their efforts to hide, immediately fell prey to savage attacks by the uncivilized warriors. Remarkably, somehow the pact between the two leaders concerning their boundaries held, and when Ej Tauk-Zar's men were appeased, there were no attempts by tribesmen to break through the curtain wall. Furthermore, at the command of Ej Tauk-Zar, there was no burning and despite the raping, killing and pillaging, destruction of buildings was kept at a minimum. In the aftermath of this chaotic spectacle, the tribesmen, loaded down with their booty, started home. This, of course,

20 - Ej Tauk-Zar

alarmed Haczlok greatly, for he still anticipated the return of Kaine and saw his number of defenders dwindling. Ej Tauk-Zar, however, simply shrugged it off by saying, "It has been a long war. What is to keep them here? They care nothing for this city. The north is now ours for the taking whenever we want."

Miles away, as Ej Tauk-Zar's army moved off to the north, events were unfolding south of the city that would drastically shift the balance of power once again. In the days immediately following the fall of Attalia to Haczlok and his allies, Engrid had secretly sent out a patrol to set up camp far from the city but close to the main road by which Kaine's legion would have to return. Their mission, regardless of how long it took, was to intercept the Royal Army and alert Kaine of the danger that awaited him upon his return to Attalia. Many months after they were sent out, these loyal men were finally able to complete their vital task when they caught sight of the tired and battered legion slowly making its way up the hard-packed dirt road toward Attalia.

The leader of the patrol, a man named Stellan, was well-known by Kaine. However, the commander, always suspicious, initially had a slight foreboding about this bedraggled-looking group as it rode toward the main column. They were out of uniform, and the clothes they wore were torn and dirty. Their hair and beards were long and unkempt, and they had the look of men that had been living in the woods for months, which, of course, they had.

"Stellan, what has happened?" Kaine addressed his old Sergeant.

"Forgive our appearance, sir, for we have been away from Attalia for many months now awaiting your arrival. Can I speak with you in private?"

This, of course, heightened Kaine's anxiety as the two rode away from the others. When they stopped, Stellan hesitated before

The Winds of Wharhalen

speaking, even though he had rehearsed in his mind many times what he would say when this time came. "Almost five months ago, Attalia fell to an alliance of rebels under Haczlok and the tribesmen of Ej Tauk-Zar."

"Five *months* ago!" Kaine resisted his first impulse to ask about Myleia. "What has happened to the Queen?"

"She and Cecel went into hiding with those loyal to her and organized a resistance."

"And my wife…?"

"She is with the Queen."

Kaine sustained these blows to his stomach, regained his composure, and then continued. "How did this happen? Where is the First Legion?"

"Captured."

"Captured? How could Joal have let that happen?"

"Joal is dead, assassinated by Haczlok."

Joal dead! Kaine's mind was reeling. "Who was in command of the Legion when it was captured?"

"Lord Braslon."

"Braslon? What has happened to him?"

"Braslon conspired with Haczlok. He delivered the First Legion into the hands of Haczlok and Sharnov."

"Sharnov! We should have killed him when we had the chance! Why didn't the Queen send word to me in Ritola before things came to this?"

20 - Ej Tauk-Zar

Stellan hesitated again. "The Queen..." he started slowly, "I'm sure the Queen did what she thought was best for the Empire. Any more answers, I think, should come from her, sir."

"Stellan. Why didn't you take it upon yourself to come to Ritola and report this to me?"

"The Queen specifically gave me orders not to."

He sighed. "What is the situation in Attalia now?"

"We don't know. We haven't been back since leaving under the Queen's orders five months ago. Our mission was to avoid capture by the enemy and make sure that you knew of the occupation before you returned to Attalia."

"So we really have no idea what size of force we are facing," he said, almost to himself. "Where is the First Legion now?"

"My men and I have been able to determine that they are being held at Torin, do you know it?"

"Yes, it is about eight miles from here. What is the size of the force that guards them?"

"We estimate it at about four hundred."

Kaine thought silently for a minute. "All right, we must first free the captured troops. Under the circumstances, our chances of recapturing Attalia with this battered army are not good."

Kaine then rode back to the main column and gave the order to make camp. He then called his Officers-at-Arms together to plan the attack on Torin.

The Winds of Wharhalen

CHAPTER TWENTY ONE

Torin

Locke and the other men shared a sense of anxiety as they gathered for the meeting. They had been anticipating a triumphant return to Attalia within two days. After traveling for over three weeks and being away from their homes for almost two years, they were weary of fighting. Despite all this, Locke was regaining his strength with each passing day. He sat his horse with more confidence now, and the use of his left arm had gradually returned. Only twenty-one years old, his experiences had shaped him into a man who could have passed for thirty. His hair and beard were long like the rest of the soldiers and he bore many scars. The taut chords of muscle in his arms and legs were like steel. He had begun to gain back a little of the weight lost during his rehabilitation in Ritola, but his face was still gaunt.

Kaine, flanked by Stellan and the other men of the Queen's patrol, didn't waste any time in addressing the group. "Attalia has fallen into the hands of the rebel Haczlok and the warlord, Ej Tauk-Zar. They are allied with two other traitors, the exile Sharnov and the noble,

The Winds of Wharhalen

Lord Braslon. These four men are enemies of the Queen and, therefore, must be defeated. There is no alternative if we ever want to return to our homes. We don't know how many men they have to defend the city, but it's likely more than we can overcome at our present strength. The First Legion infantry is being held captive at Torin by a force of only four hundred men. We must first free them and then together we will retake Attalia." He spoke with conviction, and none of the men assembled here doubted in the least that they could accomplish the plan he'd laid out. In spite of Kaine's personal demons, outwardly, he was a leader without peer.

Stellan then told the assembled Officers-at-Arms what he and his men knew about the layout of the compound at Torin. The captive legion had been divided into four groups and placed in separate enclosures, each guarded by about one hundred soldiers, mostly archers. The enemy also had about fifty horses in its possession. The four groups of prisoners were held out of range of communication with each other on the north, south, east and west sides of the village. It would be possible to approach to within about three hundred yards of the compound before being seen, but after that it would be all open ground from then on.

Again, Kaine addressed the officers. "We will strike the east section first with the mounted archers leading the attack. At the same time, the heavy cavalry will attack the south. The infantry will follow the cavalry, freeing the prisoners and using them to secure the captured areas as we go. Locke, after the south area is in our control, proceed through the village and establish a blockade to prevent any retreat to the west. Once the east is secured, the mounted archers will move on to the north. As soon as possible, the infantry will move on the west area. If, at any time, the enemy wishes to surrender, let them. A hundred archers can do a lot of damage and we can't afford to lose many men. Our best chance is to take them by surprise and overwhelm them quickly."

21 - Torin

In the pre-daylight hour of the next day, the sentry on the edge of Torin dozed in and out of a shallow sleep. The sound of distant hoof beats mingled with his fleeting dreams and went unheeded. When he did finally rouse himself from his fitful slumber, and he looked out across the bare tabletop approach to the small village, he saw what appeared to be shadowy horsemen emerging from the morning mist. At first he thought he was still dreaming, but as he shook the murky confusion from his head, he could see that the charging warriors were bearing down on his position. His warning cries had barely begun when he was the first to go down, an arrow passing through his chest. The small force guarding the east section, many of whom were still sleeping, was quickly and completely overwhelmed by Kaine's mounted archers. A third of their numbers were initially cut down as they tried to resist, and within minutes, the rest meekly surrendered.

At the same time, Locke was leading the knights of the heavy cavalry against the guards at the south section. Resistance was light and scattered since half of the guards were just rising for the day and weren't at their posts yet.

By the time the infantry arrived at the compound, many of the guards had already surrendered to the better-armed knights on their powerful warhorses. As the foot soldiers began to free the prisoners, they, in turn, took the weapons off the guards. As the bulk of the infantry moved on to the west, Locke then took his knights out past the western perimeter to wait. Since the west was the last area to be attacked, it followed that any of the enemy that escaped the net thrown by Kaine would flee in that direction. It wasn't long before the lookout that Locke had sent out to his left flank signaled that the exodus was indeed coming in their direction. Approximately fifty riders, trying to escape capture in Torin, were intercepted by the Queen's knights about four miles out. Outnumbered and at a serious weapon and armor disadvantage, they too surrendered. The swift and decisive victory at

The Winds of Wharhalen

Torin was a minor one, but the significance of regaining the First Legion could not be overestimated. Kaine now commanded an army larger than the one that had taken Ritola. He just hoped that it wouldn't take two more years to recapture Attalia.

As the army began its forced march toward Attalia, Kaine's anxiety over the fate of Myleia was becoming nearly unbearable. It seemed to him that somehow fate had deemed that they would always be pulled apart. Their first separation, which lasted nearly five years, had ended shortly after the overthrow of Zironon. Kaine still looked back on the events surrounding that reunion with a sense of wonderment. As he rode toward what he hoped would be a second, the events of the first came pouring back to him.

Moussaud, Myleia's father, had died, and the girl's mother traveled to Toulussia, where her daughter had been taken against her will years earlier. Marceila hated Moussaud but was powerless to do anything about the sale of Myleia while her husband lived. Hers had been an arranged marriage like her daughter's, and Myleia was her only joy in life. Now free and possessing great wealth by virtue of her inheritance from the merchant, she set in motion a plot to provide an opportunity for the girl to escape her unhappy fate. Marceila arranged for Myleia to be abducted from the prince's house and brought to her, and, together, they boarded a ship that took them to Velesko, a seaport on the north coast of Wharhalen. Months later word got back to Kaine in Attalia that they had been seen there, and he immediately embarked on a journey to search for the girl that had once seemed irretrievably lost.

After Kaine left Attalia, he rode north toward the Karpoans, along the Veral River. It took him nearly a month to reach Velesko. It was a lonely ride for Kaine, across the barren plains that stretched endlessly in every direction. The foothills brought some relief from the

21 - Torin

monotony and soon he was negotiating the narrow passes of the grim Karpoans. Loneliness was nothing new to the dark and brooding Kaine. Although he took refuge from his personal demons in his camaraderie with the reckless and carefree men that he led, his life otherwise had been one lacking hopefulness or promise. Many times in battle he would have welcomed a swift death to bring an end to his torment. Yet he fought on because his hatred refused to let him acquiesce and make it easier for his enemies.

The air was cold in the high mountains, and the wind swept through the canyons. In another month there would be snow, closing the passes until spring. Unlike the Catalosas with their warm westerly winds, the Karpoans had harsh weather in the winter months. When Kaine reached the highest elevation, he paused for a moment and looked back toward Killarassee, which, for the first time in his life, was free from Zironon's tyranny. He had taken no satisfaction in killing the warlord; in fact, he was surprised at how little emotion the act had evoked. Hate had smoldered inside him for so long that he felt it had consumed his heart. There had been a time when the light of Myleia's love had temporarily driven out the darkness, but even that once glorious flame had since been extinguished. Moussaud's infamous deed of using his own innocent daughter to advance his position had embedded a cynicism in Kaine that would always be a part of him. The assassination of Zironon had set in motion changes that gave the people of his country reason to hope that their lives might get better as well as affording him an opportunity to personally avenge the terrible injustice done to his mother. He now rode to find the only person whose existence could reveal if there was still any part of his dying soul that was worth reviving. With that in mind, he wheeled his mount around and started down the mountains toward Wharhalen.

Kaine traveled down through the plateaus on the seaward side of the mountains and onto the wide coastal plain. In spite of its great physical beauty, Wharhalen was an inhospitable country. The

The Winds of Wharhalen

indigenous people were split into tribes that constantly fought among themselves. Zironon had tried to keep outposts there, and his soldiers spent all of their time putting down little insurrections. Velesko, however, was a relatively peaceful oasis in the midst of a turbulent land, its tranquility based on the economic necessity of always keeping at least one center of commerce open to trade with the rest of the world.

Kaine's journey across Wharhalen was, for the most part, relatively uneventful. However, he did have to avoid confrontations with two groups of bandits that he came upon. Kaine carried with him a considerable amount of gold, as he wanted to be prepared for whatever would be necessary to bring about a successful conclusion to his quest. The gold might be needed to buy information, transport by ship, horses, weapons as well as food and lodging. He wasn't about to risk failure because of losing his assets to bandits.

In late morning on the twenty-seventh day after leaving Attalia, Kaine arrived in Velesko and found it alive with activity. Vendors' stalls were open for business, produce from nearby farms was in abundance, and the streets were filled with people and livestock. He proceeded immediately to the inn where Myleia and her mother were last reported seen and questioned the innkeeper. The man was cooperative and gave Kaine the information he had hoped for. The two women had been there and had stayed for nearly two weeks waiting for a ship that would take them to Castellonia. He had helped them arrange passage on a merchant vessel that was bound for the port of Acadarian. He was certain they were delivered safely to the ship and placed in the care of the Captain, for he had seen to it himself. Kaine had seen no reason to doubt the accuracy of this story, so he gave the man a gold coin and went directly to the docks to find a swift vessel that could take him down the coast to Acadarian. His ability to pay whatever price was necessary aided him in finding a willing ship owner almost immediately. The voyage was not a long one due to favorable winds. A trip that

21 - Torin

would have taken Kaine a month traveling overland across the Valdanes was, therefore, accomplished in only eleven days.

Arriving in the port city of Acadarian, Kaine at once began making inquiries concerning the arrival of the ship that had carried the two women he was looking for. His years as a trader in cities reaching far up and down the coast had made it possible for him to communicate in some of the languages and dialects used throughout the Empire. Although it had been many years since he had been in Acadarian, he found it little changed. He soon learned the ship that had sailed from Velesko had indeed brought a Castellonian woman and her daughter there many weeks ago. When he was told that they had hired a cart to take them to the village of Torbagos, Kaine bought a horse, obtained directions, and set out immediately. His eleven days at sea had left him rested and he was eager for action. He was further encouraged by his success in having been able to find the trail of those he pursued so quickly, and his anticipation nearly drove him to ride the poor animal into the ground. The village was three days ride from Acadarian, and there was no way for a man on horseback to make it in any less. But, after two sleepless nights and miles of dusty roads, Kaine came to the little village of Torbagos.

He rode into the little collection of hovels amidst the stares of the few villagers that he saw. There was no inn, Torbagos not getting many visitors. A man he questioned gave him directions to a house outside the village where he'd heard that two women, who had recently arrived, were said to be staying. Trying to contain his emotions, Kaine was soon at the end of a narrow lane that led to a stone house surrounded by vineyards that stretched far into the distance. At the entryway to the house, he was met by a thin, elderly servant who greeted him politely, but suspiciously.

"I wish to speak with a young woman who I believe is staying here. I know her by the name Myleia."

The Winds of Wharhalen

A grave look came over the face of the man. "I regret to inform you, sir, but the person you seek is dead."

The words staggered Kaine. "But...how?"

"She became ill during a sea voyage. She just kept getting weaker and weaker. She died about a week after arriving here."

This sudden turn took Kaine completely off guard. The excitement that had continued to grow in him during his journey now suddenly drained away as he sunk into despair. "Can I see her grave?" he finally asked after a long pause in a voice barely audible.

"Her body was cremated, as is the custom in the family," answered the man in pitying tone.

After another somber pause, Kaine asked, "Can I speak with her mother then?"

"She is very ill. She came down with the fever soon after her daughter died."

Kaine thought for moment. "Could you give her a message for me? Tell her...tell her that Kaine came to find Myleia, regretfully, too late." He turned and walked out of the house, thinking that his unfortunate life had met yet another tragedy. He was untying his horse and preparing to mount when a voice came from behind him, "Sir, wait."

He turned to see a woman whose name he could not remember, but whose face he could not forget—for its visage bore a reminder of the girl from whom he had been separated five years ago. Myleia's mother had aged greatly, her features drained of their youth by the strain of adversity.

"Myleia is alive!" She said these words quickly, as if she sensed the need to quickly relieve the pain she saw in his face.

21 - Torin

At the moment, there were no other words that could have dragged Kaine back from a despair so deep it felt that he, himself, was already among the dead.

"We had received word that someone was searching for us," the woman continued. "We thought you had been sent by the Prince. When I saw you in the house just now, I remembered seeing you at our home in Kuensah. There has been no joy in my daughter's face since that time. The wrong committed by her father against her has over the years taken a grievous toll. Go to her. She fled to my brother's house just before you arrived. It is three miles down this road to the east. You will know it by the row of fig trees bordering the lane. Perhaps it is not too late for her wounds to heal and for her to still find happiness."

Kaine was struck mute by this revelation. Without saying a word he sprang into the saddle and started down the lane. After only about a hundred feet, however, he pulled his horse up and shouted back to the woman, "Thank you!" She was still standing there as he turned and galloped away.

Once again, Kaine was charged with anticipation. How many more times would his hopes be able to rise to dizzying heights only to be crushed like dry and brittle leaves on the ground? He saw no other houses until he reached the one with the fig trees along the lane. It, too, was of stone construction but in this instance, it was situated in the midst of grain fields, which were nearly ready for harvest. Kaine tied his horse and strode to the front door. A dark, bearded man, who would only open the door slightly, answered his knock. "I have come to see Myleia." He said this in a voice loud enough to be heard inside.

The man answered sternly, "There is no one here by that name."

"I have had enough of these deceptions!" Kaine boomed, as he pushed his way into the house, despite the protests of the man at

The Winds of Wharhalen

the door and several servants that tried to bar the way. Kaine quickly brushed them aside and immediately began trying doors. One after another, he found only empty rooms. Finally, he burst into a bedroom to discover a young, dark-haired woman backed defiantly into a corner with a large knife held to her breast. "Myleia!" the word escaped from his mouth with the finality of the last note of a song.

The girl stared back at Kaine with a combination of fear and bewilderment. Slowly, recognition crept into her tear-filled eyes. The knife dropped to the floor as she rushed toward him and threw her arms around his waist. Her head buried in his chest, she sobbed uncontrollably.

Kaine had vowed that day to never let them be separated again, and so it was a crushing sense of guilt he now carried with him back to Attalia.

CHAPTER TWENTY TWO

The Return

Inside Attalia, the resistance had gone dormant for a time while Ej Tauk-Zar's men were rampaging through the outer city. Now that the warlord's army was gone, the resistance fighters of Engrid and Cecel stepped up their activity. During the course of the occupation of Attalia, the tough Gruenlander had had time to almost fully recover from his injuries and at the same time had grown leaner and fitter. He still walked with a slight limp, but the urgency of the situation had brought out the best in the grizzled warrior. He had assumed command from Attuis, and his group had proven themselves to be just as effective in wreaking havoc among the occupiers as the Queen's. Haczlok's loyal followers, weary of fighting their fellow citizens, began to stay closer to the relative safety of the castle while the general lawlessness in Attalia continued to escalate. Braslon's knights, used to fighting battles in the field on horseback, were ineffective at this type of duty and grew increasingly discontented.

When Kaine's legions appeared on the hill overlooking Attalia, word spread quickly throughout the city. Sequestered in the caverns, the

The Winds of Wharhalen

Queen's rebels were among the last to hear the news. When mobs began to gather in the streets, there was little Sharnov's men could do to disperse them since they had to focus their efforts on preparing to defend the walls against the impending attack. Engrid, once she did learn of Kaine's proximity, immediately summoned Skauld and instructed him to contact his most trusted informer among the citizens of Attalia. "Tell him to get the people organized but to wait until the attack comes. When Haczlok is occupied with defending the walls, overwhelm the guards at the gate and get it open."

Meanwhile, outside the walls, Kaine crossed the river and rode out from their encampment with Drobek to demand the surrender of Haczlok and Braslon and the return of Attalia to the crown. Haczlok, as expected, refused to negotiate and remained in the castle while Braslon, with his disgruntled knights reluctant to stay confined inside Attalia, was busy making plans to escape.

Kaine knew his army was not well-equipped for a siege. They had left all of the heavy machines of war behind them at Ritola. And during the occupation, Haczlok had put his men to work rebuilding the wall that had been breached during the last siege. The only vulnerable place along the entire perimeter of the city was the gates. Kaine set about cutting down large trees to serve as battering rams. He also decided that before he exposed so many of his men to the barrage of arrows that was sure to come from the walls, he wanted to create a distraction to test the strength of the defenses. And so he sent out four hundred bowmen, all he had, each protected by a pair of infantrymen with shields. This forward excursion stretched itself out in a single line that ran along the entire length of the south wall. This spacing was designed to prevent the defenders from being able to concentrate their projectiles on a clustered group. And, as Kaine had anticipated, when the arrows did come from the walls, they were largely ineffective. While most glanced harmlessly off the shields, during each lull between

22 - The Return

volleys, the royal bowmen lobbed flaming arrows over the barrier, a few of which started fires in the buildings behind the walls and drew the attention of many of Sharnov's men. Soon a cloud of smoke was choking and blinding the defenders of the walls and gate.

At this point the plan that the Queen had set in motion, but Kaine had no reason to expect, went into effect. The crowd of townspeople, organized by Skauld's confidant, began to attack the already harried guards and soon had the main city gate open. With no moat surrounding the vast extent of the Attalia wall, it now appeared that the city was wide open to Kaine's army. Kaine had expected Haczlok's army to emerge to take the field against them, but when that didn't happen he began to suspect the truth: that he was somehow being assisted by supporters inside the city. Seizing this opportunity that had been handed to him, he ordered half of his heavy cavalry to lead the charge for the open gates.

Sharnov's Officers-at-Arms tried to mass their troops at the breech, but were hindered by the angry mob whose long pent-up fury was now being unleashed against the occupiers. With little resistance, the heavily-armored knights of the Queen's army poured into the city, and, aided by the "citizen army," began fighting their way toward the palisade. They, in turn, were followed by the infantry who quickly took control of the outer wall and lower town. Kaine, anticipating that the conspirators might attempt to flee, had held Locke and the other half of his knights in reserve for containment.

The defenders, whose allegiance to Haczlok and Sharnov had been eroded by months of conflict with their fellow countrymen as an occupying army, and the constant harassment of the resistance fighters, yielded ground quickly when it became apparent that the balance of power had shifted. Their resolve was further weakened by Sharnov's disappearance shortly after the commencement of the attack.

The Winds of Wharhalen

Braslon and his knights attempted to escape by using the west gate, which was far away from the concentrated fighting. Informed of this, Kaine sent Locke and his men in pursuit. "Braslon must be brought back to Attalia to be judged for his crimes. If his knights try to protect him, kill them!"

Braslon had hoped to buy some time by reaching his castle and making a stand there. He figured his serfs still owed their allegiance to him and would provide some support in addition to his knights. He also held out hope that the other nobles would come to his aid once they became aware that he was under attack. The knights that accompanied him, however, considered themselves warriors, and, as such, had an extreme distaste for fleeing. And so, once the Queen's knights caught up with them and demanded that they stop, their honor would not allow them to continue their flight. Having made their decision, they selected a spot, pulled up their horses, and turned to fight.

Braslon rode out with his second, Sir Wyant, to meet with the representative of Kaine's forces. Locke was accompanied by Marchek. "Lord Braslon. You must return to Attalia to answer the charges against you."

"I will not be arrested by one of Kaine's peasant soldiers. I don't even know you."

"I am Sir Locke and I have orders to take you by force if necessary."

"My knights and I are going to continue to my castle. If the Queen has a grievance against me, she can address it through the council of nobles."

"Sir, my orders are clear. If you continue to try to escape, we will be forced to spill the blood of your brave knights here on this field, and you will still be brought back to Attalia."

22 - The Return

"Sir Wyant. Kill this man so that we may be on our way."

Braslon's knight dropped the visor on his helmet and drew his sword. Marchek drew his sword, but Locke placed his hand on his friend's arm. Locke lowered his visor and unsheathed his own sword as the two knights approached each other. Wyant spurred his horse into a gallop and raised his sword upward and across his body. As they passed, Wyant brought his blade down hard but it was deflected harmlessly by Locke. Turning to face each other again, this time Braslon's knight charged with the point of his sword directed at his opponent. Like the flickering of a candle, Locke lightly brushed Wyant's blade aside and made a quick thrust. It happened so fast that neither Braslon's knights nor even the ones on Locke's side of the field knew that the fight was over. Sir Wyant swayed briefly in his saddle, and then fell heavily to the ground.

Locke circled back and came to a stop in front of Braslon's knights. "We have three times your number. Give up your weapons and armor, and you may keep your horses and ride away from here. If you force us to fight, I swear every one of you will die. I will not see another one of my knights die without making every one of you pay with your blood."

One by one, the outnumbered knights dropped their breastplates, helmets, and swords to the ground and rode away. Lord Braslon was left alone to surrender his sword to Locke, a man born as a peasant in the Karpoans.

The Winds of Wharhalen

CHAPTER TWENTY THREE

Reunion

Kaine's dismay on entering Attalia could hardly have been more profound. Where he had left a prosperous city that should have flourished in his absence, he found instead a gutted shell that had survived rebellion, occupation, and civil war. Smoke hung over the city in thick clouds, and bodies were strewn throughout the commons beyond the outer gate. Pockets of fighting still raged in other parts of the city, but the path to the castle had been secured. The citizens that had comprised the street mob, so instrumental in allowing the Royal Army to retake the city, were still taking out their pent-up fury on the former occupiers. As word spread of Kaine's arrival, crowds began to line the commander's route. The mood was both raucous and jubilant in spite of the visible carnage.

However, Kaine felt no joy in the victory that had come more easily than had been anticipated. There were so many questions to be answered, but foremost in his mind was the fate of his young wife, Myleia. He had never before felt such helpless fear and dread as he contemplated what she might have suffered at the hands of an invader

The Winds of Wharhalen

like Ej Tauk-Zar. As he continued towards the castle, he saw no one that he could ask, even if he could somehow manage to summon up the courage to do so. Then, the sea of faces parted and he recognized Cecel. His old friend was thinner than when he last saw him, and pale, like someone who has seen little sunlight for a long time. But the old soldier stood tall, a bloody sword still clutched in his huge hand. When he saw Kaine, his keen eyes flashed in recognition and a broad smile spread across his face.

In the midst of this terrible wreckage, where so many lives had been lost on the battlefield over which the warring factions had struggled to decide the direction of the Empire, Kaine climbed down from his horse, walked over to his fellow warrior, and the two old companions embraced.

"I didn't think I would find you alive," said Kaine, still holding his friend's massive shoulders.

"I probably would have died months ago had it not been for Engrid's guile."

"How then did you manage to survive the occupation without leaving the city?"

"We lived in caverns waiting for you to return, which, by the way, certainly took long enough. We fought the occupying forces using hit-and-run tactics just like we did in the old days; only this time we didn't have to run so far to escape."

"I heard that Joal died."

Cecel nodded sadly. "That is how it began."

"Why didn't Engrid send to Ritola for help?"

Cecel hesitated. "I don't think I should answer for her."

Kaine nodded. "Where is she now?"

23 - The Reunion

"At the castle. She told me to bring you there as soon as you arrived."

"All right, let's go."

Cecel put his hand on Kaine's arm. "Joal's death wasn't her fault. She made some mistakes after he died, but her leadership since then has been smart and courageous."

As the two men walked toward the castle, Kaine continued to ask questions. "Where is Haczlok now?"

"We haven't found him yet."

"How about Sharnov?"

"He has vanished, too."

"Cowards," said Kaine, his teeth clenched. "What became of Ej Tauk-Zar?"

"He became impatient when there weren't more spoils for his men. He wanted to sack the city but, for a long time, Haczlok wouldn't let him. Finally, Haczlok couldn't restrain him any longer. So, after Ej Tauk-Zar's men took what they wanted, they left and moved north. His army is still intact though. We're going to have to deal with him eventually."

Finally, after a long silence, Kaine summoned up the courage to ask what he wanted to know the most. "What…what has happened to Myleia?"

"She stayed with Engrid when we divided the resistance into two groups. I saw her a couple of days ago and she was fine then. She is…a little different now."

Kaine looked at Cecel inquisitively. "What do you mean, different?"

The Winds of Wharhalen

A wry smile appeared on Cecel's face. "It's nothing bad. You'll see."

Kaine's spirits were elevated to know that Myleia was all right, but he tried not to betray his emotions by any outward sign. Cecel noted, though, that his friend's step quickened after that as they continued toward the castle.

As Kaine and Cecel entered the castle, Kaine could feel the changes that had taken place there since he had been away. The grandeur that Engrid had restored to the heart of the Empire of the Old Kings had once again been sullied by a careless tenant. Like one's house after the departure of drunken party guests, it wasn't beyond repair, but it would take time to make it feel like home again.

Engrid was standing with Skauld when Kaine entered the throne room. The commander didn't take long to examine the expression on her face, though, as his eyes darted quickly around the room to find the one he was so desperate to see. The dark eyes of Myleia were bright even as they glistened with joyous tears. Kaine started toward her, but he could only manage a few steps before the girl ran to him and threw herself into his arms in an uninhibited display of enthusiasm. The only person in the course of Kaine's unhappy life that could ever bring him joy was finally back in his arms. The familiar contours of her body brought back the warmth that had previously been missing from his desolate existence. Neither wanted the embrace to end, but gradually they began to relax and soften their hold on one another. Finally, confident that their long separation was over and the reunion wasn't imagined, they held each other at arm's length. Kaine, still in battle dress and covered in the grime of the campaign, looked frightful with his long hair and beard. Still, Myleia basked in the light from his eyes that only she could bring out. For the first time, Kaine became aware that his wife was dressed like a man, and a warrior at that when he saw a sword strapped to her waist, and an empty arrow quiver

23 - The Reunion

hanging over her tiny shoulders. There was a different look to her face as well. She was still stunningly beautiful with her dark, almond-shaped eyes and skin more perfect than a new flower petal. That certainly hadn't changed. But her smile was now more self-assured and her eyes, always lovely though a little melancholy, now exuded a glowing contentment that even Kaine had never seen before.

Concern spread quickly over Kaine's face. His expression hardened, and his eyes flashed toward Engrid. "What is this manner of dress for the women of Attalia?" he asked, struggling to contain his anger.

Myleia intercepted the accusation that had been directed at the Queen. "It's not Engrid's fault. I gave her no choice. It was a fight that involved us all, and I wanted to help."

"But I left Attalia with the understanding that you would be under *her* protection. I would never have gone to Ritola if…"

"I know. And no one could have been a better friend and protector than Engrid." And then, under her breath, Myleia said, "If we must continue this discussion, let us do so in private."

"But…"

Myleia then reached over and gripped Kaine's hands tightly, and her expression grew firm.

Kaine relented. Whatever the issues involved in the conflict, the important thing was that Myleia was safe and back in his arms.

Engrid intervened. "Now that that the commander is back in Attalia, there are some matters that we need to discuss in private."

Cecel, Skauld, and Myleia left the room, and finally Kaine stood alone before Engrid. The old comrades, whose relationship had been forged in the fires of the revolution, both felt the need to repair the rift that had recently formed. Theirs was the most important

The Winds of Wharhalen

alliance in the Empire. Engrid was the unifying symbol that could hold together the many factions of the feudal, warring land. But Kaine was her strength, the powerful leader necessary to eradicate those who would dare to rise up against her.

Kaine was angry over Engrid's mistakes in letting Attalia fall to the insurgents, and even more angry that she hadn't tried to recall him from Ritola to help. He was also angry that Myleia had been put in danger and especially that she had actually been involved in the fighting. But seeing his wife safe and holding her in his arms once again had done much to stem the tide of his anger. He could forgive almost anything knowing that he still had Myleia. Thus, he waited for the Queen to speak first. She eventually broke the uneasy silence by saying, "Well, Commander, is Ritola now secure?"

"It is. Vartan is dead and so is his brother. Their army has been disarmed and dispersed. We left a detachment there to help maintain order. You will need to appoint a new Regent soon though. The city will rebuild and the southern region should remain quiet…for awhile."

"You see, Kaine, if you had been recalled from Ritola before completing your mission, you would not have been able to give me such a satisfactory report," she said, anticipating his criticism.

"You are lucky that you are still alive to receive the report," was his caustic reply.

"It was a gamble, I will admit. But if I had let you abandon Ritola, and you had been unable to get here before Attalia fell, we could have lost both cities, and your army would not have been able to overcome the combined strength of Haczlok and Ej Tauk-Zar. As it worked out, our enemies began to fight among themselves after a while, and you faced a weakened opponent upon your return."

Kaine knew that, because things had worked out the way they did, he could not justify arguing the point any further. The two

23 - The Reunion

remained silent for a moment, and then Engrid spoke again. "I am sorry about Joal."

"No one has really told me how he died," said Kaine in a somber tone.

"You know that he always took too many risks. Men like Joal don't die of old age. With you out of Attalia, Haczlok went after him. It wasn't in Joal's nature to be cautious. He had gotten out of dangerous jams so many times before, but somehow Haczlak's soldiers managed to corner him in the lower city late one night and..." Engrid's voice trailed off.

Kaine contemplated for a moment, and then said, "Cecel looks better than the last time I saw him."

"Cecel needs a good fight. He grows stale without one. He has been a great help in the fighting recently."

"What about Braslon?"

Engrid sighed. "I made a mistake. Among all the nobles, he seemed the most loyal. He had helped overthrow Zironon, and I also thought it would be a good way of helping to unify Killarassee by bringing the nobles into the process. I knew he was ambitious, so I thought this would satisfy him. Obviously, he had even higher ambitions."

"Ours was always a peasant revolution. The nobles will never accept the fact that it was the people who put you in power. They will continue to undermine you and seek to gain more and more power for themselves. When we catch Braslon, you must make an example of him."

The Queen nodded grimly.

The Winds of Wharhalen

Kaine then broached the subject that was really on his mind. "I left Myleia in your care. I understand there were bigger concerns that came up while I was away. But allowing her to fight?"

"I tried to keep her out of it. For a while I was successful. But then one night she went out on her own into the midst of Sharnov's camp and burned down his armory. She threatened to continue going out by herself if I didn't let her join us. I decided it was better to have her with me than running around fighting the enemy by herself. What else could I do? Tie her up? Keep a guard on her twenty-four hours a day?"

Kaine couldn't keep a smile from softening the grim expression that he had worn since entering the room. "She burned down an armory?"

"She's not as fragile as you think, Kaine. She's a tough, strong, and extremely clever woman. I am proud to count her among my friends."

Kaine shook his head, keeping it turned downward to prevent the Queen from seeing the smile. "It's just fortunate for you that she wasn't hurt," he said, returning to his gruff demeanor.

"I know."

By nightfall, the fires were out and all pockets of resistance from what were left of Haczlok's supporters had been stamped out. The enemies of the Queen that survived, and they were not many, would literally be branded as traitors and banished from Attalia forever. Reconstruction of the ravaged city would begin immediately, and the army would be replenished with new recruits. The reign of Engrid had been severely tested, but because of her resourcefulness and the loyalty of her friends, it would survive for three more decades.

That night, while Engrid slept in her own chamber for the first time in many months, Kaine returned to the quarters he shared with

23 - The Reunion

Myleia. When he entered, the room was dark with the exception of a few candles that cast a warm flickering glow on the walls. Each object cast its own unique shape in shadow, but the shape Kaine most wanted to see was that of his beloved Myleia. As she emerged from the darkness on the other side of the room, he could see that she had shed the garments of the warrior and now wore a loose, gossamer gown that lightly brushed the floor as she walked. As she passed by the luminescence of the candles, Kaine could see the outline of her body silhouetted beneath the sheer material of the dress.

Kaine wanted to scoop the girl up in his arms and rush over to the bed with her, but still in partial armor and stinking of battle, he hesitated to soil this delicate vision before him with his coarseness. Myleia came over and stood close to him and then standing on tiptoes, lightly kissed his cheek. Her soft touch and sweet smell stirred the passion deep within him, but still he refrained from clutching her body to his.

Myleia then slowly undressed her husband and as she did she gently touched each of the many scars on his battle-weary body. Next, she took him by the hand and led him to a basin of water that sat on a table in the corner of the room. When they reached the basin, she untied the single ribbon that held her gown at the waist, opened the garment and let it fall to the floor. Kaine had seen his wife's body in his mind many times over the past two years and had often wondered if he would ever again have the opportunity to stand so close to her as he was right now. She was, without question, the most beautiful woman he had ever seen.

Kaine's body tensed slightly as Myleia touched it with a sponge that she took from the basin. She slowly, caressingly, moved it over his torso and then let it travel below his waist. His desire rose higher within him than he thought he could endure, but still he waited for the girl to complete her loving task. Kaine had spent his adult life suppressing his

The Winds of Wharhalen

emotions so as to best be able to coldly exact his revenge on an unjust world. Only with Myleia had he ever let himself feel the uninhibited joy of the kind he was feeling at this moment. So different, so rare, was this heightened sensitivity that he wanted to see just how high it could soar.

Next, Myleia dried Kaine's body with a towel and took a bottle of scented oil from the table. She poured a small amount into her hand, and then warmed it by rubbing her hands together. Ever so lightly, she spread the oil across his shoulders and then down over his torso. Not an inch of Kaine's body escaped her touch, and she finished the gentle oil massage with her hands lingering on his inner thighs. Only then did Kaine allow himself to touch the girl and his hands quickly found every wonderful curve of her supple body. They began at her elegant neck and moved across her shoulders and down her slender arms. They next lightly brushed the curve of her breasts on their way to her sleek waist, then glided over her smooth, firm hips. Everywhere they traveled, they left a trail of tiny goose bumps as Myleia reveled in his touch.

Eventually, they made it over to the waiting bed. Long after the last candle in the room had burned itself out, Kaine and Myleia fell asleep, holding each other close and hoping never to be separated again.

CHAPTER TWENTY FOUR

Toulon

Locke returned to Attalia with the captive Braslon. He immediately sought out Kaine, and when he found him, the commander said that only the Queen could decide what the traitor's fate should be. However, Kaine insisted that Locke accompany the prisoner since he was responsible for the capture. Queen Engrid, informed that Braslon was in custody, was waiting in the throne room. She had resumed wearing her feminine attire and looked every bit the royalty that she was. Locke had heard that she was beautiful, but was surprised at how young she looked. Indeed, she was hardly older than he was. Kaine introduced him to the Queen by saying he was one of the heroes of Ritola and had recently been knighted during that campaign. "Sir Locke is also fully responsible for the capture of the Queen's enemy, Braslon, who was caught fleeing Attalia two days ago."

Locke bowed deeply, but Engrid surprised him when she came down from her throne and offered her hand to the young man. Locke took it nervously and bowed again.

The Winds of Wharhalen

"I am grateful for the services that you have performed for the crown. You will be rewarded with productive land and given the finest weapons and armor that we can provide so that you may continue to help protect the Empire."

Locke was dumbstruck for a moment. Finally, he managed to say, "Thank you, Your Majesty."

Engrid then turned to Braslon, who stood before her, proud and defiant.

"Lord Braslon, you have conspired with a known traitor and a barbarous warlord to destroy the Monarchy. You have tortured and killed citizens of Killarassee to advance your own evil cause. You lied to me when I trusted you with one of the most important posts in the Empire. What do you have to say in your own behalf?"

"The Monarchy that you speak of is illegal. It was put into place by a gang of peasants led by a thief. Only the nobles can name a ruler in Killarassee, and the nobles answer only to the one they choose to rule over them."

The Queen stared coldly at this arrogant representative of his social class and pondered how long this resentment must have been festering among the nobles at being constantly by-passed. She paused to compose herself before she replied. "It took that gang of peasants to rid the Empire of Zironon while the nobles meekly submitted to his tyranny for thirty years. I proudly align myself with the peasants, for it is their country that they have chosen to let me rule. As for you, Lord Braslon, you made your choice, and now you have to face the consequences. I hereby confiscate your lands and sentence you to die by hanging. You will stay in prison until a gallows is built, so that you may have time to contemplate all that you have given up. A part of your lands shall be given to this worthy knight who stands before us today, for he has demonstrated his loyalty to the crown. Take this prisoner away!"

24 - Toulon

Locke did not, at first, realize that the Queen was referring to him until Braslon's protests rang out in the chamber. "You can't do this! My family is one of the oldest in Killarassee! You can't give away my ancestral lands to a common mercenary!" His voice faded away as the guards dragged him away down the hall.

After the throne room was cleared and Kaine was alone with Engrid, he said, "That was a very impetuous thing you did, giving Braslon's land to young Locke."

"Yes, I guess it was. But it felt good," she said, smiling a contented smile. "Tell me more about this young knight that I have just made so wealthy."

"I really don't know a lot about him. He came to us as a horse trainer with a herd of remounts. He told me he had been cheated by a noble named Toulon and he was sold into slavery after trying to buy a girl's freedom. He worked his way up through the ranks with extraordinary bravery and intelligence. However, he still seeks revenge on this Lord Toulon."

"I know Toulon. He would be one of the nobles that shares Braslon's feelings that my crown is illegitimate. I can't say that I would be sorry to see him die, but we can't just go around killing all the nobles that disagree with us. Try to talk Sir Locke out of this. I don't want to lose such a valuable knight."

Later that day, Kaine talked with Locke. "The Queen wants you to reconsider your plan to get revenge. She thinks it is foolish to go after Toulon by yourself."

"Is she planning to bring him to justice herself?"

Kaine hesitated. "It's complicated. About the only thing that unites the nobles is a mutual distrust of the crown. Executing Braslon will anger them. Going after Toulon as well will make it appear that she is waging war against them. She doesn't want to provoke them into a fight."

"I didn't think so. It's my fight anyway. I don't need any help. Was she serious about the land?"

"Of course she was. And land is power. You can have a very bright future."

"I never thought I would hear anyone say that about me," said Locke, shaking his head.

"If," Kaine continued, "you don't get yourself killed."

The next morning, Locke left Attalia to settle matters with Toulon. He headed south riding on the mare that he had taken possession of after the fall of Ritola. She had served him well since that time, her battle wounds having healed along with those of the young man who rode her. She was placid when there was no action, but would respond with a fiery determination when combat was imminent. She was dun-colored and sturdily built, not as tall as Arawae, but extremely agile with explosive speed. She performed her job well, like so many other horses men routinely used and eventually discarded like pieces of equipment.

The route that Locke traveled was a familiar one, having just been over it on the return from Ritola. In a few days, though, he knew he would have to turn west toward the region that held so many mixed memories for him: the race in Callanco, the treachery of Toulon, the cruel treatment in the quarries. The place where fate had stepped in and snatched him away from a certain death and placed him near Kira. The once fevered passion that he had felt for her just before he was wrenched away to Ritola had, of late, cooled, but his feelings toward the dark-haired beauty had remained pleasant. Although he could now acknowledge that it was her physical attractiveness that had clouded his thinking when he was with her, she still remained something of an enigma. Initially, she'd acted spoiled and arrogant, but as they became friends he found her to be sweet and vulnerable, as if the haughtiness was nothing more than a defensive façade. Of course, he considered the possibility she was being nice because she was attracted to him, but wasn't that one of the great mysteries of the female? Could a man ever completely unravel the complex workings of a woman's mind? Regardless, he felt a degree of sympathy for Kira, since, in a way, she was almost as much a prisoner as Eylese.

Eylese. Sweet, sad Eylese. What had become of her since he had been away? Most of his thoughts made him fearful. He knew that she was beaten. He had seen the bruises. Locke tried not to think about the possibility of rape. Would her desperation have led her to try to escape? And if she tried and failed, he was certain her punishment would be terrible. She might even be dead. In any case, Locke vowed that Toulon was going to pay for his crimes.

Locke had an abundance of time to think on the long ride to Toulon's lands. During the ride, his thoughts often turned inward. He had ridden this way before, more than two years ago, as a youth burdened with sadness from his parents' death and the tragedy of Jocar. He was just beginning, at that time, to learn about mistrust and cynicism. His experiences since then had only served to reinforce his feelings. He had aged quickly, becoming a man forged in the fires of combat, cruelty and betrayal. Hatred and vengeance still burned inside him, but rather than consume its host, it had become the catalyst to survival.

When he left the Karpoans, he was wandering aimlessly, with no idea how to restart his life after it had been shattered. His fateful meeting with Eylese, however, had renewed his spirit and had given him

The Winds of Wharhalen

an unexpected opportunity to help someone whose future looked equally hopeless. But over this very ray of light that initially seemed to shine so bright for both of them came the cloud of treachery that sent Locke on an odyssey that only now was about to come full circle. During his long journey, he often mused over what might have been had he not stopped to talk with Eylese that day. He also wondered if perhaps the fate that had spared him death on so many occasions was like the waves of an ocean current simply carrying him along to this point.

The road eventually branched away toward the vast, forested lands of Lord Toulon. A few more days of riding brought him, finally, to the grove of majestic trees where he and Eylese had spent those few happy days together. They seemed so long ago now that it was almost as if they'd happened to two other people. Certainly, Locke's appearance had change markedly, and he wondered if Eylese would even recognize him now. His hair was much longer, and a beard had replaced the smooth cheeks of his boyhood. His face was thinner, accenting the angles of his face to a greater degree; and his lanky teenage body, although still lean, had given way to a more powerful build. The clear blue eyes were still recognizable but had seemingly receded deeper under his brow creating a cynical, contemptuous look where once there had been trust. But these were just the external changes. Locke was more concerned with how he had changed within the hardened shell. Was he still capable of love? Of gentleness? Had his soul been eroded away by the act of killing? Whenever these questions unsettled him, he tried to remove them by evoking the feelings that he once had for Eylese. However, with all that he'd endured they were becoming frighteningly faint, as if they were being buried under layers of anger and hatred.

It was mid-morning when he arrived at the edge of the woods, and he approached carefully, not wanting to alert any of Toulon's rangers of his presence. He tied the mare and went the rest of the way on foot. The sun was beginning to peek through the stately trees and poke shafts of light into the dark grove but there was no sign of any other person in it. Locke realized at that point that he had foolishly anticipated Eylese being in the grove like she had been the first time he'd seen her. He wanted so badly to see her there, but after all the time that had passed, he realized it was silly for him to think that she would, at that exact moment in time, be there waiting for him. Perhaps, he thought, she didn't come there at all any more.

As Locke entered the dark, cool grove, a part of his consciousness saw in the trees troop formations deploying for battle. In his mind, every gap needed to be filled; every weak line needed shoring up. Then the flickering leaves of the canopy became flaming arrows raining down on his position. He struggled to shake the images out of his head. He had been this way since Ritola. It wasn't as if he couldn't see things the way they really were. It was just that a part of his brain now constantly saw things strategically arranged in battle terms, and the terrible images of war would always be seared deeply into his consciousness.

Overcoming the landscape of conflict and killing, he was finally able to see the grove in the way he preferred: a place of quiet refuge, where the memories of time spent with Eylese still lingered. The smell of damp leaves and tree bark filled his nostrils while the cool, still air made him shiver a bit, and he sought a log bathed in penetrating sunlight to sit on. Quickly, the chill left him and the warm memories of sitting with the girl came flooding back. Even without the memories, this would have been a magnificent place, with its cathedral-like canopy and soft carpet of moist leaves. But the memories were there nevertheless, eternally interlaced in Locke's consciousness with what his eyes saw, and all his other senses felt. Another grove, in another place, in another time, might evoke similar feelings. But this particular one

The Winds of Wharhalen

was powerful in the way it pulled him in. Even knowing that it belonged to Toulon couldn't diminish its aura. Could a mortal man really own a piece of the earth? Long after Toulon's death, these magnificent trees would endure. Even if the next landlord cut all the trees down, it would take only the blink of an eye in the chronicles of time for them to grow back.

The thought of Toulon brought Locke back to the purpose for his being here. He withdrew from the woods, taking one last look back and imagining he saw Eylese under the giant trees picking mushrooms. Sighing softly in resignation that he would have to delay seeing her, touching her, for just a little longer, he returned to the place where he had tied the mare.

Locke's attire was that of a knight and Officer-at-Arms of the Queen, and he believed that his appearance would be sufficient to gain him an audience with Toulon. The two guards at the outer gate, who on his last visit had been so suspicious, let him pass this time with barely a look. Locke assumed, then, that knights and nobles came and went routinely from the castle. He rode his horse through the bailey this time and was met at the castle gate by another guard.

"I wish to see Lord Toulon on business from the Queen," said Locke, in his best "official" tone of voice. While on his previous mission here he had been treated with disdain and ridicule, this time the guards did not attempt to engage him in conversation, but rather acted toward him with polite formality. A page was immediately sent into the castle to announce his visit and soon returned to say that the Baron would receive him. Locke's horse was then taken by a stable boy who headed off in the direction of the stables.

As Locke entered the inner courtyard through the massive gate, the memories of his first visit to the castle instantly began to flood his mind. The last time he walked this way he was with Eylese and he cursed himself for having been so naïve as to think Toulon would allow his servant to bring a peasant into his castle to ask for her freedom. Her cries still echoed in his brain, and he also remembered how the guards had beaten him, and he could still feel the blow to the back of his head that stunned him.

    The great hall where he now waited for the arrival of Toulon was the same one where all these previous horrors had taken place. The tapestries on the walls, the iron candleholders and the heavy, wood furniture only served to bring his memories into clearer focus. He was aware of his heart beating faster, and a wave of nausea passed over him at the thought of coming face to face again with the man who had stolen his gold and had sold him into slavery. Before the day was out though, thought Locke, either he or Toulon would be dead. He would not let himself be captured again. Locke studied the room carefully as he waited, noting the number and placement of the doors, the distances to each, and the placement of furniture, or other potential impediments. Most importantly, there were two guards positioned at the main door to the corridor, armed with long pikes.

    The Baron purposely made Locke wait a long time before he made his self-important entrance into the hall. Still large and red-faced, he now seemed much older and less imposing to Locke than in their first meeting. The dark, piercing eyes remained the same, though, as they studied the envoy from the crown. Locke hoped that his momentary uneasiness at this scrutiny had gone undetected as he tried to maintain his composure. Apparently satisfied that he hadn't seen the younger man before, Toulon looked away carelessly and said, "My guards tell me that you come from the Queen."

    "Yes," answered Locke with as much bravado as he could summon. "I have ridden here directly from Attalia."

    "How could that be when Attalia has been controlled by the rebel Haczlok for almost a year now?"

The Winds of Wharhalen

"Not quite true, sir. Indeed, the fight for control of Attalia had been a continuing one for the time period that you mention. However, it is only within the past several weeks that order has been restored and Queen Engrid is now firmly in control of the city once again."

At this news, Toulon glanced up and raised an eyebrow. "Indeed. Well, we are far from the throne here, and what happens in Attalia affects us little. What is it, then, that brings you here to our remote region?"

The arrogant tone of the Baron's words and his condescending attitude clearly indicated disdain for submitting to any laws other than his own.

"The Queen wishes to establish outposts throughout the Empire to enhance security for all her people and to better be able to deal with problems before they get out of hand. As the leading landholder in this region, it is hoped that you would be able to be a major supplier to the local post."

Locke thought he detected a glimmer of interest in the Baron's eyes as he momentarily contemplated the profits this arrangement would bring him. Apparently losing some of his initial suspicion of this rare visitor from the Queen, Toulon's demeanor changed slightly. "I was about to have my mid-day meal. Please join me, and we can discuss the particular needs of this new outpost while we eat."

The two men sat at opposite ends of a long, heavy wooden table as a male servant brought goblets and poured some wine. Locke had hoped to see Eylese once he was inside the castle, but he knew that right now it was more important that he not be distracted so he could more effectively concentrate on deceiving Toulon until the time came to strike. He had prepared meticulously during his long ride for the conversation that now took place, and so he was able to give detailed plans for the outpost, complete with all the logistical needs. The noble

24 - Toulon

listened quietly without interrupting, trying not to seem too interested but there was unmistakable greed radiating from his dark, beady eyes.

Suddenly, Locke's carefully rehearsed discourse was interrupted in mid-sentence when his eyes caught sight of a familiar figure entering the room carrying a platter of food. The girl, shoulders rounded submissively and eyes downcast, moved quietly and unobtrusively around the table. Locke tried to recover his thoughts but momentarily stumbled over his words. When he looked up he could see Toulon's eyes studying him suspiciously.

"My apologies sir; involvement in the campaigns of the last two years have left me easily distracted as I sometimes lapse into memories of the battlefield." Maintaining steady eye contact now with the Baron, Locke continued with the details for supplying the fictional outpost. Toulon's gaze gradually became less intense as he turned his attention back to the food being laid out on the table. With great difficulty, Locke struggled to avoid looking at Eylese as she went about her duties serving the meal. He forced himself to eat, although sharing a meal with this detestable man was making his stomach churn.

Toward the end of the meal, Eylese came near Locke to clear away his plates. He placed his hand gently on her wrist, and when she looked into his face to ascertain what he wanted from her, the girl's eyes became riveted on his. The audible gasp that next emanated from her mouth attracted the notice of Toulon.

"Has my servant offended you in some way, Sir Knight?"

"On the contrary, Baron, I find her quite attractive. Can I purchase her from you?"

Now Toulon's eyes studied the soldier's face even more intently to determine whether or not he should be taken seriously. Apparently satisfied, he said, "The girl is like a daughter to me. I practically raised her. But in the interests of goodwill with the crown, I would sell her to you for seventy-five gold pieces."

"A girl so lovely would be a bargain at twice the price, but I happen to know that this one is not yours to sell."

Toulon's expression darkened. "What did you say?" he asked, incredulously.

"This girl cannot be sold by you or anyone else, because she is not a slave. The indebtedness that she once had to you has already been paid."

Toulon continued to study the young man's face, which now revealed the hatred that had been smoldering for two years. "You've been here before. You're a thief!"

At that point, the guards posted at the door, on a signal from Toulon, rushed at Locke with their pikes lowered. Locke drew his sword and with a sweeping motion redirected the first man's pike upward. At once he was inside the long reach of the awkward weapon thereby rendering it ineffective. The broadsword struck and one guard was cut down. Locke evaded the point of the second man's pike, again the sword flashed, and the other guard was dealt a mortal wound. Stunned by the swiftness of this action, Toulon shouted for more help. The scream had barely left his lips when Locke agilely bound across the room and slipped in behind the door. Toulon's warning came too late. Wielding the broadsword with two hands now, Locke nearly decapitated the first man through the door. The second man, now more alert, stayed clear of Locke's deadly blade and circled his adversary cautiously. Meanwhile, Locke held his sword high with both hands and waited. As his opponent thrust, Locke retreated. A second thrust, another step back. When the third thrust came, deeper than the other two, Locke held his ground this time and skillfully knocked the pike aside with his blade. The sword claimed a fourth victim. Without hesitation, Locke

24 - Toulon

picked up the pike and jammed it through the handles on the doors, barring the hall from further intrusion.

Locke now turned and faced Toulon, who'd armed himself with a sword taken from one of several displayed on the walls. Eylese, who had hidden herself behind the heavy wood table during the fracas, moved around the perimeter of the room in the direction of Locke. The young knight lowered the tip of his blade. "Lord Toulon, you took fifty gold pieces from me and sentenced me to a slow death as a slave in the quarries. How many others have you wrongly treated just because they were poor peasants? For this crime you should pay with your life. But I will let you live if you repay the gold that you took from me and allow this girl to leave here with her debt to you finished."

"Do you really think I would allow a common thief masquerading as a knight to come into my castle and take what is rightfully mine?" The nobleman attacked with a strength and ferocity that initially drove Locke back. The clash of swords echoed throughout the great hall as the two enemies fought with desperation, each knowing that one mistake would be fatal. Toulon proved to be an expert swordsman and he fought with great skill. However, after several minutes of this unrelenting combat, Locke sensed that the noble was tiring. He stepped back momentarily, yielding ever so slightly to the pressure of Toulon's blade, thereby drawing him into an attack. The Baron took the bait and lunged toward his adversary. Whereupon, Locke deflected the assault and ran his own blade through Toulon's throat. As blood spurted from the wound, the nobleman's sword arm dropped to his side. Locke stepped back as his enemy toppled like a tree. "You pompous fool," said Locke to the prostrate, dying Baron. "I gave you a chance to live."

Unable to call for help, Toulon stared silently with terrified eyes as the life oozed from his body.

The Winds of Wharhalen

"Locke, this way!" implored Eylese, jolting the young man from his contemplation as he stood over the victim of his anger and revenge. She led him out the servants' door and down a narrow hallway, through the buttery and into the kitchen. Several times they passed servants who stood and watched silently as the two fugitives hurried past. After going through three more rooms and then descending a flight of stairs they came to a door. Eylese turned to Locke and said, "This leads outside the castle. But we'll still be within the curtain wall. How are you going to escape?"

"Can we get to the stables in the bailey? My horse is there."

Eylese nodded. "Along the east wall there is a walkway that isn't used very much anymore. Once we get to the other side of the keep there is a passage we can use to get down into the bailey without having to go through the gate from the courtyard. It is used by the servants to bring provisions into the castle."

"That sounds like our best chance. Do you still want to leave here with me?"

Eylese smiled, tears beginning to form in her eyes. She put her arms around Locke's neck and kissed him on the lips. Without saying a word, the girl then took him by the hand and pushed open the door. Once outside, they followed the walkway along the wall until they came to the passageway Eylese had described. They continued along its sloping stone floor that led through the fifteen-foot thick wall and down to ground level where it emerged into a storehouse. Coming back out in the daylight, they were less than a hundred yards from the stables, which were situated along the outside wall. "Maybe it would be better to have you wait out here while I get my horse," cautioned Locke.

"It will be all right. Most of the people who work down here are my friends."

24 - Toulon

So they went into the barn together in search of the mare. When she saw Locke she stuck her head out of the stall door and nickered. They led her out into the aisle and were searching for her saddle when an old man came in. He was leathery and wrinkled with white hair and bushy brows. His gnarled hands seemed too large for his body, and he walked with a bit of a limp. "I would have gotten your horse ready for you if you had asked," he said, somewhat annoyed.

Eylese walked over to the man and said something to him in a hushed tone.

The old man looked surprised and said to Locke, "I thought you were dead."

"Actually, I've never been better."

"I need to borrow a horse, Mikas," exclaimed Eylese enthusiastically.

"You can ride?" asked Locke, a little surprised.

"Of course I can ride. Do you know so little about me?" she teased.

"To be honest, I know almost nothing about you," said Locke, matter-of-factly.

"Does the Baron know you are planning to take one of his horses?" asked Mikas.

"It won't matter to him; he's dead." answered Eylese.

Mikas's eyes brightened. "Well, in that case, take any one you want."

As Locke saddled his mare, Eylese and the old stable keeper prepared a second horse, a stout, gray mare with shaggy fetlocks and a sleepy disposition. Mounting proved a bit awkward for the girl in her ankle length dress. With a bit of a blush, she hiked the skirt up, pulled the hem between her pale thighs, and tied it at her waist with a length of rope. Locke thought of Kira and her tight-fitting riding pants.

Little notice was taken as the two rode down the long lane that led away from the stables toward the palisade. The people who worked in the bailey were peasants like Eylese and cared little for the personal business of the noble. Life was hard for them as they struggled to scratch out an existence under the feudal system. The guards at the outer gate paid no more attention to Locke and Eylese than they had earlier when Locke first arrived. The knight with the girl trailing behind him rode across the bridge over the dry moat without even glancing back. Locke had no way of knowing how long it would be before someone would discover what had happened in the great hall, or even then what would be done about it. All he knew was he wanted to get Eylese as far away from Toulon's castle and lands as quickly as he could. Locke headed in the same direction that he'd come from, north being the direction that would get them out of Toulon's fief the fastest. However, when they reached the forest, the girl suddenly shouted for him to stop. "I'm sorry," apologized Locke, "am I going too fast?"

"No. I have something to show you." Eylese then turned and started off in the direction opposite of that which would take them to the main road.

"Where are you taking me?"

"You'll see. Just trust me," came the reply from the girl. Her voice had a playful ring to it.

The path continued to grow narrower, until finally they had to dismount and lead the horses. The way was seldom used and would not have appeared to be anything more than a trail used by deer. Eventually, they emerged into a small clearing, and at the other end of it was an old, weather-beaten shed. Eylese whistled loudly, and the signal elicited a throaty response. Rounding the corner from the other side of the

24 - Toulon

shed came a beautiful bay mare. It was Arawae. Incredulous, Locke stammered, "How…"

"After they took you, I found her in the grove. I have been keeping her here all this time, for when you returned."

"You thought I would return?"

"I admit there were times when I almost lost hope. But I always knew that if you were alive, you would come back for me someday." There were tears in her eyes as she said these words, and Locke took her in his arms and hugged her tightly. All the pain and suffering and atrocities that the boy had been through in the past two years were suddenly pushed aside by the softness and warmth of the girl's body as it pressed against his.

Eylese held the two mounts while Locke had his reunion with Arawae. As he stroked her neck and spoke softly to her, the mare nuzzled his chest. He thought back to helping his father when she was foaled and of riding the hills with Jocar and swallowed hard to keep his composure.

Locke then led Arawae back to the girl and said, "Let's get moving again. Even now, there may already be rangers looking for us."

"I didn't think you would want to leave without Arawae."

Locke just shook his head, emotion choking his voice. "Thank you for keeping her for me."

Late in the afternoon, after having covered many miles at an urgent pace, the two travelers stopped to rest their horses. Locke and Eylese sat together for a little while at the edge of an isolated meadow while the three mares grazed peacefully before them. "So, where do we go now?" asked Eylese.

"Where would you *like* to go?"

The Winds of Wharhalen

"I don't really know. I've never had a choice before. I wouldn't even know where to look for my family." With her head on his chest and her arms wrapped around his waist, she purred contentedly, "I only know that I want to be with you."

After a few minutes, Locke offered, "I have recently acquired some land near Attalia. We might consider living there."

Eylese gave the boy a puzzled look.

"I know. None of it really makes sense to me right now either. The important thing is that we're together."

Later they left the meadow to put even more miles between themselves and Toulon's fief. As darkness came and brought to a close that eventful day in their lives, Locke and Eylese stopped to rest for the night. They tethered Arawae and the mare which still had no name but left the gray on her own, knowing that she wouldn't stray far without the others.

It was a warm night, late in summer, and after the last glow of the sunset had left the sky, a nearly full moon rose on the horizon. In the dim moonlight they knelt down in the soft grass under a huge, spreading oak tree. All day Locke had been observing his companion. He'd studied the lines of her body, the features of her face, all the perfect contours and proportions. She smiled coyly whenever she happened to notice him scrutinizing her. He decided that there was nothing more important that he could do with the rest of his life than take care of this girl who had put her trust in him. As he now gazed on her beautiful face, bathed in the soft light, he tried to commit to memory each lovely detail. It had bothered him during their separation that he was sometimes unable to recall the features that, at this moment, seemed so familiar. The girl's enchanting eyes, so expressive, looked slightly upward into his. Moving slowly at first, then holding back momentarily to heighten the expectation, he kissed her waiting lips

24 - Toulon

as gently as he could. The kiss turned more fervent as Eylese responded eagerly. Locke's long-imprisoned passion had filled up every space in his body, but this was their first time, and he proceeded cautiously. The brutality of the past two years had certainly hardened the fortress that was the shell of the man, but there still remained within him a gentle nature. The dark shadows in the recesses of his soul might never disappear completely, but they would always pale in the light that had now been brought back into his life by Eylese. Soon their clothes were left on the ground along with their initial shyness. Locke's touch left not an inch of the girl's body unexplored that night, and each smooth, supple region willingly surrendered.

The next morning, Locke and Eylese set out on the road to resume a journey that had started two years earlier. Before they would return to Attalia, though, they would go to Sebastian's farm to retrieve the remainder of the gold that Arawae had won at Callanco.

"So," started Eylese, "How did you get to be a knight?"

"It's kind of a long story."

"We have a long ride ahead of us."

The Winds of Wharhalen

About the Author

 Tom Nelson lives on a small horse farm in central Ohio with his wife, Carolyn. They have been married for 33 years and have two grown daughters. Tom has worked as a teaching tennis professional and coach for the past 40 years and has published many instructional articles in tennis magazines and professional journals. He also presents professional development seminars to other coaches, tennis professionals, and teachers.

In addition to tennis, Tom has a passion for horses. He has owned horses continually for the past 40 years and still rides regularly. He is also a licensed harness trainer and driver.

Tom enjoys reading books from the great authors of the 19th century. Robert Lewis Stevenson, Alexander Dumas, James Fenimore Cooper, and many others have provided the inspiration for Tom's writing. He likes the medieval genre because it provides the colorful,

The Winds of Wharhalen

romantic escapism of fantasy, but he doesn't rely on magic or spiritualism to resolve conflicts between good and evil. Tom's characters must summon their own resourcefulness to overcome the challenges of a harsh life in the middle ages. In a continuing effort to inject authenticity into his writing, Tom travels to destinations in Europe to research castles.

Did you like this book?

If you enjoyed this book, you will find more interesting books at

www.CrystalDreamsPublishing.com

Please take the time to let us know how you liked this book. Even short reviews of 2-3 sentences can be helpful and may be used in our marketing materials. If you take the time to post a review for this book on Amazon.com, let us know when the review is posted and you will receive a free audiobook or ebook from our catalog. Simply email the link to the review once it is live on Amazon.com, your name, and your mailing address -- send the email to orders@mmpubs.com with the subject line "Book Review Posted on Amazon."

If you have questions about this book, our customer loyalty program, or our review rewards program, please contact us at info@mmpubs.com.

a division of Multi-Media Publications Inc.

Prophecies of the Ancients

By Weslynn McCallister

Swept away in a disaster by a devastating emerald eyed Prince, Jennifer Harper awakens, star bound to cities beyond her wildest imagination. Falling desperately in love with Prince Karo, their romance is interrupted by Drona, the Sorcerer who vows to make her his or destroy her. While Jenna is stricken by a deadly virus, Karo undertakes a mission to the Isle of Beasts to search for the antidote. Unaware of the ancient prophecy, Jenna and her rival, Elena soon find themselves within the heart of it.

Inadvertently cast into the future by his irate mistress, Drona joins Queen Michelle, a white magician, in an effort to defend the Red Moon from Vincent 11, the most evil sorcerer the galaxy has ever known.

When his archenemy, Prince Karo, arrives from a century past on an errant time machine, they gather strength as they combine their unique talents. Only by their joint efforts and Drone's brilliant inventions of unique androids can they hope to prevent the prophesied war of 2112.

ISBN-10:   159146014X
ISBN-13:   9781591460145

Price: $13.00

Available from Amazon.com or your nearest book retailer.
Order direct from the publisher at www.CrystalDreamsPublishing.com.

The Necromancer

By Kevin Dunn

Salem, Massachusetts - 1692: The witch hunts begin. Neighbors are turning on one another. A smallpox epidemic has broken out. People are dying. One man is responsible, a warlock of great power - the Necromancer - and he has just seduced one of Salem's purest women into a perdition that will haunt her the rest of her life.

Using actual historical evens as the backdrop for the fictional story of Reverend Ambrose Blayne and Susanna Harrington, it is a novel of passion, horror, love, and the cruelty which man is capable of. It is a deeply disturbing, often graphic depiction of those brutal and uncertain times.

The novel, while primarily set in Salem, sprawls across Europe from witches being burned at the stake in Scotland to spiritual awakenings in the Roman Amphitheater and depraved Witches' Sabbats in the Harz Mountains of Germany. The series of events culminates in the warlock's summoning of a Lovecraftian demon which threatens to unknit the fabric of the world and an ending that will chill the reader's blood.

ISBN-10: 1591460719
ISBN-13: 9781591460718

Price: $15.00

Available from Amazon.com or your nearest book retailer.
Order direct from the publisher at www.CrystalDreamsPublishing.com.

Printed in the United States
136577LV00002B/4/A